"Grab the ladder!" someone shouted faintly.

Nissa grabbed it with both hands and wrapped her legs around the rope, hanging on with superhuman strength she didn't know she possessed. God bless adrenaline.

A big green shape came up the ladder. It didn't stop at her feet, though. It moved up behind her until the SEAL's head was at her waist.

"Keep going!" Cole shouted.

Not. A. Chance.

No way was she letting go of the rope to keep climbing.

He climbed until his head was level with hers, his body spooning hers, his longer arms grasping the rope ladder around her slender frame. Warmth from his body penetrated the back of her wet suit as he plastered his entire body against hers.

"One foot. Just put your right foot up one rung for me," he shouted into her ear as another huge gust of wind buffeted them. "It'll be calmer on the deck of the ship." His breath was warm against her exposed cheek. He felt alive. Vital. Real in the midst of this unreal nightmare.

* * *

Code: Warrior SEALs: Meet these fierce warriors who take on the most dangerous secret missions around the world!

* * *

If you're on Twitter, tell us what you think of Harlequin Romantic Suspense! #harlequinromsuspense

Dear Reader,

I'm super excited to finally give you Commander Cole "Frosty" Perriman's story! You've waited through a bunch of books for him to get his very own happily-ever-after, and you've totally earned this one.

Nissa Beck is a CIA psychological operations officer, and the only woman I can imagine giving Cole a run for his money. But can she break through his icy reserve to find the passion lurking beneath? I don't envy her the task...

And may I take this moment to apologize for the opening scene? It positively gave me the shivers to write. You might want to get a few bland crackers and nibble on them as you start this book. I recommend a hot beverage of your choice, too. And maybe a cozy chair next to a warm fire. Oh, and a blanket. There. Now we're all ready to settle in and enjoy the wild ride as Cole and Nissa chase down one of the most dangerous men in the world and dare to love each other.

Happy reading!

Cindy

HER MISSION
WITH A SEAL

Cindy Dees

PAPL
DISCARDED

HARLEQUIN®ROMANTIC SUSPENSE

Recycling programs
for this product may
not exist in your area.

ISBN-13: 978-1-335-45628-1

Her Mission with a SEAL

Printed in U.S.A.

www.Harlequin.com

New York Times and *USA TODAY* bestselling author **Cindy Dees** is the author of more than fifty novels. She draws upon her experience as a US Air Force pilot to write romantic suspense. She's a two-time winner of the prestigious RITA® Award for romance fiction, a two-time winner of the RT Reviewers' Choice Best Book Award for Romantic Suspense and an *RT Book Reviews* Career Achievement Best Author Award nominee. She loves to hear from readers at www.cindydees.com.

Books by Cindy Dees

Harlequin Romantic Suspense

Code: Warrior SEALs

Undercover with a SEAL
Her Secret Spy
Her Mission with a SEAL

The Prescott Bachelors

High-Stakes Bachelor
High-Stakes Playboy

Soldier's Last Stand
The Spy's Secret Family
Captain's Call of Duty
Soldier's Rescue Mission
Her Hero After Dark
Breathless Encounter
Flash of Death
Deadly Sight
A Billionaire's Redemption

HQN Books

Take the Bait
Close Pursuit
Hot Intent

Visit Cindy's Author Profile page at Harlequin.com for more titles!

Chapter 1

Nissa Beck had done some crazy things in her life, but sailing into the teeth of a rapidly intensifying hurricane in a tiny dinghy—in the dark—with a trio of Navy SEALs was right up there on the stupid scale. They'd actually strapped her into the boat so she wouldn't get tossed out as their craft went nearly vertical climbing the wave faces towering overhead and then plunged nearly vertically down the waves crashing into black troughs of icy seawater.

Throat-paralyzing terror was the only reason she hadn't screamed herself hoarse already. The horror of being out here at the mercy of the wildly tossing ocean was indescribable. As was the sheer size of the waves. They were small mountains. Literally. Except for the ones that periodically collapsed on top of them, burying them in frigid seawater for endless seconds until they popped back up to the surface and could breathe again. In short, it was a living nightmare.

She'd swallowed more seawater than she could fathom and thrown most of it back up along with the last meal she'd consumed three hours ago. A lifetime away in a safe place. On land. Not in the path of Hurricane Jessamine.

But her target had fled the United States and was out here somewhere in the Gulf of Mexico making his getaway on a container ship call the *Anna Belle*. The ship wasn't one of the super giants, just a relatively small cargo ship. The manifest said she sailed with a crew of twenty, was loaded with wheat below decks and carried 120 containers stacked above decks.

What the manifest didn't say was that she also carried a passenger. A man named Markus Petrov. One of the most elusive spies ever to operate on American soil. A colleague of Nissa's, an American spy named Max Kuznetsov whose mother had been killed by Petrov, had spent nearly a decade tracking the guy and had spent most of the past three years undercover in Petrov's criminal organization learning his true identity.

It was a brilliant setup, actually. Petrov ran a Russian crime gang and used its proceeds to finance his extracurricular espionage activities. In the meantime, he hid behind the Russian mafia, who fiercely protected his identity.

Max and a team of Navy SEALs had destroyed most of Petrov's criminal organization last week in a spectacular shoot-out deep in the bayous of south Louisiana. But Petrov had disappeared.

Unfortunately, Max also needed to go to ground,

along with his fiancée, a psychic who had helped him identify Markus Petrov at long last. Until Petrov was apprehended, the two of them were in extreme danger and had been whisked into federal protective custody. This left no subject matter experts on Petrov except Nissa to help with the manhunt.

She'd been tracking Max's progress in the Petrov case for years and was the CIA's second most knowledgeable analyst when it came to the Russian spy. Which was why she was out here tonight doing her darnedest to drown. The SEALs needed someone who could make a positive ID on Petrov when they captured him on the *Anna Belle.*

The cargo ship had gone silent the moment it crossed into international waters, and the only reason they knew where it was now was compliments of a hurricane hunter aircraft that'd made a visual sighting of the ship on its last pass through Hurricane Jessamine that afternoon.

Were it not for that chance sighting, nobody would have any idea where Petrov and the ship he'd fled on had disappeared to.

The ship's manifest said it was bound for the Dominican Republic with food and humanitarian supplies. Perhaps that part was true, at any rate.

One of the SEALs had a radio headset plastered to his ears. He shouted a course correction back to the muscular man wrestling the tiller, the team leader, Commander Cole Perriman.

He was easily six foot three and built like a god. The high-tech wet suit currently clinging to his torso was an exercise in truth in advertising. Every beautiful, perfect muscle was clearly outlined for her viewing pleasure. Thank you, God.

At the moment his hood was pushed back, and his short dark hair was plastered to his skull. Still, his face was handsome and rugged. She knew from earlier that his eyes were pale, icy blue and practically glowed against his darkly tanned skin.

The members of his team called him Frosty. Although the nickname initially made her think of cheerful snowmen, after two minutes in his presence, she understood the moniker. The guy's nerves were made of pure ice.

Their pitifully small craft topped a massive swell, and she thought she caught sight of a black shape looming ahead. But then the rain squall around them intensified, and they slid down the back side of the swell into a black trough bordered by massive walls of water on all sides. Lord, the ocean was *big*. She felt tiny and insignificant in the face of these gigantic waves. She was not a particularly religious person, but a prayer entered her head now to whatever deity might hear her plea to please save them all from this insanity.

The only good part about being down in the troughs was they got a momentary break from the screaming winds trying to tear their faces off. The rain, blowing at a hundred miles per hour or more, felt like a power washer trying to scrub the flesh off her bones.

She would be more inclined to whimper in fear were it not for how unconcerned these guys seemed about the storm. They were self-possessed and untalkative, exuding a certain cool self-confidence.

"There's the *Anna Belle*!" the one called Bass shouted as they topped another huge, heaving swell.

"Where are its lights?" she shouted back.

Commander Perriman answered from behind her, "Good question. They may have lost power. If they've taken on enough water, they could have flooded their engines and backup electric generators."

"That sounds bad" Nissa ventured to reply.

The SEAL called Ashe responded, managing to infuse his voice with dry irony, even while shouting over the storm, "It would suck to be them in a storm like this without power."

The big twin motors on their rigid inflatable boat powered them up a half dozen more mountain-steep swells before they finally drew close to the darkened container ship. It was actually the scariest moment of the journey so far when a swell tilted the *Anna Belle* way over on its side toward them, a huge pile of containers looming overhead, threatening to topple the ship and kill them all.

"Suit up!" Perriman ordered the team. All the hoods came up. Nissa already had hers up, and it held in place the earbuds and throat microphones the team would use to communicate once they boarded the *Anna Belle*. She covered her eyes with the night-vision goggles that had been stowed around her neck. The three men beside her leaped into lime-green relief against the heaving black sea.

"Ship's listing pretty bad," Perriman commented over their discrete radio frequency.

"Fifteen to eighteen degrees to the port side," Ashe replied. He sounded like an expert sailor. "She's looking top-heavy, too. With those containers stacked high like that, they act as a wall to catch the wind. Hurricane could blow the ship over if they get crossways of a big enough gust."

Okay, that sounded *really* bad.

"Let's get on and off her as fast as we can," Perriman ordered. "I don't like the looks of her seaworthiness."

Great. The ship they were about to board was on the verge of capsizing and sinking. Just how every girl wanted to spend her Saturday night.

They tied off their craft to a cleat low on the hull of the *Anna Belle*, and then Bass, using welded rungs on the hull, climbed the side of the ship like a freaking monkey. He lowered a rope ladder from the deck down to them.

"Up you go, Nissa," Cole ordered. He clipped a rope that Bass threw down onto the body harness they'd made her wear and which they'd used to lash her into their boat.

She looked up at the rope ladder swinging around over her head and gulped. He must have seen her hesitation because he moved up behind her and leaned forward to shout in her ear, off microphone, "I'll be right behind you."

Right. As if that was reassuring. At least she knew to grab the rope ladder from the side and not to try to go up it facing the rungs head-on. With one rope of the ladder against her cheek, she turned her feet pigeon-toed to climb the ladder.

It was okay for the first ten feet or so. But then the ship got sideways of a swell, and it tilted toward her sickeningly. The rope swung out into space. She wasn't even over the SEALs' boat anymore. Black water yawned below her. *I'm going to die.* Frozen in terror, she squeezed her eyes shut and clung to the ladder for dear life.

The ship tilted back the other way, and the ladder swung back toward the ship, slamming her into the cold steel hull. She lost her grip on the wet ladder and swung out to the side on the safety rope, smashing into the ship's hull hard enough to knock the wind out of her. She screamed, but the sound was ripped away from her by a huge gust of wind and rain that hit her with the force of a fire hose.

"Grab the ladder!" someone shouted.

She opened her eyes and swung sickeningly out in space as the ship rolled again, black water reaching up to her and the listing ship looming above, as if it was about to come down on her head and drag her to the bottom of the sea.

Panic paralyzed her so completely that she couldn't even form thoughts, let alone take action. She bumped along the hull of the ship as it tilted away from her, and by some miracle, she banged into something hard and rough. The rope ladder. She grabbed it with both hands and wrapped her legs around the rope, hanging on with superhuman strength she didn't know she possessed. God bless adrenaline.

A big green shape came up the ladder. It didn't stop at her feet, though. It moved up behind her until the figure's head was at her waist.

"Keep going!" It was Cole.

Not. A. Chance.

No way was she letting go of the rope to keep climbing.

He climbed until his head was level with hers, his body spooning hers, his longer arms grasping the rope ladder around her slender frame. Warmth from his body penetrated the back of her wet suit as he plastered his entire body against hers.

"One foot. Just put your right foot up one rung for me," he shouted into her ear as another huge gust of wind buffeted them. "It'll be calmer on the deck of the ship." His breath was warm against her exposed cheek. He felt alive. Vital. Real in the midst of this unreal nightmare.

He patiently talked her through the rest of the climb, one hand and one foot at a time. Bass kept tension on her safety rope from above, helping her make the climb, and Cole steadied her with his big body and strong arms, protecting her from the worst of the storm.

It took a lifetime, but eventually Bass hauled her onto the deck beside him. She lay on her belly and although there was nothing left in her stomach, she dry heaved anyway, so terrified she didn't think she was ever going to be the same again.

Of course, Ashe jogged up the ladder as if it was a walk in the damned park. The party all aboard, they knelt together in the shadow of a pile of containers, shadows among the shadows in their black sea-land suits and black facial camo grease. Of course, she looked the same, her blond hair tucked under her neoprene hood, her skin blackened like theirs.

"Any sign of movement out here?" Perriman asked.

Bass replied, "Negative."

The deck tilted steeply beneath her, and she looked down at water as the ship listed worse than ever.

"Man, she feels top-heavy," Cole remarked.

Ashe replied, "She looks violently misloaded. Death

trap. This storm gets much worse, and she's going down."

"Then let's get our guy and get the heck off her," Perriman ordered. "You have your orders." He glanced at Nissa huddling miserably against a container and said off mike, "You're with me."

The team split up and ran off in different directions to search the ship. She and Cole were supposed to make their way to the bridge. He was going to have a word with the captain and obtain the guy's cooperation—at gunpoint if necessary. The other team members would go below decks, searching the ship and making their way to the bridge by other means.

Hanging on to the deck rail with both hands, she followed Perriman aft toward the conning tower. In a storm this bad, they didn't expect to see any crew above deck, and indeed, the open area between the tall stacks of shipping containers and the ship's superstructure aft was deserted and dark.

Perriman stopped in front of a hatch, and she endured a nauseating roll by the *Anna Belle* way over to one side, the sickening pause while the ship teetered on the brink of capsizing, and then the roll back the other way.

How Cole unlocked the steel door, she had no idea. But she was relieved when he threw it open. She dived inside and helped him haul the heavy door shut against gravity as the ship rolled again. He threw the handle and latched the door behind them.

The relative quiet and the relief from the hammering pain of hurricane-driven rain was intense. The ship still rolled like a big dog beneath her feet, but in here, she couldn't see the ocean and had less of a sense of being ready to capsize.

Perriman hand-signaled her to follow him. She nodded and fell in behind him as he raced silently up a set of metal stairs. He paused at the doorway to the next deck, peering through a tiny window before opening the door. Bracing herself against the wall as the ship rocked, she followed him into what looked like a small dining room.

"Stay here," Cole breathed.

Gladly. She nodded and he disappeared behind a swinging door into the kitchen, according to the ship's diagrams that they'd studied on the helicopter ride out here. Perriman swung back into view, staggering a little as the ship heaved.

"Clear," he announced.

Deck by deck, the two of them cleared their way up the superstructure toward the bridge. Oddly, they didn't run into a single crew member. Maybe the captain had sent everyone to strap themselves in the sleeping quarters below decks to ride out the storm. Cole had mentioned that such a thing was possible, so she wasn't completely freaked out by how deserted the command portion of the ship was.

They turned the corner to the last flight of steps leading to the bridge. Unlike the living areas below, this space was guaranteed to have crew members in it. Cole paused, checked over his shoulder that she was ready with her pistol drawn and then he charged the bridge.

She went in on his heels, awkwardly spinning left as the deck tilted underfoot to cover Cole's back as he spun to cover the right half of the space.

"What the hell?" he exclaimed.

The bridge was deserted.

From up here, she could see outside again, and the ship rolled dangerously far over onto its side as she glanced out. From this high up in the air, the list was even more pronounced, and she all but froze again in panic.

Perriman jabbed at his throat mike. "Bridge is abandoned. I repeat. Abandoned. Report if able."

Bass and Ashe both reported immediately that they'd been unable to find any crew members aboard the vessel.

"Complete your search and join us on the bridge," he ordered.

She looked over the panel of controls. Every needle was at zero. The ship was completely shut down. This could not be good. "Can we start the engines or something?" she asked.

"Diesel engines are not as simple to start as flipping a switch. But maybe I could get a generator online." Perriman fiddled with a set of controls to one side of the ship's wheel, and then swore quietly. She gathered that meant they weren't going to get any lights on.

"Batteries are dead, too."

"Has the crew abandoned ship?" Nissa asked.

Perriman frowned. "They sent no distress signals."

"Maybe there was no time to send one?"

"The ship's still afloat. Granted not for long the way she's listing, but still. We could send a signal right now if we had even an inch of battery power. I can't believe they ran the batteries all the way down before they got out a call for help."

The door opened behind them and Nissa spun fast, jumpy as heck, weapon drawn. It was Bass and Ashe.

"Funny thing, boss," Bass said. "The generators looked like someone took a sledgehammer to them. The batteries were pulled free of their moorings and smashed up, too."

"The engines?"

"I couldn't see any damage at a glance," Ashe replied. "But I got nothing when I tried to start up the diagnostic panel at the engineer's panel. I looked under the console and found a bunch of ripped out wires beneath it."

Curious, Nissa dropped to her knees to take a peek under the dashboard in front of her. "Uh, guys. All the wires and conduits I'm seeing down here are trashed, too."

"So the ship's been sabotaged," Cole responded. "Why?"

The ship leaned particularly far onto its port side just then and everyone grabbed on to something to stay upright. She stared in dread at the tall stacks of containers tilting perilously.

"I've being doing weight and balance calculations on ships my whole naval career, and I've never seen a ship this badly loaded. The manifest showed the cargo spread out in three layers over the entire deck, not stacked six high all afore midships like this," Ashe complained. "She feels too light in the water for the weight listed on the manifest, too."

Cole looked at him keenly. "What are you saying?"

Ashe shrugged asking instead, "Hey, Bass. Are the holds full to the brim with wheat like the manifest said?"

"Negative. All the holds are empty."

"Holy hell," Ashe breathed. "Sir, we have to get off this ship immediately. She's in imminent danger of capsizing."

"In case you hadn't noticed, the storm's getting worse. Fast. The idea was to turn this ship around and sail it back to New Orleans with the prisoner in custody."

Ashe replied urgently, "Even if we could get the engines running, this ship is top-heavy as hell and has no ballast below decks. I can't believe she hasn't gone over already. I'm telling you, sir, we have to get off the *Anna Belle now*."

"And you're sure no one but us is still aboard?" Cole asked.

Bass and Ashe both nodded and murmured in the affirmative.

Perriman ordered tersely, "Let's get out of here, ASAP."

After that, it was all elbows and assholes as they raced downstairs, Ashe's warning ringing in Nissa's ears.

The trip back down the rope ladder of doom wasn't nearly as bad for Nissa because she was so bloody relieved to be getting off the *Anna Belle*. She'd had enough of those rolls and those endless, breathless pauses while the ship debated capsizing.

She landed in the SEALs' tiny boat with relief. They might be a cork in this vessel, but it was better than being aboard the doomed *Anna Belle*.

They untied their mooring lines and motored away from the big ship. Nissa had never breathed so big a sigh of relief to be away from the *Anna Belle*.

"Nearest land?" Cole asked from his position at the tiller.

"Louisiana coast. Nearly a hundred nautical miles," Bass answered.

Yikes. Even traveling at twenty knots, it would take them *hours* to make shore. Hours for the storm to intensify around them.

They'd been lucky to catch a ride outbound on a big Coast Guard cutter heading into the gulf to take measurements of the approaching storm, but they'd made no arrangements for a lift back to New Orleans. The plan had been to sail the *Anna Belle* back.

"Do we have enough fuel to make it?" Ashe asked practically.

Oh, hell. Now she had running out of gas to worry about.

"Close, but enough," Cole replied casually.

Jeez. What else could go wrong?

"Give me a course heading for the nearest land," Cole ordered Bass.

While Cole steered, the other two men put up a framework of curved poles and stretched a tarp over them, lashing it down tight. It created a low clamshell covering over the vessel. It didn't keep out all the rain, but it knocked down the worst of the water and wind. They still had to use a motorized pump to empty water out of the hull, and the ride was rough as all get-out. But after the rolling of the *Anna Belle*, this freezing-cold misery was a boon. And their boat wasn't trying to capsize.

Until Bass, on the radio again, shouted something directly into Cole's ear off headset that put a grim look on the man's face.

Cole ordered over the radio, "Everyone don a life vest and let's go ahead and put Nissa into an exposure kit."

An exposure kit turned out to be a body-sized pouch of some slick neoprene-like material that encompassed her entire body and attached to the donut-shaped life vest the guys inflated around her neck.

"What's this for?" she asked as Cole checked the connections around her neck.

He paused at his task to gaze at her from a range of about one foot. Lord, he was gorgeous with those lean cheeks and firm jaw. His voice rumbled comfortingly. "If you end up in the water, the kit provides a layer of insulation to extend how long you can survive hypothermia by hours or days. It also protects you from sharks. They can't smell you through the material. In pockets attached to the interior of the bag are water, rations, a small desalinization kit, a GPS locator beacon, a mirror and an emergency radio. My team and I know how to climb into one in the water and bail out any seawater. But since you haven't had the training, we're popping you into yours now, to be safe. Try to think of it as a sleeping bag, and it won't freak you out so bad."

"Thanks."

How did he know that being wrapped up in this giant condom was scaring her half to death? She'd always struggled with claustrophobia, and this situation wasn't helping matters one little bit. She fought like crazy not to hyperventilate and hung on by a bare thread to the ability to breathe.

She muttered under her breath, "Please, God, don't let me need this stupid contraption."

Cole cracked the first smile she'd seen from him. Even in the dark, it was dazzling. "It's purely a precaution."

But when he had all four of them lash their safety harnesses together with rope and bungee cord, she had to wonder just how unnecessary a precaution it really was.

They finished the Boy Scout knot project before she asked on radio, "Does someone want to tell me why we're suddenly preparing for disaster, here?"

Bass answered, "Jessamine has gone from a Category 1 to a Category 3 hurricane in the past few hours. Weather service is now forecasting that she'll spin up into a high Cat 4 or Cat 5."

"Isn't that just special?" she responded sarcastically.

Everyone laughed.

Seriously? They could laugh while sailing around in the middle of a hurricane in a rowboat with motors?

The SEALs took turns at the tiller, wrestling the ocean until they became exhausted and had to switch out. The interminable journey settled into a steady-state nightmare, and the team chatted on headset to pass the time. The good news was the hurricane wind at their backs was blowing them landward at an impressive clip, shaving hours off their journey.

Ashe took the radio from Bass and had an earnest conversation with someone at the other end that culminated in him saying, "Let me know when you've run the numbers."

Ashe piped up after a few minutes, "The Coast Guard has pulled the *Anna Belle*'s manifest and compared it against what we saw on the ship. She definitely left New Orleans with a belly full of wheat. But sometime in the past twenty-four hours, the ship's crew must have dumped all of it overboard."

That made everyone frown. The weight of the wheat low in the ship's belly would have been critical to making the ship safe and stable.

"And," Ashe continued, "the Coast Guard checked with the harbormaster. She left the port of New Orleans loaded three deep in containers across her entire deck, not six deep, all fore of the beam, like we found her. The crew of the ship *moved* the containers after they sailed. They intentionally built a high-profile stack that would catch the most wind."

"Were they trying to sink the ship?" Nissa blurted.

Cole answered grimly. "Seems so."

"And then there's the missing crew and sabotaged engines," Bass piped up.

"And no distress calls," Cole added. "The crew definitely intended to scuttle the ship."

"Oh, they'll succeed," Ashe responded. "Once Jessamine cranks up another ten feet of seas and another twenty knots of wind, that huge wall of containers is going to catch a gust and take the *Anna Belle* right over."

"Assuming she doesn't drift crossways of a couple big waves and break her beam first," Bass commented. "Either way, that ship's going down in the next few hours if she's not already sunk."

"But *why*?" Cole asked.

Nissa had an idea why. The others speculated, but discarded every idea they came up with. When they all fell silent, she spoke up reluctantly, "What if this was all an elaborate scheme to fake Markus Petrov's death?"

The team turned as one to stare at her. "It's a hell of an expensive ruse," Cole replied. "Twenty million dollars plus or minus for the ship, several million dollars' worth of wheat, and who knows what other cargo in the containers. Then there's the cost of paying off the crew, and of making them all disappear. Something like a fifty-million-dollar escape route? That seems pretty improbable."

"But that's the point," Nissa replied. "Markus Petrov is obsessive about secrecy. And goodness knows, he has fifty million bucks lying around to burn. The man has been a mobster for thirty years. My CIA colleague who got inside his outfit said the man was clearing a million dollars a week."

Bass swore, then drawled, "I'm in the wrong business."

"I thought all you cops are on the take," Ashe teased the Cajun. Apparently, Bass had been called off military reserve status and reactivated as a SEAL recently. When he wasn't on active duty, he was a civilian police officer.

"New Orleans Police Department has cleaned up its act in the past couple of decades, thank you very much," Bass retorted.

"Indeed. They kicked you out, didn't they?" Cole quipped.

The guys laughed, apparently oblivious of the monster storm spinning up around them. She envied them their ability to find humor in this nightmare.

Cole looked over at her in her exposure pouch. "The only problem with your theory that Petrov engineered the sinking of the *Anna Belle* is that no one knew he was aboard her. We were lucky to get a tip from one of Petrov's guys we captured in the gun battle last week."

"Or maybe that tidbit was intentionally leaked to us so we would believe he died when the *Anna Belle* turns up missing or is found sunk."

"The ship will be tough to find," Ashe offered. "We're in close to eight thousand feet of water right now."

Aww, jeez. She did *not* need to know that.

"What's the next move Petrov will make, Nissa?" Cole asked.

All of a sudden, everyone was staring expectantly at her.

"I have no idea. I was only sent out here with you to make the ID on Petrov."

She was one of the few people on earth who'd seen even a photograph of Markus Petrov, and it had been taken twenty years ago. The tech gang at Langley had run an aging simulator on the image, though, so she had a rough idea of what he would look like now. More important, she knew every detail of his life that the CIA had uncovered and could ask the right questions—and furthermore know if she was getting the right answers—to make the identification. And, of course, she was a trained psychological operations officer. She could probably manipulate the guy into talking when most other people could not.

Cole gave up his position at the tiller to Ashe and flopped down beside her, breathing hard. It took a minute or so for his respiration to return to normal, but then he said to her, "My orders are to capture Markus Petrov with extreme prejudice." Meaning he had authorization to do whatever it took to catch the guy, no holds barred. He continued, "I'm going to need you to stay with my team until we catch up with him."

But this was supposed to be a quick out-and-back mission for her. Fly to New Orleans. Make the ID. Fly back to Langley, Virginia, and resume her regularly scheduled life. She didn't *do* field operations. At least, not this kind. As it was, the trip into the Gulf of Mexico to catch Petrov had been well beyond the scope of her orders. She definitely didn't run around with Navy SEALs trying to get herself killed.

"I'm an analyst, not a field operative!" she protested. She didn't even like being outdoors, let alone playing soldier.

"You're a field operator now. Welcome to the big leagues, kid."

Chapter 2

Even Cole had to admit he was glad to see land as the coast of Louisiana came into sight, a low black line on the horizon. The hurricane was stalled offshore at the moment, and the last hour of motoring north had taken them out of the heart of the storm. For now. As long as Jessamine parked over the warm, shallow waters of the northern Gulf of Mexico, she would only grow in strength.

The breathtakingly huge swells had diminished to merely god-awful seas, and the first faint light of dawn was barely visible in the east.

What a hell of a night. Cole had never seen a ship so close to capsizing before. Climbing aboard the *Anna Belle* had wigged him out worse than he would ever admit. Every time she'd rolled onto her side, he'd been sure that was the one where she would keep on going and drag them all down to a watery death.

"So. Anyone got reward points at a decent resort along the coast we can cash in?" Bass asked drolly as they approached a line of cypress trees and grassy wetlands.

The guy was the team's clown and great for morale. Cole had missed working with the Cajun. But then Cole had missed working in the field, period. This was his first op back as a team commander in four long years.

It figured that the mission had not gone to plan. At all. The target wasn't where he was supposed to be. Cole had had to put his team in extreme peril to search the *Anna Belle*, the civilian with them had completely panicked and their egress plan had been shot to hell by the sabotage to the ship.

They'd caught a minor break when the hurricane stalled offshore, but he didn't have any illusions that riding out a major hurricane in whatever improvised shelter they could find was going to be anything but ridiculously hazardous. They were far from clear of life-threatening danger. It was Cole's job to adapt to whatever came their way, but he had to wonder if he was too rusty to be out here in the field anymore. Should he have anticipated these contingencies and planned better for them?

Right now, he had to get them as far inland and on as high ground as possible before Jessamine came calling. He put Bass at the prow to guide the Rigid Inflatable Boat ashore. Bastien "Bass" LeBlanc was native to this area and more familiar with these coastal waters than anyone else on the team.

To his surprise, Bass called back to Ashe to turn the RIB and parallel the coast. "What are you looking for?" Cole asked.

"Inlet. The storm surge is already flooding the edges of the bayou. If we motor ashore now, we'll hit a submerged cypress stump and rip the bottom out of the boat."

Nissa piped up. "What will an inlet look like? Can we help you spot one?"

"Two roughly parallel rows of trees leading inland," Bass answered absently, staring shoreward through a big pair of binoculars.

"Weather report, Ashe?" Cole asked over the radios.

"Cat 3 and growing. Expected to start moving due north in the next few hours. Winds should hit before noon, and the eye wall should make landfall by evening."

Damn. They could not catch a break on this mission! He checked the fuel gauges, which were perilously low, flirting with the red empty line.

"Is that an inlet?" Nissa called, pointing from inside her survival bag.

Cole squinted through a rain squall that had just sprung up, obscuring his vision. "What do you think, Bass? We're getting way low on fuel and we need to make land before we become a cork out here."

"Let's give it a try, sir."

The RIB slowed to a crawl, and they all kept their gazes on the water before them, looking for submerged hazards. The storm surge was already a good ten feet above normal and all sorts of stumps and small trees that would normally be above water were now covered—treacherous traps waiting to destroy their vessel.

Dawn arrived in a thin strip of color beneath the ominous overhang of clouds forming one of the storm bands of the hurricane. The rain abated just long enough for them to see the line of sky streaked with every hue from palest pink to fiery red. The CIA asset, Nissa, turned to stare at the sunrise as the brilliant ball of liquid red crept over the edge of the gulf and then nearly as quickly disappeared behind the roiling cloud line.

"Wow," she breathed.

One corner of Cole's mouth turned down cynically at her innocence. It had been a long time since a sunrise had been enough to cause him wonder. Almost twenty years in the SEALs in one capacity or another had made him a hard man who didn't look for beauty in the world anymore.

"We've got an inlet!" Bass called. "Come right five degrees."

In another minute, two rows of cypress trees rose on either side of them. They looked more like truncated bushes in the early morning light, much of their height below the floodwaters.

They proceeded cautiously up the inlet for perhaps twenty minutes, buffeted by the choppy water almost worse than when they'd bobbed on the open ocean's big swells. Cole went back to spell Ashe, who shook out his noodled arms as he moved up front to pull stump watch.

The right engine sputtered then caught again. Its fuel needle lay on the peg to the far left side of the gauge and didn't budge. At least the left needle was still bouncing off the peg with each wave.

"Find us a spot to land, Bastien. This is about as far inland as the RIB's going to take us."

"Roger that, Frosty." Bass scanned the lines of trees

on either side of the canal they were following. In about a minute he hooted in excitement and yelled, "Bring her hard right!"

Cole complied, following Bass's instructions for the next minute or so, aiming for a particularly tall cypress looming over the edge of the flooded canal. They made it past the big tree when the right motor cut out entirely and the left engine started to sputter.

"Just a few more yards," Bass called.

That was probably about all they had before they turned into drifters.

"Cut the motor!" Bass called.

Cole complied with alacrity, just before the bottom of the boat scraped hard on something that sounded like gravel. A rain squall was rolling in on them, and Cole barely saw Bass and Ashe jump out of the boat into what turned out to be knee-deep water. They'd run aground.

Ashe fought to steady the RIB as a huge wind gust tried to shove it sideways off the spit of land, while Bass ran ahead with a line and tied off the prow to a tree.

Cole moved over to Nissa in her waterproof bag. "We've got to get you out of that thing so you can walk."

She was already flailing around inside the sack to no avail. He realized with a start that she was panicking. Poor girl had been through a lot in the past fifteen hours.

"Easy, Nissa," he murmured. "Sit still so I can get you out."

His words had no effect on her. And now that he was within arm's length of her, he realized her eyes were glazed over and unseeing. She was lost in a full-blown panic attack. Only one fix for that. He wrapped her up in a bear hug, survival bag and all. She thrashed wildly in his arms, but her small frame was no match for his iron strength. He hung on grimly and let the panic attack run its course…and tried hard not to notice how great her body felt writhing against his. He was a total jerk for even registering it, given how panicked she was. He did his best to project calm and comfort to her through his silent touch.

As quickly as she'd freaked out, she went still in his arms.

"You done?" he asked.

"Get me out of this thing," she mumbled in chagrin. "I can't stand being confined."

"Yeah, I noticed," he replied drily. Using the tip of his Ka-Bar knife, he pried loose the water-soaked knot at her neck. Finally, the cord gave way and the top of the survival bag popped open. Nissa shoved it down her body and jumped clear of the thing, giving it a dirty look. She gave the piled bag a swift kick with her combat boot for good measure.

"It's dead. You killed it," Cole commented.

"Good riddance," she declared.

"It would have saved your life if we'd gone down at sea."

A shudder passed over her. "I'd have gone crazy if I had ended up floating around in that thing."

He shrugged. "You would have done what you had to in order to survive. It would have sucked, but you'd have pulled through." In his experience most people were a lot stronger than they realized. It was just that most people were never put into actual life-and-death situations.

"I dunno. I have pretty bad claustrophobia," she disagreed.

"Then last night sucked worse for you than I realized."

She threw him a bleary glare that said he didn't know the half of it. His respect for her notched up a bit more. She had been brave as hell to go out with his team into the storm and then to crawl around the *Anna Belle* in the dark with the big ship trying hard to capsize.

"C'mon. Let's get you onto dry land," he said, offering her a hand to steady her as she crawled forward around the saddle seats to the prow.

"It may be land but it won't be dry," she snapped.

She'd earned the right to be a little testy after the past night. He helped her over the edge of the boat into Bass's arms. The big Cajun set her down into the water and helped her wade ashore to join Ashe, who was depositing a bag of gear on the soggy ground.

Cole passed the remaining gear bags out of the RIB and Bass retied the boat using a loose hurricane tie that would allow it to stay afloat as the storm surge rose.

"Now what?" Nissa asked Cole as he joined the others.

"Now we find shelter."

"Any chance we can find a phone for me to report in to my boss?"

"Don't hold your breath on that. Where there's no electricity, there's usually no phone service."

"Can't the Coast Guard or whomever you guys have

been talking to relay messages to my people?" she asked.

He shrugged. "Your call. Personally, I wouldn't be broadcasting that Markus Petrov got away on an open frequency. No telling who's listening in. The way you talk about him, I gather Petrov has spies and informants all over the place."

"Good point. I'll need a secure phone line to make a full report."

"You may have to wait awhile for one of those. Right now, the priority is shelter from the storm."

"Isn't the Coast Guard going to come pick us up?"

He snorted. "Not with that monster storm bearing down on us. Besides, they'll have their hands full with rescues already. We're on our own to ride this thing out."

Nissa was already pretty pale, but he thought she went a shade or two whiter with that revelation. He said bracingly, "It's just a storm. At least no one's shooting at us. We'll be fine."

"Promise?" she asked in a wobbly voice.

"Yeah. Sure." It was a lie, but he needed the civilian female not to freak out. If they didn't find solid shelter and *soon*, they were in serious trouble.

"And then we can get some sleep, yes?" she asked hopefully.

"All the sleep you want."

He and his guys could go five days without much more than a nap now and then. But he realized that most normal mortals were not aware that they, too, could match the feat. It was all about motivation. Find the right one, and anyone, man or woman, would die rather than give in to mere exhaustion.

Cole continued, "Once the worst of the storm passes, we'll make our way back to New Orleans and figure out how we're going to acquire our target and take him into custody."

"I have some ideas—"

"Later," he said, cutting her off. "The core of the storm will be here in a few hours, and we need to be under cover before then. How do you feel about running?"

Nissa stared up at him, her blue eyes even bigger and wider than usual. She was a looker, all right. The sea-land suit the Navy had lent her clung to her slender legs and girly curves, showing off a slight body any Hollywood starlet would be proud to have. Her blond hair was French-braided back from her face, but it only accentuated her elfin features.

"As a rule, I'm not fond of running as a form of exercise."

"That's too bad," Cole replied.

"I don't have any choice about the running thing, do I?" Nissa asked mournfully.

"Nope. Let's move out." He grabbed the extra pack of gear meant for her and shouldered it on top of his own pack. It meant he was carrying close to sixty pounds of gear, but no way could Nissa keep up with his team if she were carrying any weight at all. As it was, he suspected she was going to slow them down badly.

It turned out that Nissa could go for about fifteen minutes at a time at a steady, but slow, jog if she got a three- or four-minute break to catch her breath in between. A SEAL team was only as fast as its slowest member, and right now, that was she. But as egress-ing with a totally untrained civilian went, she wasn't doing half bad. He'd had missions where they'd had to carry out the principal.

The trek was miserable. What solid ground they could find was saturated and spongy, giving way without warning beneath their feet, sinking them knee-deep in black muck and pitching them on their faces. Everybody took at least a few such spills.

Even when they remained upright, the going wasn't great. They caught blowing tree limbs in the face, thorny brambles clutched at their bodies and backpacks, and bouts of driving rain pecked at them like angry crows. The only good news was that the gusty wind was mostly at their backs.

They jogged and rested, jogged and rested, for almost two hours. How Bastien was finding his way through the swampy bayou country, Cole had no idea. The rain was whipping around them now on fifty-mile-per-hour gusts, and the brief hint of dawn had faded into twilight gloom as the hurricane roared ashore. They had to find high ground and some sort of shelter before long, or they were going to be in deadly peril.

They jogged maybe another ten minutes before Bass veered suddenly to his right. They had to hack their way through a veritable wall of kudzu vines and brambles, but when they popped out the far side, Cole spotted what had made Bastien change course. A house. Or more accurately, a dilapidated-looking shack.

The one-story dwelling was raised on stilts that, as they approached the structure, turned out to be two dozen massive cypress pilings. The exterior badly needed a coat of paint, and rust from the metal roof stained the gray wood siding orange. But as they climbed the stairs to the wraparound porch, the building looked sturdier than his first impression. They might just survive the storm, yet.

Bass pounded on the front door loudly and long enough for them to be sure no one was inside. Ashe picked the door lock and dead bolt with quick efficiency, and in under a minute, they had all piled inside the cabin.

The dwelling was as rough inside as out with a log-framed couch sagging in front of a small wood-burning stove. What looked like handmade chairs and a crude table were tucked in one corner of the main room. A huge alligator skull hung on the wall above the stove. Cole would have hated to see the live beast it had come from. That gator had to have been twenty feet long or better.

A dilapidated stove and refrigerator flanked a rust-stained sink, and a few cabinets rounded out the kitchen corner.

Ashe called from down the short hall to their right, "All clear. One bedroom, one bathroom."

"How hurricane-proof is this place?" Cole asked Bass.

"Windows could use some plywood or at least some boards over them. There's no time to check out the roof. We'll just have to hope it's nailed down tight. The pilings look sturdy and they'll take a fifteen-foot storm surge easy."

"Is Jessamine forecast to surge that high?" Cole asked no one in particular.

Ashe, just returning to the main room, replied, "That's right about what the forecast calls for. Fourteen to seventeen feet."

Cole glanced back at Bass, who said grimly, "Lemme go out and take an exact measurement from the canal behind this place to the bottom of the porch."

The door opened, and wind and rain howled inside until Bass wrestled the door shut once more. Meanwhile, Ashe moved over to the kitchen cabinets to poke around. "There's some canned food in here. Should hold us for a few days."

Nissa surprised Cole by speaking up. "Drinking water's going to be the problem. The storm surge will bring in filthy, polluted salt water that no amount of purification will make drinkable."

She had a point. Give the intelligence analyst credit for common sense on top of her book smarts.

She asked, "Is there a tub in the bathroom, Ashe?"

"Yes. A small one."

"Let's see if there's running water," she suggested. "If so, we need to sterilize the tub and fill it while we still can."

Cole set Ashe to scrubbing the tub with a jug of bleach they found under the kitchen sink, while he went outside to check for a water well and possibly a pump for it.

He met Bass coming up the steps. "Seventeen feet, sir. That's what this place can take before the house floods. Even with a lower surge than that, we may see wave action pushing some water inside."

"Good to know. Any sign of a well and a water pump down there?"

"There's a well. But the electricity's already out. Pump won't work."

"Generator?" Cole asked.

"Maybe. Whoever owns this place has it decently

stocked. There's a shed, and that's where I'd look for a generator. It's locked, but we can break in and have a look around."

They ended up using an axe they found sitting on a ledge over the shed door to break the rusty hasp and get inside. They didn't find a generator, but they did spot a small lawn mower whose gasoline motor Bass thought he could jerry-rig to run the water pump. And they found a toolbox. Armed with a hammer and pocket full of nails, Cole scrounged under the house for pieces of scrap lumber that he hauled up to the porch and nailed across the windows. They weren't as good as sheets of thick plywood, but they were better than nothing. The boards would break the worst of the wind pummeling the glass and should catch large pieces of flying debris.

He and Bass stumbled inside an hour later, wet, cold and exhausted. Construction in hurricane-force winds turned out to be strenuous stuff.

Ashe and Nissa had been busy inside, as well. They'd hauled in a big pile of firewood from the porch and stacked it beside the wood-burning stove, in which they had started a fire. Baked beans were heating in a pot atop it, and the sound of running water came from the bathroom, where Ashe poked his head out to announce that they should have enough water for several days. He'd also filled a dozen empty moonshine jugs he'd found with water for flushing the toilet.

As they pulled chairs around the wood-burning stove to warm and dry themselves, Nissa asked in a small voice, "Are we going to be safe here?"

She looked fearfully at Cole for an answer, and he replied, "This old place is sturdier than it looks. Jessamine won't be its first hurricane." He forced himself to give Nissa a smile in hopes that it would encourage her. "We'll be fine. And even if something unexpected does happen, we're SEALs. We take problems as they come and deal with them."

They'd battened down the hatches in the nick of time, for within the next half hour, the winds outside rose from a roar to a howl and then to an ominous scream. The entire structure shook alarmingly, but it held.

For now.

Chapter 3

Nissa crawled into the only bed in the cabin at the unanimous insistence of the guys. They assured her they were perfectly comfortable sleeping on the floor. Cole set up a watch rotation for himself and his men, and then he urged her to get some sleep before the storm got bad.

This wasn't bad? The walls shivered every time a big gust hit, and she shivered right along with the tiny cabin. The glass in the windows rattled, and she flinched every time something hit the boards nailed over them, sure that this was the time the window was going to shatter and let in the full fury of the storm.

What had she gotten herself into, volunteering for this insane mission? It wasn't supposed to be like this at all! She was supposed to hang out with some super hot Navy SEALS and catch a notorious bad guy, thereby advancing her career, which was rapidly threatening to die of boredom in a beige cubicle. Although, she had gotten the super hot SEAL part of the deal. All of the men with her were extremely easy on the eye. But the one she couldn't look away from was their leader.

Cole Perriman was totally hunkalicious. She'd tried really hard not to fantasize about crawling all over that spectacular physique and keep her mind on business, but it had been rough listening to the inbriefing he'd given her and his two guys. She kept getting distracted by how big and rugged he was, but how he had movie-star looks, too. He was a perfect blend of raw masculinity and sheer beauty.

Her friends back at Langley wouldn't believe she got to work with him. She vowed before she headed back to Virginia to get a few pictures of him to show to the girls around the watercooler…and maybe to fantasize over when she returned to her bland, dull, colorless life.

The wind got so loud it hurt her ears, and it was relentless, moaning and roaring like nothing she'd ever heard before. She finally resorted to pulling the covers up over her head in a futile effort to block out the noise. And maybe she was also hiding like she had as a little girl, when monsters had come calling in the dark of her bedroom at night. She always had been a giant thunder-chicken.

As exhaustion overtook her body, her thoughts drifted, replaying the horror of the past twelve hours: sailing into the teeth of a hurricane, the nightmare climb aboard the *Anna Belle*, the frantic search for shelter as Jessamine roared ashore. She'd been so certain she was going to die a watery death, drowned at best and bashed to pieces by the stormy sea at worst.

When she finally fell asleep, it was no surprise she dreamed of water. Except in her dream, the ocean was not black and angry…

The sea was brilliant turquoise, light and warm and lazy, and she swam below the surface easily, breathing water. She swayed gently as surf rolled past overhead, untouched by the cheerfully churning surface of the sea.

Her hair drifted in pale wisps around her, and she was startled to realize she was naked. The sea caressed her body lovingly, and she felt safe. At home down here.

She became aware of a large shape moving toward her, knifing forward with strong strokes of humanoid arms. She started to backpedal in alarm, but as the man drew near, she recognized his beautiful, chiseled face and stilled. Cole.

He stopped before her, righting himself until he floated vertical, as naked as she in this underwater dream world. He smiled at her and the temperature of the water around her rocketed up. She looked down and was captivated by his body, more spectacular than she'd imagined in her waking state. His skin was smooth and supple, the musculature rippling beneath it nothing short of spectacular. The man was sculpted like a god. Poseidon would be the correct one, she supposed, given that they were underwater.

His long legs kicked lazily, the deeply-cut muscles of his thighs powerful even underwater. And those abs. Washboard stomachs like that should not be legal. They were certified lethal weapons. Fascinated, she stared at his torso, her underwater breathing coming fast and shallow as her gaze followed the V-line of his obliques downward to the dark curls and his manly parts, which were impressive even at rest.

If possible, her breathing accelerated even more, sounding loud inside her head. The current nudged her toward underwater deity Cole and she let it carry her close enough to feel the heat of him radiating to touch her skin. Everywhere his warmth caressed her, she burned for him.

His silvery blue gaze captured hers, igniting with desire as he stared at her. Suddenly, the water around them was boiling hot, and he willed her even closer to him. Their feet and knees tangled together as they treaded water, only inches separating them now. Each accidental bump sent her pulse a notch higher until her heartbeat pounded like a drum in her ears.

Her belly tied in knots by the intensity of his stare, she looked away, her gaze drifting to his mile-wide shoulders and the bulging wreaths of muscle tapering to powerful arms. His right hand moved forward slowly toward her free-floating breast, giving her plenty of time to splash away from it. But she only watched with breathless anticipation as his big, tanned hand approached her pale flesh, visibly quivering with desire. She needed him to touch her like she needed to draw her next watery breath.

His fingers were strong, his palms heavily calloused. A warrior's hands. Capable hands. Hands that knew how to kill and—oh, my—hands that knew how to give pleasure. His thumb rubbed across her taut nipple as he cupped her weightless breast, kneading it gently. Her back arched as she strained toward him, desperate for more of his drugging touch. Every inch of her body ached to be his. To be taken by him. Claimed and possessed by him.

He must have read her thoughts for, all of a sudden, he surged against her, his legs entwining with hers, his erection pressing into her belly as hot and hard as a branding iron. His left arm captured her waist, his other hand still making magic on her breast.

Her left hand traced the lean indent of his waist, and slid around to his back, tracing the deep ridge of muscle running along his spine. Down, down, she followed the path of it until her palm filled with the stone-hard bulge of his behind.

Hers. He was all hers, to hold, to touch, to take. Her right leg snaked up around his hips, and using her right foot and left hand, she urged the hot steel pressing into her belly lower, closer to her core. Yes. Right...there...

His mouth closed upon hers, and the kiss was as hot and carnal as the rest of him, as commanding and untamed as a proper sea god should be. Her entire body molded to his and she gave all of herself to him, opening her mouth and feminine core to receive him.

She projected the thought into his mind, "Take me. Take me now—"

"Holy crap, Nissa. Wake up." The voice was distant and desperate, barely touching her dream, hardly scratching the surface of her raging desire for her underwater god.

Just like that, her turquoise paradise was replaced by the cold blackness of an ocean at night, thick and suffocating. She thrashed in the darkness, weighed down by something confining and heavy.

Must be that damned survival bag. She'd fallen overboard and gotten separated from the others and was going to die out here in the vast abyss of the ocean, cold, scared and alone—

"Wake up. For the love of God," someone ground out. The man sounded like he was in pain.

Wait. She wasn't in the ocean. She wasn't wet at all, in fact. Groggily, she climbed a little closer toward consciousness.

Something powerful grabbed her in a viselike grip.

No! They said a shark wouldn't attack through the bag! But she was going to die torn in two by one. She fought then, kicking as best she could through the heavy material.

A spate of swearing erupted in her ear, low and irritated. Gods shouldn't take themselves in vain, should they? Confused, she registered that no saw-sharp teeth penetrated her flesh. Not a shark, then.

The grip turned into mostly a heavy weight immobilizing her, still suffocating her, though. Death by drowning or death by asphyxiation? What a choice. Something primitive within her refused to give up or give in, and she flailed her arms and legs, stubbornly fighting not to be shark bait without at least giving the damned fish a bloody nose before it ate her.

"Oww! Jeez, that's some right hook you've got," the male voice complained.

Had they found her? Had the SEAL team and its smoking-hot leader, the same team she'd insanely agreed to help, come back for her, after all? She started to shout for help, but bright light broke over her, and her scream went unuttered. She squinted up, blinded by the piercing light shining directly in her eyes from a range of about twelve inches.

She shoved at the light, trying to get it out of her

eyes, and her hand encountered cold metal and very warm, very human flesh and bone.

Wait. Was this real? Was she actually awake?

"You can stop trying to kill me, already."

She recognized the voice. Cole. In the flesh.

"Huh? Where am I? Am I alive?"

"Yes, you're alive. And you will stay that way if you'll quit trying to bludgeon me."

Talk about disoriented. She looked around and made out a tiny bedroom in some sort of rough shack.

The cabin on stilts. The hurricane. The *Anna Belle*. That god-awful run through the bayou to find shelter. It all came back to her in a rush. The danger, the terror, the certainty that she was going to die. No wonder she was breathing hard already.

"Are we safe from the storm?" she rasped, her voice hoarse as if she'd been shouting forever. Oh, wait. She had been. To be heard over the storm, they'd pretty much had to shout all of last night.

"So far, so good," Cole murmured cautiously.

"What time is it?"

"A little after eight o'clock."

"At night?"

Behind his flashlight's glare, she thought she caught a hint of a grin. "Yes. At night. You've been asleep about seven hours."

"Wow. I don't feel as if I got that much sleep."

"You did get more of a workout in the past day than I imagine you're accustomed to."

Now there was an understatement. She checked in on her body and was not surprised to feel ominously sore muscles and pain setting in. She was shocked, however, to register that Cole Perriman was sprawled on top of her, and that her right leg was wrapped around his hips and her left hand was clutching his, umm, rather delectable tush.

She let go of his behind with alacrity, but then had the problem of where to put her hand. She ended up settling for resting her hand lightly on his waist, which was every bit as hard and lean through his close-fitting turtleneck as she'd dreamed it. Her pulse lurched alarmingly. She was *in bed* with the hot SEAL!

Details of her lurid dream flooded into her mind, and she inhaled sharply. The reality of this man's big, muscular, rock-hard body mashing hers deeply into the worn mattress was all too close to her dream for comfort.

Cole stared down at Nissa, and unfortunately, her eyes were adjusting enough to the low-light conditions to stare back at him.

Oh, no. Awareness was every bit as intense in his gaze as it no doubt was in hers. The crackling attraction from her dream wasn't a dream anymore. He was right here, real and hot and alive, his thighs tangled with hers, his hard erection pressing against the yielding softness of her belly, his massive arms forming a cage around her upper body.

He moved restlessly against her and her breath hitched. So. This was lust, huh? Everything she'd experienced in her inexperienced life to date was a pale shadow in comparison to this heat and desire raging through her. She wanted this man in every way she could have him, preferably starting with the naked, hot and sweaty ways.

He stared down at her for a moment more, reciprocal

desire lighting his eyes from within until they blazed like stars above her.

With a curse, he rolled off her abruptly. But given the narrowness of the bed, his arm was still plastered against hers from shoulder to wrist. "I'm sorry," he muttered.

"For what? It takes two to tango," she replied practically.

He laughed, but the sound was more about pain than humor. Of more interest to her was the fact that he didn't answer the question. Didn't want to put his attraction to her into words, huh? A ribbon of hurt wound its way through her heart, leaching away the intense pleasure of her dream, stealing her confidence, reminding her mercilessly that she was a mousy desk jockey who worked in a cubicle jungle, not a sexy, adventurous temptress who could capture and hold on to a man like Cole Perriman.

"I'm cold," she mumbled.

"Yeah, this place was light on blankets. There's only the one quilt on this bed. Can't fault the owner, though. He had everything else we needed. Here. Let me warm you up." He rolled against her, his legs tangled with hers, belly to belly, groin to—ohmigosh—groin.

"What are you doing?" she squeaked.

"Hypothermia care 101. Body-to-body contact is the fastest and safest way to bring a person's body temperature up to a safe level."

"I said I was cold, not freezing to death."

"One leads to the other," he murmured disconcertingly close to her ear. His breath was warm on her earlobe and a shiver passed through her entire body. And it was emphatically not a shiver of cold.

His arm fell across her stomach and curled up her side, his hand tucked under her armpit mere inches from her breast. She about leaped out of bed in her shock. If not for the easy strength of his arm pinning her down, she might actually have bolted. But as it was, she merely lurched hard enough against his forearm to register that she wasn't going anywhere if he didn't want her to.

His leg slid across hers, his thigh resting intimately across both of hers. Under the wet suit the Navy had given her to wear yesterday, they'd also given her a skimpy pair of stretchy running trunks and an equally skimpy tank top. Those were all she was wearing now. And apparently, he was wearing pretty much the same thing.

She registered the general muscularity and hairiness of his leg against her smoothly waxed legs, and something shifted in her gut, a sharp awareness of Cole Perriman not as her mission commander and temporary boss, but as a Man. Capital *M*. With a side of hubba-hubba thrown in.

Other details registered. The hardness of his stomach against her right arm, trapped at her side. The width of his shoulders towering over her as he lay on his side facing her. The sheer mass of the man. He was all muscle. There was nothing soft about him. No flab to ease the hard contours of his muscles, not even a thin layer of fat beneath his skin to cushion the bulging veins and corded sinews in his arms or legs.

And good grief, he was as hot as a furnace. She was going to break out in a full-blown sweat if he stayed like this for much longer.

He muttered, "How does your hair smell good? You

just spent all night swimming around in the ocean and wading through a swamp. You should smell like seawater."

Bemused, she replied, "I got hot during our minimarathon to run here. I pushed back my hood and the rain rinsed out my hair. And, while you guys were getting the well's pump running, I used the first water that came out of the pipes to take a quick sponge bath. Salt's bad for your skin. You shouldn't leave it sitting on your flesh for any longer than necessary."

"Thanks for the beauty tip."

"I'm serious. It can cause rashes and even burns."

"I know. It's not an uncommon form of torture to rub salt into a person's skin."

Eew. She might be a collector of seemingly useless trivia as part of her work as an intelligence analyst, but torture was not one of her fields of expertise.

"Warming up?" Cole murmured against her temple.

"Umm, yes. I'm toasty warm now." He didn't move, so she added, "Thanks for sharing some of your heat with me."

It was a blatant invitation to leave her bed, but he didn't accept it. Instead he remained spooned around her.

His hand, the one thrown across her body, slid up her arm toward her shoulder, dragging the quilt higher to tuck it in around her neck. At least his hand hadn't headed toward her chest…which was throbbing disconcertingly at the moment.

She would love to pull her right arm out from between them, but she was vividly aware of how close her hand was resting to parts of his anatomy that could easily be encouraged to throb, also.

Cole didn't move, and goodness knew, she wasn't about to move. But they might as well have been crawling all over each other the way the electricity built between them. She was excruciatingly aware of every inch of his body against hers, and it didn't help that she could picture his body encased in that insanely sexy sea-land suit of his.

She'd tried really hard yesterday to keep her mind solidly on business, but there'd been no missing the fact that he'd looked like a statue of a Greek god wearing a wet suit.

A particularly violent gust of wind slammed into the wall beside her, and even the light fixture overhead rattled. Terrified, she rolled against Cole and buried her face against his chest.

His arms swept around her, drawing her closer, creating a living bulwark of protection around her. "I've got you. Hang on to me," he muttered.

The shaking around them diminished, but her insides still quaked like mad. "You must think I'm the biggest scaredy cat you've ever met."

She felt the smile against her scalp. "I've met worse."

"How much longer is this storm going to last?" she asked.

"The rest of the night, I should think."

She groaned into his pectoral, which flexed in an impressive display of bulging muscle.

"Hungry?" he asked her.

"No. You?"

"I ate a little while ago."

They lay together in silence for a moment, listening to the storm. Then he said quietly, "Try to get some sleep."

She almost confessed that she didn't want to go back to sleep because she was afraid of a repeat of her dream from before, but she bit it back.

"Do you need me to stay with you?"

"I'm a CIA analyst on a mission with a Navy SEAL team. I can survive my nightmares."

He chuckled. "You don't have to prove how tough you are to me."

Another gust struck the cabin and she stared worriedly at the rafters overhead. "Is the roof going to stay on?"

"I think it is. This place may look like a dump, but it's solid."

"We're going to have to find out who owns it and send a thank-you note."

Cole grunted as if thank-you notes weren't part of his job description. He shifted his weight, turning fully onto his back, and Nissa found herself rolling toward him as the mattress sagged beneath his greater weight. She braced herself to stop the roll and froze in dismay as she realized she'd planted her hand on his stomach. Ridges of carved marble formed beneath her palm before she managed to jerk it away from him. Good grief. Touching him was like sticking her hand into a volcano.

Sharp awareness of how much bigger than she he was, in every dimension, made lust shoot through her nether regions, hot and liquid, and nearly as disorienting as her dream.

Had they actually kissed, or had that been part of her dream, too? Nissa could swear she still felt him on her mouth, still tasted him on her tongue. And her face around her mouth definitely felt razor burned. Or maybe that was just chapped skin from the wind and salt water. Confused, she stared at the silhouette of his lips barely visible beside her.

He clicked his flashlight on and shined it up at the underside of the roof, exposed beyond the rafters. Methodically, he ran the light over every inch of the ceiling.

"How does it look?" she asked.

He turned toward her, turning the flashlight with him, abruptly blinding her in its brilliant LED beam. "So far, so good."

"Could you get that light out of my eyes, please?" She threw her hand up to shield her face.

It clicked off and total blackness descended over them, making her lurch in alarm. Even as a kid, she'd been scared of the dark. She'd mostly grown out of it as an adult. Mostly.

"Easy, Nissa. I've got you." He rolled toward her, and she was swept up against his delicious body, his arms firm and protective around her.

Oh. My. God. He felt every bit as amazing in real life as he did in her dream.

Out of the darkness, Cole murmured against Nissa's temple, "I promise I'll keep you safe. No harm will come to you on my watch. You don't have to be afraid." His low voice was raw silk, caressing her skin and sending cascades of shivers down her spine.

They lay like that for several minutes, neither one moving, Nissa barely daring to breathe. The sexual tension between them stretched tighter and tighter until she thought it had to snap. Terrified of what that would mean, she cast about in her mind for something to say. Something to distract both of them from this endless, insane moment of raging mutual lust.

"I had the strangest dream," she blurted.

"How strange?"

"You and I were swimming underwater. And we could breathe the water. You were some sort of sea-god. Poseidon, maybe."

"I like this dream. And I do have a trident. Although mine is only on my SEAL pin and not real."

He'd been all real in the dream, that was for sure. Just remembering the way she'd burned for him made her forehead break into a sweat now.

"Tell me more about this dream."

Hah. As if she would confess in a million years about them being naked and crawling all over each other.

"That's all there was. We were underwater, but we weren't drowning. The water was clear and warm and bright turquoise. It looked as if we were near a tropical shore, not the Gulf of Mexico in the middle of a hurricane."

"Good choice. Yesterday, those were the roughest seas I've ever seen."

"So I'm not crazy to have been scared out of my mind?"

"Not at all. That was a daunting ride, and climbing aboard the *Anna Belle* with her so close to capsizing would have scared the bravest soul."

"Were you afraid?"

His features twitched into a frown. "We're trained during a mission to set feelings like fear aside. They get in the way of the work. But I did register that it was a dangerous situation in which we all could easily have died."

She turned his words over in her mind, applying

the filters her years as a CIA analyst had honed to a fine edge. It was probably as close as she would ever come to hearing a SEAL admit to being scared. And she had heard that SEALs were taught techniques for fear and pain control.

Cole murmured, startling her out of her analysis, "There had to be more to your dream."

"How do you know? It was my dream."

His low voice was soft like suede caressing her skin. "I know because you all but tore my clothes off and had your wicked way with me."

Hot shame flooded her face. He *knew*. Cole knew exactly what she'd dreamed. Every sordid, sexy detail of her unconscious fantasy. She was never going to be able to look him in the eye again. Ever. Humiliation tasted sour in the back of her mouth, and an urge roared through her to curl up in a little ball, pull the quilt over her head and never come out from under it.

Without warning he rolled off the bed and the quilt lifted off of her abruptly, letting in a rush of cold air. She squeaked, but just as suddenly, the quilt was tossed back over her. She yanked it up around her neck, not that it would shield her from what he knew about her now.

"Where are you going?" she choked out.

"Back to the main room to check the water level outside. It's my turn on the watch. I only came in here because I heard you making…sounds." He added in a rush, "I wanted to make sure you were all right. That's all."

What kind of sounds had she been making? The way his voice had hitched over the word had suspicions leaping to mind that heaped embarrassment on top of her humiliation. Horror poured over her, her own personal ice bucket over the head. Some of that smoking-hot embrace had been real? Oh, God. How much of it? "What did I...what did we..."

"Do?" Cole murmured down at her. "Enough to seriously consider doing it again someday but not so much that you need to go looking for a shotgun just yet."

She pulled the quilt up over her head then. But it didn't stop her from hearing Cole's quiet laughter as the bedroom door opened and he slipped out of the room, leaving her alone with her new best friends Shame and Self-recrimination.

Chapter 4

Cole made it out to the living room before he let go of the breath he'd been holding. Damn, that had been a near miss with total disaster. When he'd tried to wake up Nissa and she'd grabbed him, pulled him down on top of her and then all but crawled down his throat, he'd been in grave danger of succumbing to his attraction to her.

He abruptly understood the saying about a person's world tilting on its axis. He felt off-balance, physically and emotionally, but also on some deeper, more fundamental level. As if his world would never be quite the same again. Which was doubly strange given that he considered himself to be the most thoroughly grounded of men, stable, unshakable and sure of who and what he was.

But that woman…throwing herself at him like that…

the way she'd felt in his arms…the things she'd made him feel… This was uncharted territory for him.

Hell, any living, breathing man couldn't fail to notice how fantastic she'd looked in that curve-hugging wet suit. Even with the hood up, she'd still been beautiful, and not many people could claim that. It wasn't just the delicacy of her facial bones, either. It was those eyes. Huge and sapphire blue, they were impossible to look away from.

And when she'd wrapped her entire, slender body around him, drawing him into her, opening all of herself to him—

Stop it, he commanded himself. She was a job. Correction, a colleague. He would tear a new one in any of his guys who messed with her on the job. He had to hold himself to the same standard. He prowled around Bass, sprawled out on a bedroll in front of the stove, and went over to the window beside the front door to peer out a crack between the boards.

The water was coming up far too close for comfort. Hour by hour, the floodwaters had been swallowing the steps up to the raised platform. Only two steps were left. Jessamine had better pass on by soon, or they were going to be swimming in here.

He'd thought Bass's suggestion to put a bunch of long planks up in the rafters had been overkill, but now he saw the logic. If the cabin flooded, they could climb up on the makeshift perch and pick up another six feet of protection from the storm surge.

Bass had also insisted they stow the ax up there, too. Apparently, it wasn't uncommon for people to drown in their attics when they didn't have the tools to break through their roofs. Lord, he would hate to have to go out in the storm, though. The wind had howled like a banshee for most of the day.

Cole glanced at his watch. Almost time for another update from the weather service on the storm. He went to the kitchen table where Ashe had set up the field radio and put on the headphones. He powered up the unit and listened in relief as the hourly report indicated that the eye of the storm had passed just west of New Orleans and Jessamine was beginning to weaken as it moved inland. They should get heavy rain and wind through the night, but sometime tomorrow, the worst of the hurricane should spin itself out and move on.

Praise the Lord and pass the potatoes. It had been no joke to get caught out in a major storm like this. Had they not found this sturdy cabin, they would likely have died, if not from drowning or exposure, then from flying debris.

The report went on to say that the eye wall had spared the city the worst of the wind damage, but unleashed a deluge of rain upon the hapless city. The new and improved levees, post-Katrina, were holding, and the city's pumping system was dealing with the worst of the floodwater so far, but the city was without power and expected to be that way for days. Civilians and evacuees would not be allowed to return to their homes for at least another seventy-two hours.

He moved back to his post peering out the window. His flashlight beam turned the rain into a sheet of crystal particles flying past him horizontally. Everything beyond the porch was swirling, angry water. In the past hour or two, he'd started imagining that he felt the cypress pilings swaying slightly in the killer currents.

The foundation of the home only had to hold a little while longer. High tide was due in another hour, and then hopefully the water would start back down. Hopefully.

His lonely vigil gave him way too much time to think about his sexy encounter with the hot CIA analyst. He couldn't shake the feel of her lithe body beneath his, her arms wrapped round him like she never wanted to let go, her mouth moving restlessly against his as if she couldn't get enough of the taste of him.

He was by no means a monk. But he never had found a woman who was intelligent enough to hold his interest for the long term and who also was mellow enough to deal with his more autocratic tendencies. It was hard to break old habits, and he'd been a team leader for a long time. He was used to giving orders and having them followed. Even he knew that made him rotten husband material.

So over the years he'd settled for occasional friends with benefits, women he saw between missions and who wouldn't question him about when he might leave or might return. He'd closed off the part of himself that would have enjoyed a family and a home, and he had become the job.

Which was all well and good as long as he had the job. But he was coming up on twenty years of active duty service and eligibility for retirement. In the current environment of budget cuts and force restructuring, he had no reason to believe he would be allowed to serve more than twenty years. This was his last year, and he'd decided to spend it in the field with his brothers and the missions he loved so much.

Midnight came and went, and he let Bass and Ashe sleep through their shifts on watch. They were both excellent operators and fine men. Asher Konig had found the woman for him and was deliriously happy with her, and Bass loved the cars he restored as much as any woman. Neither of them seemed to feel a hole in their lives.

And neither had he until Nissa Beck wrapped herself around him and all but begged him to take her in every sexy, dirty way he could think of. All of a sudden, he was vividly aware of the sacrifices he'd made for his work over the years, the loneliness, the coldness of the life he'd chosen. Sure, he had all the camaraderie he wanted with his fellow SEALs. But they didn't comfort a guy in the dark when the nightmares came calling, and they didn't make a home.

More disturbed than he cared to admit to himself, he watched the storm pass by. It was just outside, inches away, on the other side of a thin pane of glass and a few boards, but it didn't touch him. It raged all round him, but he stayed safe inside this shell of a cabin, isolated and alone.

The rest of his life yawned before him, as lonely and isolated as this, and for once, he couldn't push his fear of it away with an admonition to himself that he had years left before the end of life as a SEAL.

Now the end was only a few months away, looming bigger and more terrifying than the hurricane outside.

It was nearly morning before Bass woke with a start, looked at his watch, and swore. "Why didn't you wake me up, boss? I missed my watch."

Cole turned to him. "I was wide-awake, so I decided to let you guys sleep."

The quiet conversation roused Ashe, which was no

surprise. SEALs were notoriously light sleepers. He asked, "How's the storm doing?"

"The worst of it has passed."

"Did it hit New Orleans?" Ashe asked quickly.

His wife, Sam, was a native and had refused to evacuate. But Ashe had convinced her to go to the naval station to ride out the storm in a hardened building close to the base hospital. Sam was seven months pregnant, and Ashe was having no part of anything bad happening to her or their baby.

"Jessamine slid west of the city. New Orleans is still taking a lot of rain and some wind damage, but the levees are holding."

"Thank God," Ashe breathed.

"She's fine," Cole replied. "Sam's tucked into SEAL Ops, and none of the guys will let anything happen to her."

Bass chimed in, "A bunch of them know how to deliver babies, too."

Ashe scowled. "Sam's under strict orders not to have this kid until I'm there to deliver it."

Cole grinned. "And did you have a conversation with your son about that? Did you explain to him that he's not supposed to come until you get home?"

"Yes, as a matter of fact. I did."

Bass and Cole both laughed and ribbed Ashe about what a pushover of a father he was going to be as dawn broke outside. They ate tuna fish straight from the can—it wasn't the most appetizing breakfast Cole'd ever had, but it was a whole lot better than some of the swill that had passed for food in his career.

Nissa wandered out of the bedroom around the same time the rain stopped, around nine in the morning. "Is it over?" she asked, her voice husky with sleep and sexy as hell.

Dear God, she was irresistible with her hair—which turned out to be wildly curly when released from its braid—tangled around her face, the formfitting leggings and turtleneck she'd been given to wear under her wet suit leaving nothing to his vivid imagination. His gaze slid up her body hungrily, taking in every detail of her figure, before lifting to her face and—oh, sh—

She was watching him examine every inch of her. Her eyes were wide and startled, but as he gazed into them they went dark and sultry.

Dammit. She was thinking about her dream and that smoking-hot embrace they'd shared. And she knew darned good and well that he was thinking about the exact same thing. He tore his gaze away from hers, but that wasn't much better. He looked down and couldn't help but notice her chest rising and falling in short little gasps. Did she have to get so turned on every time she looked at him? It was really starting to mess with his head. And he wasn't going to be able to stand up without embarrassing himself for too much longer.

In fact, he moved over to the couch and sat down just in case.

"Hungry?" Ashe asked her from behind Cole.

"Yes. What've you got?"

Ashe put on a cheesy fake French accent. "I have for zee mademoiselle a delicious tuna fish on zee half can. Or I can offer to her zee beans of later making music."

Nissa's laugh was as musical and appealing as the rest of her. "I'll take the tuna, thanks."

"Good choice," Bass commented, opening the stove door to add more wood to the fire.

Nissa settled on a chair that put her knee about six inches from Cole's. Was she *trying* to torment him? He was supposed to be the ice man. Nothing rattled him, and nothing ever shook his vaunted cool. He shifted uncomfortably, putting a few more inches between them, hoping he was subtle enough about it not to draw his guys' attention. He stared fixedly into the fire, determined not to give them any fodder to harass him or, more important, to harass Nissa.

The iron stove door clanged shut, startling him into looking up at Bass. The guy was smirking knowingly. Dammit. At least he'd had the decency to keep his amusement to himself and not embarrass Nissa. Cole made a mental note to have a private word with Ashe and Bass later to keep their remarks to themselves and be respectful of her.

"How much longer until we can get out of here?" she asked no one in particular.

He glanced at Bastien, who was the local and more accustomed to hurricanes than the rest of them.

Bass shrugged. "Depends on how long it takes the water to go down. Could be a day, could be a week. When we can move out will depend on where we plan to move to."

"Meaning what?" Cole asked.

"Are we heading back to the boat, or are we going to hike inland until we hit civilization?" Bass responded.

"What are the odds of stumbling across a marina out here where we can refuel?"

"Low," Bass admitted. "Even if we had a water navigation chart, when a big storm comes through the bayou, the scouring action of the tides and the storm surge cut new waterways and clog others till they're impassable."

"So our best bet is to abandon the RIB and make our way overland toward New Orleans?" Cole asked.

Ashe chimed in. "The boat was out of gas. If we use it, we'll have to row all the way back to town. My best guess is we're a hundred miles west of New Orleans."

"So far?" Nissa exclaimed.

Ashe nodded. "Weather reports said Jessamine passed west of New Orleans, and her eye wall was about sixty miles across. I figure we didn't catch the eye wall, because as sturdy as this place is, even it wouldn't have withstood a direct hit. So we're at least fifteen to twenty miles west of the path of the storm center. That puts us a good hundred miles or more west of New Orleans."

The others launched into a brainstorming session of possible ways to get back to New Orleans, but all Cole could think about was Nissa's knee so close to his. Who obsessed about *knees*, anyway? And yet, here he was, taking note of how slender hers was and how perfectly proportioned to her legs.

Eventually, Bass distracted him by saying, "What do you think, boss? Do we radio for help or try to make it back on our own?"

He answered, "The folks back in New Orleans are going to have their hands full with rescue operations. No matter how hard the government tries to convince everyone to leave, you know a bunch of the locals were too stubborn to go." The others nodded in commiseration. "We're able bodied, uninjured and capable of taking care of ourselves. We don't need to divert resources to help us when civilians are dying. What's out here by way of roads or towns?"

Bastien pulled out the laminated maps that had been provided for this mission, and Cole was relieved to move over to the kitchen table to pore over the maps with his men. Close proximity to Nissa was doing weird stuff to his blood pressure.

Cole pulled out their GPS locator. "We've only got the one battery that's in the GPS to work with. The spare batteries got wet somewhere along the way. Let's get a solid position fix and then figure out where the closest place is that might have vehicles and gasoline."

As Ashe had guessed, they were, indeed, about a hundred miles west of New Orleans along the Gulf Coast. But what shocked Cole was that they were nearly fifteen miles inland north of the White Lake Wetlands Conservation Area. "How did we get so far north?" he asked.

Bass answered, "Storm surge. All this coastal area, here, was underwater by the time we came ashore, and we motored right over it."

"We're only about three miles southwest of this town, Gueydan. Can we hike to it overland, or will the area between us and it be flooded?" Cole asked him.

Bass shrugged. "Only one way to find out."

Ashe looked over at Nissa, seated on the couch. "What about her? Do we leave her behind and come back for her once we've got transportation?"

Cole was stunned by the visceral negative reaction in his gut at the notion of leaving her behind. Aloud, he answered, "SEALs don't leave anyone behind, and for now, she's one of us. Besides, she's had a hell of a scare—several of them, in fact. Let's not traumatize her any further by abandoning her out here in the middle of the bayou."

Nissa flashed him a brilliant smile that all but had him striding across the room to wrap her in his arms and capture all that joyous relief for himself.

They ended up having to wait a full twenty-four hours for the floodwaters to go down and for the sodden land to reemerge. They passed the time making repairs to the cabin, inside and out, by way of thanks to the owner for the shelter. Bright and early the next morning, however, they packed their gear and headed out.

Cole was plenty glad to get out of the small confines of the cabin. Its four walls hadn't been anywhere near big enough to contain the towering attraction between him and Nissa, and he was on the verge of losing his mind before they finally got outside and on the move, away from the momentary insanity that had been their impromptu hurricane party.

For the first time he could remember, he was antsy as all heck to get back to civilization and be done with this mission. And it had everything to do with a petite blonde CIA analyst and her big blue eyes.

Chapter 5

The three-mile hike to Gueydan turned into a six-hour nightmare of dead ends, doubling back and wading through waist-deep water. Nissa didn't think the trek from hell was ever going to end. She was still dreadfully sore from the last hike with these guys, but she was embarrassed to complain about being too uncomfortable to go on. They were toodling along like this was a stroll in the park. Which she supposed it was for them. Bass was actually whistling—cheerfully, no less—as he led the way forward. Instead, she suffered in silence and resolved to work out for about a month solid before she volunteered to come out into the field with a bunch of Navy SEALs again.

The only thing that kept the day from being completely miserable was that every time she stumbled, Cole's hand was there to steady her. Every time she thought she couldn't go another step, he called a rest break. Every time her throat was parched, he held out a canteen to her. His attentiveness was so constant and kind that it nearly made her weep more than once.

She knew intellectually that she was holding back the team and that Cole was only making sure she kept moving. But to have a man like him even aware of her, let alone concerned about her, was a fantasy come true. She tried to enjoy the attention, but before long it was hard to focus on anything except the burning agony in her leg muscles and the way they instantly stiffened up whenever the group stopped to rest.

Cole's touch was never anything but respectful and proper, but it didn't stop her heart from racing every time his strong fingers grasped her elbow or his palm came to rest lightly in the small of her back. His presence beside her was nothing short of devastating. He filled her senses and her mind, as raw and elemental as the stormy skies and wrecked landscape around them. Trees were snapped in half like twigs, tree branches lay everywhere and every man-made structure they came across had suffered major damage of some kind or another.

As the morning passed, the temperature rose, turning their hike into a steam bath. The sun came out from behind the dissipating storm bands, and the steam bath turned into a torture chamber. She had sweated hard plenty of times in her life, but she had no idea some of the places her body could perspire. Who knew that elbows could sweat? Or that perspiration could drip into her ears?

She must look like a drowned rat with her hair hanging in wet corkscrews around her face. And she didn't even want to think about what she smelled like.

The only relief from the relentless heat and humidity was when they couldn't find a way around a flooded area and had to go cross-country through standing water. They traversed wide swamps that Bass said were protected wetlands. They were rough going, slogging through thigh-deep water covering thick muck that sucked at her boots and made each step miserably hard work.

And then there were the running streams to ford. What bridges might have crossed the gullies were long gone, and they had no choice but to go through the floodwaters. One of the guys always went first to test the depth of the water and power of the current, but then she had to go, terrified with every step that she was going to be swept away and pulled under the water to drown. Cole always tied a rope around her waist, but it was scant comfort to consider having to be hauled out of the water like a fish on a hook.

If she made it out of this mess alive, she was never, ever, going to volunteer to step away from her safe, boring little cubicle again.

Of course, crossing the flooded streams didn't seem to bother Cole or his guys. They just held their gear over their heads in a casual, breathtaking display of strength, and pressed onward. She had insisted on carrying her own pack of gear today, but she suspected that Cole had taken out everything heavy and left her with little more than marshmallows and cotton balls to haul. Nonetheless, whenever they had to cross a swamp or low-lying area, Cole lifted her pack off her shoulders and would brook no arguments from her about it.

Regardless of his help, the wet hiking was hell on earth for her. It didn't help matters that within two minutes of going wading the first time through black, hip-deep water, something big and hard and invisible had brushed past her leg. She wasn't embarrassed to have screamed her head off. That had been an alligator, or else she was the Easter Bunny.

And then there'd been the water moccasin that had swum up to Ashe, apparently looking for a ride to dry ground. To her amazement, the SEAL had grabbed the snake just behind its head and let it wind four feet of panicked black body around his arm. When they'd reached high ground again, Ashe had actually turned the snake loose. Thankfully, it had slithered away and hadn't turned and attacked them.

That had been hours ago, but her skin still crawled at the memory of that giant snake swimming right up to them.

Eventually, the trees and marshland gave way to open farmland. Cole said these were rice paddies, but they were no less exhausting to cross than the black swamps had been. The guys began to search for roads and referred several times to their laminated map. Eventually, they came to a line of downed telephone poles and what looked like a washed-out roadbed. If there had been asphalt here two days ago, it was gone now, peeled up and carried away by Jessamine.

The good news was that the straight and mostly level road, raised several feet above the surrounding terrain, made for quicker going. Within an hour, Bass, on point, called out that he had buildings in sight.

She looked where he pointed, but spotted only a dark smudge on the horizon. They walked for another half hour before the smudge resolved into a cluster of houses and trees, announcing the presence of a small town.

The damage was heavy here, with many homes reduced to rubble or washed away altogether. As they skirted around fallen trees and dodged downed power lines, she was shocked at the silence. There were no motors, no doors slamming, no human conversation, not even a bird chirping to disturb the stillness. The town was deserted. As in totally, apocalyptically empty.

"Where is everybody?" she asked. Even her quiet question sounded impossibly loud in the silence.

Bass answered, "Evacuated, no doubt. And obviously the authorities haven't let anyone back into this area."

Cole commented, "We need a vehicle. Maybe heavy tools for clearing roads. And gasoline if you can find it."

"You guys will compensate anyone for anything you take, won't you?" she asked quickly.

Cole glanced over at her, then did a double take as he apparently realized she was serious. "We're on a mission. We take what we need."

"It's not nice to steal from anybody. And these people are going to have a hard enough time recovering from this destruction without you picking over the corpses of their homes."

Cole caught her worried gaze and he inhaled sharply, as if breathing in Nissa's fiery passion like a man addicted. "Umm, sure. Fine," he mumbled. "We'll compensate the owners for whatever we take."

Ashe and Bass looked at him like he'd lost his mind,

and he threw them a quick hand signal to be quiet. Nissa didn't let on that she understood the special forces hand signal. Rather, she turned over in her mind what it meant that he was silencing his men. She'd fully expected to be the butt of these men's jokes as the newcomer to the team and the amateur civilian. Why was Cole protecting her from the standard newbie hazing?

She surreptitiously studied Ashe and Bass. They gazed back and forth between her and Cole and then at each other. Their stares lit with unholy humor, but they kept their mouths shut.

Cole muttered under his breath to his men, "We really need to have a little chat. Soon."

"Whatever for?" Bass murmured back, laughter in his voice.

So. His men had picked up on the incendiary attraction between her and Cole, had they? She wasn't surprised. They were trained observers, and she was no good at all in tamping down her visceral reaction to him any time he was within arm's length—which was pretty much constantly.

"What are we looking for in this town?" Nissa asked.

Cole answered promptly, "An operational vehicle."

Gueydan turned out to be exceedingly short on those, however. The team checked out every nontrashed car they came across, but all of them were fouled with salt water and their engines ruined. They tried the post office, but Bass quickly declared both mail trucks waterlogged and dead.

"Now where do we try?" Ashe asked the group in general.

"How about the high school?" Nissa suggested.

"That's the most likely spot for the local school buses to be parked, and buses are taller than cars. Maybe they survived the floodwaters that came through here."

"Good idea," Cole responded.

She warmed at his praise, even blushing a little. Although that reaction startled her. There was no reason for her to be acting all fluttery and insecure around him. She was a great analyst and didn't need anyone to tell her so. Of course her idea was logical.

It took them a half hour to cross the small town. Trees and power lines were downed everywhere, and although the odds were good that the lines had no power, they still couldn't take any chances and had to circle wide around the wires.

The high school looked the worse for wear, but was still standing. And sure enough, beside it stood the school bus depot and a public works building. While Bass picked the likeliest bus to check out, Ashe disappeared inside the utilities building. The impunity with which these guys got through locks would be alarming if she didn't know for sure that they were the good guys.

At length, Bass declared the bus potentially operational, and he went to work cleaning and lubricating the engine. She helped Cole siphon gasoline from the other buses' gas tanks into a couple of five-gallon gas cans that Ashe found. They filled up their bus and then refilled the cans for the road.

Ashe loaded up the bus with a chain saw, hacksaws, and rope and chain. He also threw in rubber gloves and boots, and an armload of packaged snacks that had to have come from a vending machine, given their general fat and sugar content and total lack of nutritional value.

It was nearly five o'clock in the afternoon before Cole gave Bass the order to crank up the bus. Nissa held her breath as Bass, lying on his back under the dashboard, touched a pair of wires together. She jumped as sparks flew, but cheered along with the guys as the big engine caught, coughed and caught again. Bass used his elbow to mash down the gas pedal, and the engine steadied, idling more smoothly. One hot-wiring bus achievement unlocked.

He popped upright and announced cheerfully, "We've got wheels. Let's blow this popsicle stand, folks."

Although, they didn't exactly blow anything away as they crept out of Gueydan at barely more than a walk. They had to stop twice before they even made it out of the city limits to clear downed trees from the road. Now Ashe's theft of the chain saw and rope made sense to her. Without them, they'd have been trapped in the town with no way out.

"Did you leave a note for whomever you took those tools from?" Nissa asked as they got under way again.

"Yes, ma'am, I did," Ashe answered in a droll tone.

"For real?" she demanded suspiciously.

Cole intervened. "I promise, Nissa. I'll contact the Gueydan school district when power is restored and see to it they're properly compensated."

Nissa subsided, appeased. She was no felon.

They drove north at a snail's pace until they hit the big east-west interstate, highway 10. The going was slightly faster on the highway, which was still paved. But emergency crews were just starting to work at clearing the road, and more than once, the guys got out of the bus and pitched in with tools or muscle to help make a path for emergency vehicles and their bus.

They made it to Baton Rouge as night fell and decided to stop there. It was simply too dangerous to drive after dark and risk missing an electrical wire or other tire-blowing obstacle in the road.

Cole set an armed watch, which Nissa thought was overkill until the first gang of looters approached the bus. Ashe was on watch and woke them with a quiet warning of incoming hostiles. Instantly, the SEALs' high-caliber weapons were pointed out the windows, and Cole ordered her in a low voice to lie down on the floor and cover her head with her arms.

Thankfully, the looters thought better of taking on the trio of grim-faced men staring them down from behind military-grade assault weapons inside the bus. But Nissa didn't sleep much the rest of the night. Several more gangs of looters passed by, but all of them also chose not to tangle with the busload of armed soldiers.

When dawn broke, they hit the road once more. Here and there, people had returned to their homes, or maybe stayed through the storm, and they were hard at work dragging sofas, mattresses, soggy drywall and the other debris from their flooded homes to the curb to leave in sad piles of ruined lives.

The mood inside the bus was somber as they drove through the swath of worst destruction. But eventually, they successfully passed a National Guard checkpoint just outside New Orleans, compliments of their military IDs and a declaration that they were on official business. In the suburbs of the city most of the houses had survived the storm, and flood damage seemed to be the worst of it.

It was noon before they reached New Orleans proper, and it took them nearly two hours to cross the city and reach Naval Air Station New Orleans. Nissa sighed with relief as a gate guard came aboard the bus, asked for identification and waved them through the front gate with a smart salute.

Safe. At last.

No surprise, the SEAL operations building was unharmed by the storm and fully manned when they stepped inside. Even better, it had working air-conditioning. She sighed in bliss as cool, dehumidified air blew down on her from a ceiling vent.

The room was called to attention when Cole walked in, and he waved everybody back down into their seats. Nissa braced herself for whistles and catcalls, but to her surprise, the men she passed merely nodded politely to her and for the most part didn't stare too blatantly. She followed Cole through the big open room crowded with hard, steely-eyed men, and down a short hall to a conference room.

"In here," Cole murmured. His hand touched the small of her back briefly as she brushed past him, and she shivered with delight, her toes curling into tight little knots of pleasure. Lord, what she wouldn't give to have that man all to herself for a few days with nothing better to do than get to know each other.

The door closed behind her and she gazed around the high-tech briefing facility with its video wall and banks of oversize computer monitors.

"This room's secure," Cole announced, all business.

She did her best to shake off the remnants of his touch and focus on business, but she wasn't going to lie to herself. It was hard.

Belatedly, she asked, "Can we get a secure line to Langley from here?"

"Darlin', we can get a secure line to anywhere on Earth from here," Cole drawled.

The word *darling* sent a whole new round of shivers down her spine, even if he did mean the word in jest. "Great!" she replied brightly. "Here's my boss's number." Quickly, she jotted down her supervisor's direct phone number and waited while Cole placed the call. Apparently the naval base had its own emergency generator system, or at least this building did. The call went through in seconds.

"You're on speaker," Cole told her. "Just talk in a normal speaking voice and your party will hear you."

"Hey, Harrison. It's Nissa Beck."

"Where are you?" her boss exclaimed. "We lost contact with your tracking signal in the middle of the Gulf of Mexico."

"Satellites still can't see through hurricanes, huh?" she replied. "I'm back in New Orleans at the naval base, calling from SEAL headquarters." She informed her boss that Cole and his team were in the room and had ears on the conversation.

"Did you get Petrov?" Harrison asked her tersely, cutting to the chase.

Nissa replied, "He wasn't aboard the *Anna Belle*. In fact, no one was aboard her. And she was about to capsize when we searched her. I assume she's been reported missing by now?"

"Indeed, she has," Harrison said. "She's feared lost at sea. There's a big search on for survivors. But you're saying the crew had already abandoned ship? Maybe we should call off the search—"

Cole interrupted sharply. "No, sir. Don't call it off."

"Commander Perriman? Why not?" Harrison asked, voicing the exact same question in Nissa's mind.

"We've got the tactical advantage," Cole said. "Markus Petrov thinks he has successfully faked his own death. If you call off the search too soon, he'll realize that we know nobody was aboard the *Anna Belle* when she sank."

There was a long silence from CIA headquarters. Then, "How do you propose to exploit this tactical advantage, Commander Perriman?"

"With your permission, I'd like to keep Ms. Beck down here a little while longer while we launch an off-books search of our own for the missing Mr. Petrov. We still need her to make the positive ID when we apprehend him."

"What do you say, Nissa?" Harrison's voice boomed. "Are you up for a little more action with the SEALs?"

Ashe and Bass exchanged loaded looks, appearing ready to burst into laughter, and she couldn't miss the glare Cole shot their way. Yes, indeed. She was up for a lot more action with one SEAL in particular.

She cleared her throat and managed to answer reasonably calmly, "I'm happy to help the SEALs in any way I can."

"Excellent," Harrison replied. "I figure we've got Petrov on the ropes if he's gone to the trouble of faking his own death. Let's nail this bastard before he does the United States any more harm."

Petrov was believed to have spent three decades or more engaging in espionage against America. His crime ring had been much more extensive than anyone had imagined it would be, and now no one had any idea how extensive his spy ring would turn out to be. The CIA feared he had built a spy network at least as large as his criminal organization—and that had employed a hundred people and cleared hundreds of millions of dollars per year. Hence the unusual measure of sending a paper-pusher like her out into the field to assist with his capture and interrogation.

Assuming they could find the guy at all.

"How do you plan to proceed with your manhunt?" Harrison asked the group at large.

Cole leaned forward to answer for all of them. "The first order of business is going to be figuring out how to work in a city with no power or transportation. As it was, we got here in a stolen—borrowed—school bus."

"Keep me briefed in, Nissa. This is a high-profile investigation."

"How high?" Cole asked quickly, sounding alarmed.

"It's being briefed all the way up to the White House."

Nissa caught Cole's expression of chagrin, and she understood the sentiment. Not only did the White House have a long history of interfering in ongoing SEAL operations, but it also had a history of leaks. If wagging tongues at the White House let word out that Markus Petrov wasn't dead, any chance they had of finding the Russian would be in the wind, along with the man himself.

She spoke urgently. "Harrison, I need you to do me a huge favor."

"How huge?"

"I need you to send word up the chain that Petrov went down with the *Anna Belle* and is dead."

Cole's eyebrows shot up in surprise as her boss

squawked, "You want me to lie to the President of the United States?"

"Only temporarily," she answered. "You can throw me under the bus after this op is finished and claim that I lied to you. I'll take the fall for any backlash. But we *have* to put out the word that Petrov is dead. It's the only way we'll find him."

The line was silent, her boss clearly hesitating to agree.

"C'mon, Harrison. I know Petrov better than anyone else in the agency today. And I'm telling you, this is the only way to catch him. We have to sneak up on him when he's not looking."

"I suppose I could claim plausible deniability. I could say the agency kept the president in the dark so he would be able to deny any knowledge of an ongoing operation to capture a Russian spy on US soil."

Nissa held her breath while Harrison mentally worked through the ramifications of lying up his chain of command.

Harrison sighed loudly. "Fine. But don't mess this up, Beck. Your career hangs in the balance."

"Understood, sir. And thank you."

"Huh. Thank me after you bag that bastard."

"Will do."

Cole disconnected the call, and Nissa let out the breath she hadn't realized she'd been holding.

Cole spoke briskly. "Okay. Ashe, you head over to the base hospital and check on your wife. Bass, I expect you're going to be called back to emergency duty with the New Orleans Police Department the second they find out you're back in town. Do you want to go home and try to get some rest before that happens?"

Ashe was out the door before Bass could even respond with, "Nah. I'm good. It's fun to be back in uniform. This uniform."

Cole swiveled his chair to face her, their knees practically touching. And there went her pulse again. Good grief, this man wrecked her composure completely. She was intensely aware of being in close physical proximity to him. She felt his breaths and fancied she actually felt his heartbeats.

She became aware of other details. Like how hot his dark beard stubble looked against his tanned, taut skin. Like how piercingly blue his eyes were, up close like this. They were the bright azure of the sky right after a storm.

He murmured, his voice husky enough to make heat pool low in her belly, "Thanks for sticking out your neck for us."

"No problem," she managed to choke out. "Now we just have to find Petrov and capture him."

"Leave the capturing to us. What I need you to do is find him. Have you got any ideas on that score?"

"Do any of the computers in here still have secure internet access in spite of the hurricane?"

Cole reached for a laptop on a shelf beside the table. He powered it up, logged in with a lengthy password and pushed it across the table at her. "Have at it."

She logged in to her secure documents cloud and downloaded a file she'd worked on compiling for months. "How do I project this chart on the big wall over there?"

Cole talked her through the keystrokes, and in a few seconds a messy flowchart covered most of the far wall.

"What's that?" he asked.

"A series of thirty-one nesting corporations that I have uncovered. Markus Petrov uses them to hide his financial assets."

"Wow," he commented. "That makes my head hurt to just look at it."

She rolled her eyes. "You should have seen my headaches while I tracked down all these companies. At any rate, what I wanted to show you was this little holding company, here. Magnolia Bay Real Estate Trust."

"What about it?"

"It owns and manages a single property, which is weird in and of itself. Turns out the property is a very snazzy mansion in the Metairie district of New Orleans. Which is even weirder. It's not even an office building or apartments. It's a single-family home. My guess is that this mansion might be where Petrov lives."

"Or lived until he faked his death," Cole replied. "He's probably long gone by now."

"Not necessarily. If the raid that took out most of his crime ring was a surprise to him, he may still be scrambling to move assets around and set himself up to leave the country without leaving all his wealth behind."

"Won't he already have a lot of it offshore?" Cole asked.

"Sure. But I think he's greedy. I think he wants to take all of his money with him. Furthermore, he doesn't want to leave any trace of himself behind for us to find. He fancies himself to be a ghost. I think he'll do his level best to erase himself from existence."

"Hard-core." A pause. "So. How do we find him?"

Nissa frowned thoughtfully. "I was thinking about that very thing yesterday while we drove here. What if we were to check out his mansion before the National Guard lets anyone come back to town? There may still be a few thugs hanging around the place who stayed behind to guard it, but it can't possibly be protected at full strength. He may not be there anymore, but maybe we can find a clue as to where he went. Maybe find a computer or two that hasn't been completely scrubbed clean."

"It's worth a try," Cole responded.

"Great. When do we go?" she asked eagerly.

"Tonight," Cole answered briskly. "First, we'll grab showers, a decent meal and a nap. Then we'll head out."

She blinked, startled. "But it'll be dark soon. Looters. No police," she sputtered. "Just you and me?"

"I'm a SEAL, Nissa. You do know what that means, right?"

"Good point," she conceded. "Okay. We go tonight."

Just the two of them.

She really needed to be more careful what she wished for.

Chapter 6

Cole felt immensely refreshed after he woke from a several-hour nap. Waking Nissa as well, he took her to the arsenal, a windowless room about fifteen feet wide, with double shelves down the center, forming two aisles that were lined floor to ceiling with every supply any special forces operator could ever need. Inhaling fondly the smell of gun oil and the talcum powder items were packed in to prevent mildew, he led her to the weapons locker in the back of the room.

Cole handed Nissa a clipboard to write down everything they took, then loaded up on ammo and traded in his field assault rifle for a more compact urban assault rifle, appropriate to the close quarters of city streets.

"Try this on," he said, holding out a bullet-resistant vest in the smallest size the cabinet had in stock. It was baggy and hung down onto her thighs, but it would still stop bullets. And it was cute as hell on her.

"Can you shoot?" he asked.

"In theory. I'm hell on wheels at a firing range, but I've never shot at live human beings before."

"It's surprisingly easy to do when they're shooting back at you."

"I'll take your word for it."

He held out a sturdy 9mm Beretta that was standard military issue. "Is this similar to what you've shot before?"

"Yup, that's the one."

Cole passed Nissa the pistol, a shoulder holster, spare clips and two boxes of ammunition. He ran her through a thirty-second familiarization with the weapon, making sure she remembered where the safety was, when it was in the firing position and how to load the gun and clear the chamber.

Her gaze never left his hands, and he was shocked to discover what a turn-on that was. He held the Beretta out to her and her fingertips brushed over his knuckles. He glanced at her, startled, and she was staring back at him.

His gaze dropped to her mouth, pink and kissable, her upper lip a cherubic bow, her lower lip full and plump and in need of nibbling. She inhaled lightly, revealing perfect white teeth. The tip of her tongue passed over her lips, and something uncontrollable came over him. He had to kiss her again—this time with her fully awake. He needed to taste all that heat and sexual promise. One little sip.

Damned if she wasn't already swaying toward him, her face tilted up, her eyes heavy lidded. What the hell was going on between them? Any time he was alone with her, he could only think about one thing. And it emphatically was not the mission.

"Please," she whispered.

Aww hell. "Please what?" he mumbled desperately, barely hanging on to his self-control. He was supposed to be cold. Emotionless. Made of ice. But—dammit, that ice was melting fast under the onslaught of those big blue eyes of hers.

"I don't know. I need…" She trailed off without finishing, which was just as well. They really, *really* shouldn't go there.

Then why did he sway forward himself and whisper back, "Tell me what you need."

"I need…" A pause, then, all in a rush, "Kiss me. Please. Right now."

The shell of ice around him shattered all at once, and he gave in with a groan that was half pain and half relief, sweeping Nissa up in his arms and capturing her mouth with his. She tasted as sweet as he remembered, like a bowl of vanilla ice cream he could eat all up and then lick clean.

Her mouth moved restlessly beneath his, and he reveled in her eagerness, the way she threw herself into the kiss with abandon and seemed as desperate for more of him as he was of her. She reached up and laced her fingers into his short hair, tugging his head down for an even deeper kiss. Her tongue darted into his mouth and then retreated shyly as if her hunger had startled even her.

He inhaled her then, lifting her off her feet and plastering her against him, Kevlar vest and all. Her legs went around his hips, and he backed her up against the weapon locker door, angling his head to kiss her even more voraciously. The heat of her against his bulging zipper was almost more than he could stand. He couldn't get enough of her as lust roared through him. And possessiveness. And a need to claim this woman for himself.

The realization shocked him to his core. He was a civilized man. A gentleman soldier. Intelligent. Rational. Fully in control of himself and his emotions. He didn't act like a horny teenager, and he most certainly didn't mess around with women in the middle of a mission.

And yet, here he was, practically giving Nissa a tonsillectomy in the arsenal where any one of his men could stroll in at any time and catch them in the act.

"God, I'm a jerk," he muttered, reluctantly letting her slide down his body until her toes touched the floor. He stumbled back from her and shoved a chagrined hand through his hair. "I'm sorry *again*, Nissa. That was totally out of line."

"Umm, I do believe I asked for it. So if anyone was out of line, that would be me and not you."

"Don't try to assuage my guilt. I know better than to throw myself at civilian subject matter experts who work with us."

"Damn. I'm sorry to hear that," she said sincerely.

Cole's gaze snapped unwillingly to hers. Nissa smiled crookedly, and it took all the discipline he had not to kiss her again. He turned to stare blindly at the rows of weapons in the locker before him. The taste of vanilla was still warm and rich on his tongue, making him think of warm cookies and home. And Nissa.

Work, dammit! The mission! He had to be icy cold.

He exhaled hard. "How many ammo clips would you like to carry?"

"I have no idea," she mumbled, looking as distracted as he felt.

By rote, he handed her four ammo clips and instructed her where to tuck them in convenient pouches at the waist of her vest. He finished with, "If you need more bullets than that, we're screwed."

"You want me to shoot a gun if it comes to a fire-fight? For real?" she squeaked.

He turned to look her in the eye. "Yes. For real. This won't be a full-blown war zone, and ideally, we'll slide in and slide out of the Petrov place without anyone seeing us. But if things go south, I bloody well want you able to defend yourself and cover my back."

"Why don't we take a big squad of the SEALs from the other room with us?" she asked, frowning.

"You said yourself that the idea was to sneak into Petrov's house. A full frontal assault on it wouldn't be the least bit subtle. Yes, SEALs can slide in and slide out of most places unseen, but the more guys we take with us, the more chance we have of being spotted. Thing is, the men out there have been tasked to help provide support to local law enforcement authorities in enforcing the curfew and keeping the peace. They're already pulling eighteen-hour shifts. And besides, this is a low-threat breaking-and-entering mission. I can handle it myself. It'll just be you and me."

She audibly gulped, but didn't protest. Good girl. In his experience, just about everyone was capable of doing more than they thought they were. It was all about facing the right challenge to bring out the best in a person. Not that he particularly wanted to end up in a gun battle with Nissa as his only backup. Still, he got the feeling this mission was just what she needed to gain a little self-confidence.

He passed her a stick of black grease paint and used another to start blacking up his face. She dabbed at her face tentatively with the stick, applying it daintily like makeup, but leaving big patches of her fair skin visible.

"Here. Let me do it. Close your eyes." He took the grease stick from her and efficiently ran it over the contours and delicate bones of her face. He studied her features at his leisure, fascinated by her face's heart shape and fragile beauty. His entire being yearned for her. He wanted to taste her mouth again and feel her body pressed against his, her hips undulating hungrily against his groin. Hell, he wanted to plunge his hands into her hair and have hot monkey sex with her. Right here. Right now.

As much as he would like to stare at her all night, memorizing every detail of her, they had places to go and things to do. He tucked a stray curl of her bright blond hair under her black watch cap, its silken slide across his fingertips a siren's call to him.

He cleared his throat and announced, "You're good to go." It was a struggle, but he forced himself to step back.

"Thanks," she mumbled.

They stepped out into the main room, where Bastien was fully suited up and waiting for them. "You didn't think you were going out there by yourself, did you, Frosty?" Bass asked.

"In fact, I did."

Bass shook his head. "I'm a New Orleans cop. If you run into any local police, you're going to need me to vouch for you. And believe me, all the cops are out in force right now and armed to the teeth. We learned a lot after Hurricane Katrina, and the NOPD won't be messing around. They'll shoot first and ask questions later."

He made good sense. And Cole was happy to have someone who could help protect Nissa without slowing the two of them down. "All right, then. Are you ready to go?"

Bass nodded, all business. "The police have imposed a dusk-to-dawn curfew, so anyone we encounter on the street should be considered hostile unless they are displaying obvious law enforcement identification."

They caught a ride downtown in the back of a big military flatbed truck with a ribbed canvas roof. They continued on foot toward the northwest side of the city and the wealthy section of town known as Metairie. Bass, who knew the city like the back of his hand, found them a dry route that brought them down the tree-lined avenues and past the graceful antebellum mansions. There were puddles everywhere, but the area had seen only a little flooding.

Cole was vividly aware of Nissa sticking close to his heels, her presence strong and bright behind him. He'd always relied on his intuition to feel threats nearby, but tonight it was overwhelmed by her, and all he sensed was her breath, her steps, her fatigue, her fear…

Jeez, man. Focus on the job!

Bass stopped and Cole moved up beside him as the Cajun murmured, "Your address is about two blocks ahead and one street over."

Because the naval base's main computer servers had gone down sometime after Nissa's call to her boss, Cole had been unable to obtain satellite imagery of the man-

sion and its grounds. He'd had to go old school and use
a paper plat map to get even the smallest hint of what
lay ahead of them. The property was several acres in
size with a mansion placed squarely in the middle. He
hoped the gardens included plenty of trees and shadows
he and Nissa could use to approach the house.

They found the Petrov mansion and settled in to
observe the place. The grounds were, indeed, liber-
ally planted with trees and lines of shrubs. Cole's infrared night-vision gear picked up one man patrolling
the porch and yard, sticking very close to the house,
and two men inside. At the moment, the pair was sitting downstairs, appearing to eat. He directed Bass to
stay outside and keep tabs on the trio of guards while
he and Nissa went in.

Cole led Nissa to the west side of the home, pausing
just beyond the six-foot wrought iron security fence.
"Stay right behind me and do whatever I do. If I stop,
you stop. If I crouch, you crouch. If I run, you run.
Got it?"

"Got it."

She sounded scared out of her mind. He made one
last adjustment to her night-vision goggles, tightening
the strap around her head a little. "You can do this,"
he murmured.

"You have a lot more confidence in me than I do."

"There are only three guys, and they're more scared
than you are. They don't know what's lurking in the
dark out here. We, however, have night-vision gear.
We'll wait till the guy outside is around the front of
the house and then we'll head in. As for the guys inside, they're in a front living room right now. One of
them appears to be settling down for a nap. You and

I will slip in the back door and never get anywhere near them."

"You make it sound so easy," she groused.

"It is." He didn't tell her the hard part was when plans went off-script. And they always did. SEALs earned their paychecks when it came time to improvise on the fly.

"We'll look for an office and start our search there. Bastien will keep an eye on the guards and let us know if any of them head our way. We'll have plenty of warning to hide or leave."

She nodded, but as hyperaware of her as he was, he felt her breathing too fast and too shallow.

"Take a deep breath and hold it for me," he instructed her. When she'd done it, he counted to four and then told her to exhale long and slow. He talked her through several more breaths.

By about the third repetition, Nissa had calmed down. She nodded up at him, indicating her readiness to move out. Her eyes still showed fear, but she also appeared to trust him. He could work with that.

Bass threw a stiff rubber mat over the spikes at the top of the fence, and then he boosted Cole over the fence. He dropped lightly to the ground on the other side. Because of the power outage, they didn't have to worry about motion sensors or infrared security beams. This break-in was going to be a piece of cake—

Cole checked the thought. The missions he thought would be easy always turned out to be the born-again bitches that bit his team in the butt.

He caught Nissa against him as she jumped down from atop the fence, steadying her as she landed. His body recognized hers hungrily, and he had to make a conscious effort to set her away from him.

"Ready?" he mouthed.

She nodded, and he started a slow approach to the mansion, which turned out to be a white stucco, Georgian affair that reminded him a lot of the White House. Petrov must think it was hilarious to live in a home that mimicked the seat of the American government.

They moved from tree to tree, sticking to the shadows. At one point they bent over and crept the length of a row of perfectly trimmed box hedges. They stopped, crouching behind the last of the hedge, only about thirty feet from the back veranda and its row of French doors. The far right-hand pair of doors appeared to lead into the kitchen, and it was to those he pointed. Nissa nodded beside him.

"Where's Hostile One?" he breathed into his throat microphone. That was what they'd named the guard roving the grounds.

Bass answered immediately, "Should be coming around the corner, moving from your right to left, in about ten seconds. He'll walk across the back patio and then move around the west side of the house. You'll have five minutes to get inside before he comes around again."

Cole didn't acknowledge the report. Beside him, Nissa grabbed his arm and pointed. Sure enough, here came the guard, right on cue. They held their position, frozen utterly still as he strolled past. The guy walked casually across the brick patio. Excellent. Just the way he liked security guards. Relaxed and unsuspecting. The guy disappeared around the side of the house, and Cole headed out across the lawn with Nissa in tow. It was soggy enough that they dared not run for fear of making too much noise.

It was nerve-racking to move this slowly while fully exposed, not because it bothered him, but because he worried about Nissa stumbling or panicking and making a break for it. Finally, they reached the patio, and he moved quickly across it to the kitchen door. Simple locks were all that secured the entrance. Petrov probably relied on all kinds of high-tech security measures inside the house that rendered hard-core door locks unnecessary. Too bad none of those toys were working right now.

A stopwatch running inside his head, he went to work on the door lock. He wasn't anywhere near as fast as Ashe when it came to picking locks, but he got these opened in under three minutes. He wiped off his boots carefully before stepping into the kitchen. No sense leaving tracks that would alert the guards to an intruder. After Nissa did the same, he quietly closed and locked the door behind them.

They moved across the dark kitchen to an exit that led to a butler's pantry and a dining room beyond. The good news with these old homes was they had pretty standard layouts. Living rooms in the front, utility rooms in the back. Bedrooms upstairs, bathrooms scattered where they could be retrofit into the home. And, there should be some sort of servants' stairs around here, too. He found them, opening off the butler's pantry. Bass had spotted two rooms that looked like offices, one downstairs and one upstairs. Given that the inside guards were parked in the room directly across from the downstairs one, Cole had elected to head to the upstairs office first. If they were lucky, it would be Petrov's private office, and maybe hold some clue as to where he'd disappeared to.

He moved carefully up the servants' stairs, testing each tread for squeaks. Nissa weighed a lot less than him, so if he didn't cause a squeak, she shouldn't either. He found one squeaker on a turning landing, and he pointed it out to her. She nodded and stepped over it.

Upstairs, the hallway had a thick runner rug down the middle of it that masked footsteps. But, Cole still moved slowly, wary of squeaky floors in a home this old. At the very front of the house, he turned right into the office.

A huge desk sat in the back corner facing out into the room. Bookshelves lined two walls, and a bare spot on the third wall showed where a large painting had hung until recently. Had it been moved before Petrov fled, or had it been removed for safekeeping in the face of the hurricane?

He moved over to the desk to search it quietly. Nissa, however, headed over to the shelves and snapped pictures of the books. He made a mental note to ask her why later.

The computer station on the desk drew his attention immediately. He gestured Nissa over to it and then leaned close to her ear to whisper, "Do you want me to power this up with a battery pack, or would you rather try to remove the hard drive?"

"Hard drive," she replied.

He nodded and carefully unplugged the tower before lifting it onto the desk. Using a screwdriver from his multi-tool, he opened the case. Nissa leaned forward to examine the setup.

"It's a dual drive system," she whispered. "If we

take one drive, we can rewire it to operate on the single drive. Could be a while before anyone figures out a drive is gone."

He nodded and gestured for her to have at it. Interestingly, she chose to take the main drive and not the backup. She passed him the drive, which he tucked into one of his pouches while she reconnected several plastic leaders from the motherboard to the backup drive.

Then she whispered, "Can we start it? I'll reconfigure the operating system to lie about the existence of a second drive by partitioning the one drive to act like two."

And this was why he was a special forces soldier and not a computer geek. He passed her a battery pack, and she plugged in the computer. They had a tense few moments as the system beeped once during the boot up. Cole moved swiftly to the door and listened carefully for any response to the sound. After about three minutes, he relaxed. The downstairs guards would have come by now if they'd heard the noise.

Meanwhile, Nissa was typing up a storm behind him, doing her magic on the operating system.

"Done," she whispered.

He moved back over to the desk and helped Nissa screw the case onto the computer and then put the tower back and plug it in.

"Now what?" Nissa mouthed.

"Do you want to search Petrov's bedroom?" he whispered.

She nodded, so he led the way across the hall to the large room with grand windows. His guess was that a man who lived in a home like this would take the finest room in the house with the best view for himself. And that was this front bedroom.

They stepped into the bedroom and Nissa paused just inside, examining the room and seeming to absorb its general ambience. Eventually, she nodded, and they began carefully moving about the space. There were some telling clues as to Petrov's fate. Several of the dresser drawers were completely empty. A portion of the walk-in closet had only bare hangers on the racks. The master bathroom was devoid of everyday toiletries like razors or toothbrushes. Petrov had definitely fled.

However, there was cologne in the medicine cabinet, and a row of extremely expensive shoes in the closet. He'd left in haste, then.

Nissa moved over to the nightstand beside the bed, carefully opening the top drawer. She frowned and reached inside, pulling out a photograph in a frame. Cole leaned close to peer at it, and made out a woman standing beside a boy of ten or so. The picture was not recent, but he couldn't tell how old it was.

"Get me a towel," Nissa whispered.

Though puzzled, he moved into the bathroom and pulled a towel off a rack after taking note of how it had been folded and hung.

Nissa lay the photograph on the bed and bent down close to it, pulling out her cell phone. Then she draped the towel over her head and the photograph. Ahh. She needed to take a picture and shield the flash. He put a restraining hand on her arm.

She looked up at him in alarm as he whispered into his microphone, "Location of Hostile One?"

Bass replied, "Just coming around the front of the house."

"Report when he's on the east side."

Nissa nodded in understanding. They would wait to snap the picture until the guard wasn't outside their window where he might see the muffled light. In the meantime, she removed the picture from the frame to examine it more closely.

"Clear," Bass murmured in Cole's ear.

Covering herself once more, several flashes of light came from under the towel. Nissa emerged, smiling triumphantly. He replaced the towel in the bathroom while she put the photo back in the frame and placed it back in the drawer.

"Hostiles Two and Three appear to be starting some sort of security sweep of the house, Frosty," Bass reported. "They're moving casually, but with purpose."

Nissa tensed beside him.

Bass continued, "In about twenty seconds, you'll have a clear shot at the front stairs and the front door. I'll let you know when they enter the dining room. You'll have to hustle across the lawn, but you'll have about sixty seconds with all three men at the back of the house."

Crap. Twenty seconds wasn't long to get to the main staircase. Nissa seemed to realize that, as well, for her face showed stress, and her movements were abruptly jerky and tense. There was no help for it. He had no time to calm her panic attack. They had to move or die.

Chapter 7

Nissa's mind went blank. For a while there, she'd actually forgotten they were in the same house with armed and dangerous criminals who would kill her and Cole on sight. She'd been so absorbed in learning all she could about Markus Petrov from looking at where he lived that she'd lost track of the danger of their situation.

But now those armed criminals were coming.

Cole gestured at Nissa to move out. He seemed to think her legs were actually operational. Hah. Silly man.

He gestured again, more insistently. She tried to follow him toward the door, but her toe caught on the edge of a big rug and she pitched forward. Cole lunged toward her and caught her with a grunt under his breath. He set her on her feet and they raced for the door.

He started to ease the panel open, and she winced as it let out a loud squeak. He stopped, yanked out a tiny can of lubricating oil from somewhere on his utility belt and threw three fast squirts at the hinges.

They didn't have time for this! Petrov's men would be here any second! She felt entirely too mortal and fragile right now. What had she been thinking to agree to break and enter with a Navy SEAL? Cole was a professional at this stuff. She was as amateur a thief as they came!

Cole opened the hallway door and gestured for her to go first. Nissa slipped past him, peering nervously down the hallway. At any second, she expected one of Petrov's men to jump out and kill her. In a panic to get out of this death trap, she moved over to the stairs. The front door came into sight. Escape was right there, so close, yet so far away. Nothing but open stairs lay between her and freedom. That, and a pair of armed killers.

Cole joined her in crouching at the top of the grand, curving staircase.

"On my mark," Bass said calmly. "Three. Two. One…go."

Cole ran down the stairs, apparently not worrying about squeaking treads. She followed, right on his heels, so terrified she couldn't breathe. If she didn't get out of here fast, she was going to pass out from lack of air. Given how Cole was moving, Nissa gathered it was all about speed now, not stealth. Her entire body felt unnaturally light and fast, and she practically flew down those stairs. She'd never moved so fast in her life.

She and Cole reached the front door at the same time and he opened it for her. As she slipped out onto the grand front portico—she realized she'd never been so relieved to get out of a place before, and that included the tippy *Anna Belle*.

Cole closed the front door and took off running, and she ran full-out beside him. Terror spurred her forward mercilessly, and she gave that sprint everything she had. Cole stuck to the asphalt driveway, probably so they wouldn't splash in the soaked lawn and make noise and footprints.

Bass grunted in her earpiece, obviously running himself, "I'll meet you at the front gate in thirty seconds."

Cole and Nissa arrived at the big gate just as Bass threw the rubber mat over the fence spikes. Cole bent his knee, creating a ledge with his thigh. "Step up here. I'll boost you."

Nissa climbed onto his leg, and he planted both hands on her tush. Her gut gave a jolt that had nothing at all to do with the mission at hand. He hoisted her over his head, and she scrambled over the fence, dropping into Bass's arms on the other side.

"Hostile One's almost to the corner of the house. Take cover," Bass bit out in her headset.

"Get her out of here now," Cole ordered Bass.

"No! We're not leaving you!" she shouted in a whisper.

Bass grabbed her arm grimly and started to haul her away from the gate. Panic roared through her and she shook off his hand. They couldn't lose Cole! She wouldn't let him sacrifice himself for her!

"I'm not leaving—" she tried again.

Cole cut her off in a harsh whisper. "Go, Bass. I'll meet you two down the road."

She had no choice. Bass grabbed her upper arm again, tightly this time, and overpowered her with breathtaking ease. She had no choice but to race along beside him as he half lifted her off her feet. They ran about three blocks before he stopped as abruptly as he'd started. He pulled her back beside him into the shadow of a line of tall box hedges.

"Now what?" she whispered.

"Now we wait for Cole."

"What's he doing?"

"I imagine he's standing very still in the darkest shadow he can find until the yard guard passes by."

"There was no cover at all by the gate!"

Bass shrugged. "It's not hard to hide in plain sight. The human eye spots movement easily, but doesn't discern still shapes nearly so well. As long as Cole stands perfectly motionless, the guard could probably look right at him and not see him, particularly since the guard isn't expecting to see anyone."

"Isn't that his job? To see intruders?"

"You'd think. Even soldiers who know SEALs are coming for them routinely don't see us until we're on top of them."

"Yeah, but that's because you guys are stealthy."

"Partially. And part of it is that humans are predators who spot their targets via motion."

She was skeptical, and she hated the idea of Cole's life hanging on some armed thug not doing his job properly.

"Frosty's as good as they get, Nissa. He'll be fine. And if not, we'll hear gunfire and go back to help him. Although I pity anyone who gets into a firefight with him. He's one of the best shooters I've ever seen."

"Is he a sniper?" Nissa asked in surprise.

"No, I'm talking about close quarters combat. He's a machine. Never misses. Surgical killer, he is."

A killer? It was hard for her to reconcile that with the passionate man who'd kissed her in the arsenal. Or maybe that was just her overlaying her hot dream of him onto the actual man. Perhaps she was delusional, and he really was the cold, hard killer his men thought he was. After all, they knew him a lot better than she did. Confused, she waited beside Bass in the dark and prayed for the man she knew to come back to her.

Cole watched for a moment as Bass turned and took off running into the night with Nissa. A visceral bolt of relief shot through him. *Nissa is safe.*

He glanced over his shoulder and didn't see the guard yet. But he knew the guy was out there. He could feel the man coming. Gliding backward until his spine was pressed against the brick pillar to one side of the iron gate, he plastered his weapon against his chest with his arms folded over it to minimize his profile.

There. The guard came around the corner of the house. Instead of skirting along the front of the porch as he'd been doing before, the guy swung wide into the yard this time. Cole's index finger slid into the trigger guard and rested lightly on the trigger of his weapon. Mentally, he gauged the distance—ninety-five feet. And windage—slight right to left breeze, but nothing that would affect such a close-range shot.

The target was armed, a sawed-off shotgun slung over his shoulder behind his arm, barrel facing the ground. Stupid place to carry a weapon unless a guy thought gophers were going to jump up behind him and attack his ankles.

The guy glanced toward the gate, and Cole stood perfectly still, becoming part of the brick pillar behind him, trusting the shadows to conceal him.

The guy moved on, heading toward the left corner of the house, half turning his back to Cole. The moment of crisis had passed. He was safe. It took about sixty seconds for the guard to clear the corner and disappear completely from sight. Cole gave him a few extra seconds to change his mind and come back to the front yard. But when the lawn remained still and empty, Cole moved.

He took a few steps back, away from the gate, then took a running leap at the gate, grabbing the top crossbar. It gave a huge creak, and the chains holding it shut to the second gate rattled like a truck had just slammed into them.

Swearing, he used his momentum to carry his feet up. He swung one boot over the top of the gate, catching his weight and using it to lever himself up and over the gate. He heard shouts from inside and outside the house as the guards reacted to the noise. As he dropped down the other side of the gate, he grabbed the rubber mat and dragged it down with him.

His feet hit the ground just as a shadowy figure came around the east corner of the house and two more charged outside onto the front porch. Cole melted back from the gate into the shadows on the far side of the pillar.

An amateur's impulse would likely have been to run for his life, but Cole knew better. He eased backward slowly, doing nothing to draw attention to himself.

He heard the chains rattling as they were unlocked and thrown open, and that was when he turned and ran silently down the street on his toes. He dived into the first driveway without a gate and slowed as he reached the sodden lawn. This house had a formal English garden with lots of shrubs and beds, and crouching, he wound between them in silence.

He heard footsteps pound past on the street at a run, and he risked a whispered radio call. "Incoming, Bass. Three armed men. Move or take cover."

He cut through the backyard into the property of another house a street over from the Petrov mansion. "I'm one block south running east," he reported.

"We're two blocks in front of you moving south," Bass panted. Obviously his man had chosen speed over stealth as a means of eluding the incoming Petrov guards.

"I'll angle southeast and catch up with you. Keep moving until then."

"Roger, Frosty."

He wasn't feeling very frosty at the moment. Not that he was worried about himself. He could handle three civilian thugs. But he was scared spitless that Petrov's men would catch up with Bass and Nissa. She would lose her mind with fear if she ended up in the middle of a firefight. He didn't even want to think about what a mess *that* would be. She was a terrific analyst, but SEAL material, she was *not*.

Keeping an eagle eye out for Petrov's men, he angled south and east. Moving at top speed, it still took him a solid ten minutes to catch up with Bass and Nissa. Ten endless, tense minutes of being scared as hell that he wouldn't find them in time and that Petrov's men would mow them down with their AK-47s.

But at long last, he spotted a pair of shadows flitting ahead of him, not moving fast, but sticking to the deep shadows ahead.

"Is that you closing in on a white, one-story plantation house on a four-way intersection?" he murmured into his throat mike.

"Affirmative, boss. I'm gonna turn the corner and wait for you there. Will confirm your identity before standing down."

"Roger," he replied.

He crossed the street, ran to the corner and rounded the tall hedge there slowly, with his hands held well away from his sides. The cold hard blade of a knife touched his throat.

"It's me," he panted.

The knife fell away.

But in its place, Nissa launched herself at him, nearly choking him she hugged him so tight. Her body was lithe and slender against his, and trembling violently.

"Hey. I've got you," he murmured. "Everything's fine."

"I hated being apart from you," she whispered.

"Bastien, turn your back," he ordered tersely.

His man spun away to stare out into the night, and Cole wasted no time kissing Nissa. Her hands passed frantically over his shoulders and neck and plunged into his hair as if she was reassuring herself that he was all right. He knew the feeling. He ran his hands over her arms, down her spine and finally cupped her head, drawing her more deeply into their kiss.

Her vanilla flavor soothed him as nothing else did, yet at the same time, it made him desperate to taste more of her. His tongue swept inside her mouth and she gasped, arching her body into him. He tilted his head to gain deeper access to her and chuckled in his throat as she bit his lower lip in her urgent need. He knew the feeling.

"I was so worried," she whispered.

"Ditto, kid," he muttered back against her luscious lips.

Damned if she didn't wrap one of her legs around his hips in her eagerness. He captured the leg and used it to lift her off the ground. Her other leg went around him and he backed her up against the brick wall behind her. His erection was instant and painfully needy. Her core rubbed against his groin deliciously, and he groaned into her mouth as she wriggled in the most enticing way. Need surged through him. The need to bury himself in her, to be sheathed in her heat and vitality, to feel her naked flesh, to possess her, to die in her and be reborn.

A throat cleared behind him.

Dammit.

Reluctantly, he let her slide to the ground, gritting his teeth against the wave of pleasure that pounded through him as her body slid down his. He tried to step away from her, but she grabbed his head, kissing him one last time, long and druggingly, before she regretfully let him go.

The mission, he reminded himself. The mission. Get the civilian back to the naval base in one piece.

"What's the word on our pursuers?" Bass asked as Cole stepped up beside him.

"I haven't seen them since I left the Petrov mansion. You?"

"I spotted them once, just after you called them incoming."

Cole nodded. "They've no doubt given up the chase by now. They can't afford to get pulled too far away from the mansion for fear that it was a ruse to lure them away so someone else could move in and loot the place. I'm certain they've returned to the Petrov property by now."

"Back to the naval base, then?" his man asked.

"My house is closer. I'd rather get Nissa under cover than take her all they way back to the base."

"Roger that, sir. Stealth or speed?" Bass asked.

"How're you feeling, Nissa?" Cole asked.

"Winded. But I can run a little more," she replied gamely.

"Stealth," Cole answered. "You take point, Bass. Nissa will go next and I'll take rear guard." Which was to say, if they got shot at from behind, he'd take the bullets and not Nissa. Although it was standard SEAL procedure to protect those they rescued with their lives, something felt more right than usual about using his body to protect Nissa from harm.

He pushed the thought out of his head. No time to think about what the hell that meant. Right now, they had to get her to safety. There would be time later to dissect his strangely overprotective impulses.

The three of them hiked for another half hour or so. They detoured around what looked like a group of looters trying to break into a warehouse. Bass was tempted to confront the gang, but outnumbered and with Nissa beside them, Cole vetoed the idea.

Another five minutes brought them to Cole's doorstep.

"You gonna be good, here?" Bass asked.

"Yup. You going back to take out that gang?" Cole asked. Bastien was a New Orleans native and a cop. Cole had no doubt he would at least chase off the looters, if not take a bunch of them down.

"Don't worry, boss. I won't get myself killed. I'm just gonna put the fear of God into those guys and make them think twice about felony breaking and entering."

"You need help?" Cole offered.

"Nah. I got this. You take care of your lady."

He opened his mouth to deny that she was his, but he was a firm believer in the truth. And he couldn't deny the truth of Bass's comment. He merely nodded grimly. "Be careful, Bass. I saw at least four handguns in that crew."

"Good. I'd hate for them to be no challenge at all. Killing sheep isn't any fun."

Nissa piped up in concern, "You're not going to kill them, are you?"

"Bye, Bass," Cole said drily as he took Nissa by the elbow and gently forced her up toward his driveway.

"But—" she started.

"Bass is a cop. This is his town. His turf. It's his job to protect it."

"Yeah, but there were a lot of guys in that gang—"

"Bass is a SEAL. If they turn it into a gunfight, he'll wipe them out and they won't have any idea what hit them."

"But they're citizens of the city. You guys are soldiers. You can't just go around killing people! This isn't a war zone!"

"Believe me, when word gets out that the NOPD

has teamed up with the SEALs, this city will get a lot more peaceful *fast*. Nobody will attempt to shoot at any armed law enforcement official. They'll run first."

Nissa didn't look happy about it, but he knew what he was talking about. No looter wanted to get into a firefight with the law. They were mostly in the streets to steal stuff or look for drugs, not to die.

He led her down the driveway beside his shotgun house to the detached garage behind the structure. He unlocked the garage door and pushed it up.

"Are we stealing a car now? I thought the idea was to stop criminals, not become them," she accused.

"I'm not stealing this truck," he replied.

"Then why did you break into this garage?" she demanded.

"You may not have noticed, but I used a key to unlock the garage door. This is my house, and that is my truck. I thought you might prefer driving back to the naval base instead of walking the whole way. It's about five miles from here."

"Oh."

He suppressed a grin as he opened the passenger door for her. He helped her up into the vehicle, and his hand lingered on her elbow for a moment. He would love to pick up that earlier kiss where they'd left off, maybe even take her into his house right now and make love to her—

No. The job came first.

Sometimes having self-discipline purely sucked.

Nissa buckled her seat belt without comment, and he backed the vehicle out of the garage and closed the door behind them.

"Pull out your handgun and hold it in your lap," he directed her.

"Why?"

Ah, civilians. They had no idea how to follow an order first and ask questions later. He explained patiently, "It's possible we'll run across more looters, and this truck will be a juicy target for them. If anyone approaches us who's not a cop, show them the gun through the window."

"What if they have bigger guns?"

"Then I'll show them mine. They won't have anything better than my assault rifle."

"Sheesh. This is almost as bad as a zombie apocalypse," she declared.

"Oh, I don't know about that. The problem with zombies is the sheer number of them. In war, sufficient quantity overwhelms quality every time."

"I thought SEALs operate on the notion of a few guys taking out much larger forces."

He guided the truck down the street, watching carefully for debris in the road. He talked as he drove. "We do operate on that principle. But even a highly trained special forces team can be overwhelmed if enough force is brought to bear against them. The trick is not to go into situations where that will happen."

"What are you guys trained to do if you do get overwhelmed?"

"We go down fighting. The idea is to die with no more bullets left in the guns. Take out as many of the bad guys as we can before we go down and hope that reinforcements get to us in time. We rarely operate completely in the blind. We've usually got helicopters or gunships, or maybe drones, reasonably close by for backup. SEALs are valuable assets. We don't get thrown into unwinnable scenarios willy-nilly to die. The object is for us to succeed."

"Forgive me for disagreeing, but I just went with you and your guys onto a ship that was moments from sinking to recover a bad guy. We had no backup at all."

"That was an unusual assignment. It's why I led the team myself. I refuse to send my guys into harm's way that I wouldn't go into."

"Gee. Thanks for not telling me we were on a suicide mission."

He spared a glance for her across the dimly glowing interior of the truck. "You were already scared to death. I didn't want to paralyze you completely by telling you just how outnumbered we would have been on that ship had the crew been aboard her."

That silenced her. He hoped she understood the operational necessity of his withholding information from her. But if she didn't, it wouldn't change the rightness of his decision, and he would do the same thing again.

At length, she asked, "Is there anything else you haven't told me?"

Like the fact that he was so hot for her he could hardly keep his mind on the mission? Or that she was the most fascinating woman he could recall meeting in a very long time? That he found her intelligence and plucky determination completely irresistible? That he'd been dreaming of her the past few nights and that all of his dreams had been at least as sexy as hers had been of him?

"Nope. Nothing mission related."

"Will you promise to tell me the whole truth and nothing but the truth going forward?"

He stopped the truck and turned in his seat to face her. "You're asking me not to do my job. I can't agree to that. If your life is ever in danger, I will do whatever it takes to keep you safe. *Whatever* it takes. And if that means lying my ass off to you, I won't hesitate to do it. I'm sorry if that isn't what you want to hear. But it's the God's honest truth."

She stared at him for a long time. And she shocked him by murmuring, "Okay. I can live with that. And… thank you." She turned to gaze out her side window, and bemused, he put the truck into gear once more.

His mind circled back to that moment of abject relief when he'd known Nissa would be okay even if he got shot in the back the very next second. His personal feelings had come very, very close to intruding on a mission. Way too close. Which meant he had a problem. A big one.

Chapter 8

Nissa's heart didn't stop pounding even after the front gate of the naval base came into sight. Ever since that kiss on the street, she'd been a bundle of nerves. She wanted more of kissing Cole in the worst way.

But that wasn't the only source of her jumpiness. Cole had just all but admitted to having personal feelings for her. She was no dummy, and her job was to read between the lines and see nuance and meaning beyond the words on a page.

Cole Perriman actually liked her? *Mind. Blown.*

Not that she was in any better a spot on this crazy mission. When he'd grabbed her rear end to boost her over Petrov's front gate, she'd all but had an orgasm on the spot. Even though she had been terrified she was going to get shot on her way over that fence, still her heart had pitter-pattered like crazy the second he laid his hands on her. And that kiss… Granted, she'd initiated it, but he'd been an enthusiastic participant until Bass had reminded them they were on an exposed street corner in a lawless city. No doubt about it, she was a complete mess.

Nissa *knew* not to mix business and pleasure. Not to fall for the hot SEAL who would move on to the next mission without a backward glance. Not to confuse his concern for her safety with real feelings for her. He was doing a job, and at the moment she was a useful asset for doing that job. Nothing more. Heck, for all she knew, he kissed her purely to distract her from her terror. Goodness knew, it had worked.

Thankfully, after his admission that he would do anything to protect her, Cole turned his full attention back to driving across the ruined city, and she had a few minutes to regain control of her pulse and respiration before they parked in front of the SEAL operations building.

Cole spent the next few hours accepting debriefs from his men as they trickled into the building. Nissa installed Petrov's hard drive into a desktop computer Cole lent to her and wasn't surprised to find that all the data on the drive had been erased. However, a regular disk erasure still left behind the actual data in the form of magnetized bits on the drive itself. Those were wholly recoverable.

She scrounged up cables and parts to rig up a makeshift forensic hard drive reader and attached Petrov's hard drive to it. Given that this wasn't a dedicated hard drive stripper, she figured it would take twelve hours or more to lift the individual magnetic bits off the drive. Then she would have to go through the tedious process of reassembling the raw data into meaningful documents and files.

When the data collection process was under way, Nissa went out into the ready room and caught the latest team's report as they came in. She was relieved to hear that the reports involved multiple apprehensions of looters that had subsequently been handed over to the police.

Cole made a few adjustments to the duty roster posted on a whiteboard in the main ready room, and then he finally turned to speak to her. "What would you like to do now, Nissa?"

Crawl into bed with you and spend about a week?

"Umm, I guess I'd like to send a copy of that photograph we found in Petrov's bedroom to the FBI. They can run a facial recognition search on the woman and boy. Then, I suppose I should get started on digging into the first raw data from the Petrov hard drive to see if I can reconstruct the files without help from Langley. If we're lucky, there may be some quick forensic evidence I can lift that will tell us where he went."

"You look tired. Maybe you should sleep first and worry about the hard drive tomorrow."

Nissa winced. "It's a race against time. Any clues we find from our little field trip will have a very short shelf life of usefulness. I need to get you whatever I find fast enough that we can still pick up Petrov's trail."

"How soon will you have any useful results from the drive?" Cole asked.

"It'll be a few hours at least."

He shocked her by saying, "Then come back to my place with me. Let me feed you a hot meal and a decent cup of coffee while you wait."

"Do you have power?"

"I have a diesel generator that'll power the whole house. And I really do need to check on the place and see how it fared in the storm."

She grinned. "Of course you have a generator. You live to prepare for emergencies, don't you? I'll bet you've got a year's supply of food in a nuclear bunker somewhere, too."

He shrugged modestly. "My bunker's only zombie-proof, not nuke-proof."

She snorted. Thing was, she actually believed him.

"C'mon, Nissa. Let's get out of here. You've earned a break."

The danger of going back to Cole's home with him did not escape her, but neither did the rush of excitement at the possibilities when they were finally alone, away from the prying eyes of his men.

She followed him out of SEAL Ops.

At length, they parked behind the tidy shotgun house. Though not much wider than the driveway, it was impeccably restored and in pristine condition.

Cole let Nissa in the front door and she gasped in surprise. Cathedral ceilings opened overhead, and a shocking sense of space and openness greeted her.

"This place is great!" she exclaimed, shining her flashlight around in delight. The decor was modern and industrial, but comfortable. "Did you decorate it yourself?" she asked.

"I cheated. It came fully furnished. I put on a new roof and rewired the place, but I'm not nearly this taste-ful left to my own devices."

Nissa smiled at Cole as he led the way into the kitchen past the open dining space. Both areas were as chic and comfortable as the living room they flowed from. Although the house was narrow, all the rooms ran the entire width of the house and didn't feel the least bit cramped.

"Bathroom's through that door." He pointed to a door at the back of the kitchen in one corner.

"What's through that door?" She pointed at the second door in the rear wall of the kitchen.

"Bedroom. My office and a spare bed are in the loft."

In the dining area, a steel staircase led to the second-floor space over the back portion of the home. It was all very efficient. Contained. Neat. Like its owner.

Cole headed out into a tiny backyard that was designed as a courtyard garden with geometric flower beds and a fountain in the center. She held a flashlight for him as he checked over the generator and started it. He pulled the cover back over it, and she was surprised at how well it muffled most of the sound of the engine. They headed back inside.

"I have a point-of-contact water heater, so if you want to take a shower, there will be hot water right away. I'll see what I can cook up for us in the meantime."

She'd only brought a small suitcase with her for this assignment on the assumption that she would be in and out of New Orleans in a day or two. She pulled out her lone pair of clean jeans and a plain blue T-shirt almost the same sapphire shade as her eyes and headed for the restroom.

To say a hot shower was heavenly was an understatement. Even though she'd had a shower back at SEAL Ops when they first arrived, she still shampooed her hair twice to get out the lingering scent of salt water, swamp slime, sweat and general filth. She scrubbed her skin until she was pink all over, as well.

She cracked the bathroom door to call, "Is there enough electricity for me to run your blow dryer?"

"The generator can handle the entire house. Go for it," he called back.

Bless him. Nissa dried her hair, corralling its natural curls into soft waves around her face. At least until she stepped outside and the humidity turned it into frizz central.

The kitchen smelled like heaven when she emerged, and Cole was just pulling a pair of steaks out of the broiler. "Where did you get those?" she asked in amazement.

"Freezer. The generator kicks on automatically every few hours during a power outage to run the refrigerator and freezer and to cool or heat the house a little."

"You really are Mr. Preparedness, aren't you?"

He grinned over his shoulder at her. "You have no idea."

She helped set the table and toss a salad with greens and tomatoes still fresh in the refrigerator. It seemed like they'd been gone forever, but in reality, it had been just a few days. They sat down to eat, and she released a mental sigh of relief. She was safe. They were safe.

They dug into the steaks, which of course, were as perfect as the man who'd cooked them.

"So tell me about yourself, Cole."

"Not much to tell. I grew up in Colorado. Studied mechanical engineering in college. Joined the Navy. Became a SEAL. Never looked back."

"How long have you been on the teams?"

"Seventeen years."

"Wow. That's a long time and a lot of ops."

He shrugged and carved off a bite of steak. "I didn't spend all of it in the field. I was a BUDS instructor for several years, and I've been team leader for a while."

"So it won't be long until you can retire."

His entire demeanor changed, as if she'd just asked him how long he had to live. He went closed and silent, and the muscles in his face were working too hard to just be chewing the tender steak. He finally muttered, "A few months."

Yikes. Talk about having hit a nerve. Clearly he was not the least bit happy about his forthcoming retirement.

Cole said tersely, "Tell me about yourself."

The topic change was blatant. He didn't want to talk about retiring. At all. Fair enough. Nissa played along with his diversion. "I'm from Maryland. Suburbs of Washington, DC. Went to college at Georgetown. Russian Studies. Got hired as an intelligence analyst and never looked back." Out of long habit, she didn't include that she worked for the CIA. But he already knew that anyway.

"How long have you worked for the agency?"

"Six years."

An awkward silence fell between them, and she concentrated on her supper, grateful to have something to do with her eyes and hands.

Cole finally spoke. "Tell me about Markus Petrov."

"We know very little about him, actually. The only reason he's on the radar at all is because one of our field operatives was recruited by Petrov."

"Oops."

Nissa smiled at Cole. "We got lucky. Our operative didn't, though. Petrov killed the guy's mother a number of years ago. Our agent was on a leave of absence trying to infiltrate Petrov's organization and find proof of the murder, or maybe take revenge for it, when he came to Petrov's attention and was recruited."

"If you've got a guy on the inside, why don't you know where Petrov is now?"

"We burned our guy on the inside recently in a giant raid that took down the criminal side of Petrov's operation. We decimated the crime ring. It was a sweet bust. Netted over a hundred people. Destroyed Petrov's ability to raise cash to run his spy ring."

Cole whistled. "Why didn't I hear about this on the news?"

"We squashed the story because we still need to take out Petrov's espionage network. On the off chance that some of his informants aren't aware of the takedown, we kept the story off the internet and out of the news."

"I'm impressed. It's awfully hard to keep a secret in today's age of technology."

She snorted. "Tell me about it. We scrambled for nearly a week to kill the story."

They finished eating and she helped with the dishes. Then Cole asked, "Can you access Petrov's data from here if I tell you I've got a dedicated line to SEAL Ops in my office?"

"Are you serious?" Nissa exclaimed.

"Like you said. I'm Mr. Preparedness. I've got a secure landline to Ops so my men can get a hold of me anytime and talk about classified missions if necessary."

"Dang. And I thought I was thorough."

He smiled. "You go work on Petrov's hard drive data while I brew some coffee for you."

Nissa went back up to his office and set up her laptop. The landline wasn't ideal for data transmission, so she batched in the first set of data from the drive and downloaded it to a thumb drive to analyze at her leisure.

That done, she carried her laptop downstairs and set it up at the kitchen table attaching the thumb drive containing the initial raw data. Normally, she would connect to forensic programs contained on the CIA's main servers. But tonight, she had to work manually, searching through the random information bits for meaningful data. It was tedious work, going sector by sector on the drive, looking at raw data, in some cases symbol by symbol.

Cole stayed out of her hair, silently refilling her coffee cup, and fetching her a pad of paper and a pen when she requested them.

She lost track of the time, but her eyes were gritty and her body ached when she finally pushed back from her computer.

"Find anything?"

She looked up, startled, as Cole stepped into the kitchen. "I found some financial spreadsheets. I suspect they're expenditure records for the spy side of his organization, and they may give Langley some bank account numbers and routing numbers to help us track down his informants. But there's nothing in here to indicate where Petrov has gone."

"Were there any large cash transfers to indicate that

he emptied out a checking account preparatory to his escape?"

She shook her head. "No."

"Too bad."

Nissa hated to admit defeat. Maybe they would have better luck with the next batch of data. If Petrov slipped away from them now, they would never find him again. Of that she was certain. She pulled out her phone and loaded her pictures of the photograph from Petrov's nightstand onto her laptop. "Do you have a magnifying glass?" she asked Cole.

"Coming up." He jogged up the steel staircase to the loft and returned in a minute with a magnifying glass.

Using it, she examined the picture on her laptop screen, enlarging the background of the shot. She murmured, "This looks to have been taken roughly twenty years ago somewhere in this area."

"How can you tell?"

"By the tree in the background. It's a live oak. And those are azaleas beside the building. Also the black bit on the corner of the building—here—looks like wrought iron. Porch trim, maybe. But definitely wrought iron."

"How do you know how old the picture is?" Cole asked.

"The back end of this car. It looks like a model from twenty to twenty-five years ago. The woman's hair is the right cut and her clothing is the right style to be about that old."

"Who do you suppose she is?" Cole asked.

"I initially thought it might be an older picture, maybe of Petrov and his mother. But given the actual age of it, I'd say it's a woman and child who meant something to him. Maybe a sister or a lover."

"Maybe his wife and child?"

"We have no record or rumor of Petrov being married, and our informant got the impression he was unattached."

"A mistress, maybe?"

Nissa shrugged. "Possible."

"If that's the case, what are the odds the boy is his son?"

She looked up at Cole. "That's an excellent question. If this is his son, there's no way Petrov would go out of contact with his heir. Based on his psychological profile, it's safe to say he would jump all over the idea of founding a dynasty. If we find the son, we could find the father. This may be just the lead we were looking for!"

Cole came around behind her and leaned down over her shoulder to study the image on her computer screen. "That boy looks about ten. That would put him in his thirties now."

She nodded. "If the facial recognition folks at the FBI can get us a name on the woman, we ought to be able to track down the name of her son."

"You don't think the kid's surname is Petrov?" Cole asked in surprise.

"No way. Petrov prides himself on being invisible. He may be arrogant and take great pride in having produced a male heir, but there's not a chance he would let a child bear his name. He would be far too self-centered to endanger himself by sharing his identity with the boy."

"Wow. That's cold."

"Petrov is as coldhearted a bastard as they come."

"Jeez. Makes me feel sorry for the woman."

Nissa shrugged. "Petrov is thought to have killed our informant's mother for refusing to sleep with him. The odds of the woman in the picture having never pissed him off enough to kill her have got to be low, given how quick a temper he has toward women."

Cole shook his head. "Are you sure you want me and my guys to take him alive? It's possible to take him out, particularly if he puts up a fight."

"Thanks, but we'd really like to talk with him. We'd love to know the full extent of his activities and how deep into our government his network reaches."

"You think he'll actually tell you?" Cole asked skeptically.

She nodded grimly. "I think we can play to his pride. If we scoff at him and act like we don't believe anything he's telling us, I think he'll ultimately brag about how much he knows and how highly he's got people placed. He's a narcissist and a megalomaniac at heart. Thin-skinned guys like him can always be taunted into outbursts that reveal too much."

"Sounds like a gem of a guy."

Nissa rolled her eyes. "We really need to find him and stop him for good."

"I think you've already stopped him if he's faking his death and disappearing."

She looked Cole in the eyes. "I sincerely hope you're right. This guy scares me to death."

Cole reached down, drew her to her feet, and gently pulled her into a hug. She mentally sighed in pleasure as his powerful arms wrapped around her like living armor. "I'm never going to let this jerk hurt you. I promise."

She laughed a little against his chest. "You can't watch me for the rest of my life."

"That could be arranged."

Chapter 9

Nissa was shocked to her core by his comment. No surprise, Cole froze against her, too, as if it had just dawned on him what he'd suggested.

A long-term relationship with Cole? She didn't even dare think of such a thing. She realized her breathing was coming too fast and too shallow again. Lord, she hyperventilated on a daily basis around this man!

Cole stepped back from her, turning her loose, and her heart fell. She was just a job to this guy, a pesky and nervous civilian to keep calm until he was done using her expertise to complete his mission.

"Are you done working for the night, Nissa? It's nearly four a.m."

"Really? I lost track of the time."

"If you're done, I'll power down the generator."

"Why?"

"Finite amount of diesel fuel. I don't know when I'll be able to get a refill."

"Sure. Go ahead."

In a few seconds, the overhead lights went out and Cole came back inside holding a couple of lit candles. "Take the bedroom. I'll sleep in the loft."

"I'm not kicking you out of your bed."

"And I'm not debating it with you," he said sternly.

She had to admit she liked it when he took charge like this. She loved feeling taken care of for once in her life. While her parents had been decent people, she'd been an only child born late in their lives, and they'd both had demanding professional careers. She'd been an inconvenience much of the time. She'd learned early on that if she wanted attention, she had to act like a good girl, stay out of their way and be an over-achiever whose résumé added to their prestige. She'd largely raised herself and gotten used to isolation over the years. Maybe that was why she was such a big scaredy cat. No one had ever been there to make her feel protected.

Cole was speaking again. "I'm sleeping upstairs, and you can sleep wherever you'd like—" He broke off as if it had dawned on him that she might choose to sleep with him.

It was tempting. *Really* tempting. But reluctantly, she reminded herself that her crush on the man did not a mutual lustfest make. For all she knew, he was tolerating her attraction to him purely to distract her enough to get through a mission until he didn't need her help any longer.

"Fine," she sighed. "I'll take the bedroom."

His bed smelled like him. Or at least like his aftershave. It was woodsy and green and clean. The combination of it and the smooth slide of his cotton sheets against her skin provoked wild fantasies. Groaning into his pillow, she tossed and turned, fighting to go to sleep in spite of her lust.

She had never, ever, had it this bad for a man. Not that she was the most experienced woman on earth, and not that she had ongoing relationships with men on a regular basis. Dating was hard, and being a natural introvert with a job she couldn't talk about—at all—didn't help. For that matter, she didn't usually run around crushing on anyone, either. This entire situation was an anomaly for her.

But there was something about Cole that called to her. And it wasn't just her erotic dream of him that drew her to him. It was his keen intelligence, the flawless condition of his body, his kindness, his courage, the way he took command.

And...she was back to lusting after him. Drat. She would never get to sleep now.

The sound of air-conditioning kicking on and the smell of bacon frying woke her. Bright sunshine crept in around the edges of the blackout curtains. She rolled over groggily, groaning out loud. Her entire body ached as if she'd been worked over with baseball bats.

"Rise and shine!" Cole called from the kitchen.

She grumbled back, telling him in no uncertain terms where he could put his rising and shining.

He laughed and called back, "Breakfast will be ready in ten minutes."

"Fine," she griped. "I'm bribable for free food."

Cole's hair was wet, and his cheeks rosy as she

emerged from the bedroom. "Don't tell me you've been exercising," she exclaimed.

"I just went out for a quick run and to have a look around the neighborhood."

"How did this area hold up during the storm?"

"Not bad. We're on high ground here, actually a few feet above sea level. There are tree limbs down and wind damage here and there, but it's nothing like Katrina."

Nissa snorted. "Nothing is like Katrina. Did you live here then?"

"No, but I was assigned to augment the police after the storm. We got here about three days after Katrina passed through."

"Was it as bad as everyone says it was?" she asked curiously.

"If you mean was it lawless, crazy and dangerous as hell? Yes. If you mean was it a humanitarian disaster? Hell, yes. We've learned a lot about crisis response since then."

"Thank goodness."

Their gazes met…and there it was again, the thick and insistent attraction that always hung between them, pulling them toward each other, threatening to wipe out all professional scruples in an instant.

They ate in awkward silence that she had no idea how to break without making a fool of herself. This morning it was Cole's turn to get up from the table first, carrying his dishes over to the sink.

She surreptitiously watched his muscular back and broad shoulders as he efficiently washed his plate and glass. He was almost at the end of a distinguished career. The last thing he needed was an entanglement with some woman that would destroy the outstanding reputation he'd built over many years of service. But Lord above, that man was walking temptation incarnate. Maybe after he retired he'd be open to a visit to Washington—

Stop that thought right there, missy. He's out of your league. Way out of your league. The idea of a relationship with him was pure fantasy. He was only being nice to her because he needed her not to freak out on him. That was all.

That was *all*.

The logical analyst in her knew it to be truth, but the hungry woman in her was desperate for it not to be so. She'd never met a man like him, and she had no doubt whatsoever that she would never meet another to compare to him. Being with him was like hanging out with a superhero, in the flesh. Having a crush on him and being the kind of woman who could hold a man like him for the long term were two entirely separate things.

Cole spoke over his shoulder from the sink where he was rinsing off dishes. "If you want to use your computer, I'll keep the generator running."

"Right. Work," she mumbled. She cranked up her laptop and was surprised to get a Wi-Fi connection. "Hey! The internet's working."

"The phone company must have gotten power hooked up to a wireless switch box nearby. That being the case…" He pulled out his cell phone and grinned. "Hah. Cell phone service is restored, too. They've got power going to a cell phone tower or two."

"Thank God. We're rejoining the civilized world."

"Yes, but that means our window to find Petrov's

hypothetical son and check out where he lives is closing fast."

She frowned. He had a point. "When are civilians
supposed to be let back into the city?"

"Tomorrow morning."

One day. That was all they had to find Petrov's son
and break into his home—

Good grief. Cole already had her thinking like a
SEAL. She was casually thinking about committing
a felony in the name of spying on someone. Curious,
she asked, "How do you maintain any sense of right
and wrong in the face of the kind of work you do?"

He leaned a hip on the kitchen counter and studied
her seriously. "How do *you* maintain a sense of ethics while watching surveillance footage, breaking into
peoples' email and peeking into their bank accounts?"

She tilted her head. "I keep my eye on the ultimate
goal—safeguarding my country's security."

"Same for me." He shrugged. "You look at private
information. I take physical action to obtain that information for people like you. Same difference. I keep
my moral compass by knowing why I do what I do."

Nissa nodded slowly. "But what about killing people?"

"I have to trust my superiors only to ask me to kill
when it's absolutely necessary. Once that necessity has
been determined, somebody has to do the job. Why
not me, at that point? I take no pleasure in killing, and
I don't lose myself in the wet work. I'm better suited
than most people to do that kind of a job because I dis-
like it and don't take it lightly."

It was a pragmatic attitude, but one she could respect. She'd sat in a few meetings where the deci-

sion was made to order a hit on a person hostile to the United States and who posed an imminent threat to American lives. Cole was right. No one should make the decision lightly. It made sense that no one should execute the decision lightly, either. They weren't so different, after all.

She logged in to her work email account and saw a message from her contact at the FBI to whom she'd sent the picture of the woman and boy. She opened it eagerly and announced, "We've got a name on the woman. Rosalie Martin. Deceased fifteen years ago."

"Any information on the boy?"

"Nope. But with her name, I can do a birth certificate search."

"Do you need access to local hospital servers to do that?" Cole asked.

She grinned at him. "You forget who I work for. We have acres of supercomputers that store data and information for us. With the internet up and running, I've got access to all of it." She typed rapidly, and then sat back. "It'll take a minute or two for a search of all birth records in the United States in the right time frame— say a ten-year span—but if Rosalie Martin had a baby, we'll know soon."

"How obscure does information have to be for you not to be able to find it?" Cole asked.

"If I've got the security classification to access it, there's almost no data in existence that I can't get to sooner or later."

"That's actually kind of scary."

Nissa shrugged. "It's my job. I spot possible threats to our nation and track them down wherever they might be hiding."

"Do you watch the dark web?"

"We have specialists who work the dark web and black web, but if a trail of information leads me there, I can follow it without too much trouble."

"I've always wanted to ask someone like you something," Cole said.

"Ask me."

"The Navy says it sanitizes men like me out of the system. So if you put my name into your computer, would you find anything?"

"Realizing that my system is not the usual system most other people have access to, let's find out, shall we?" She typed in his name, and in a matter of seconds was rattling off his Social Security number and date of birth. Cole looked alarmed, but she told him, "Those are a matter of public record according to the Geneva Conventions, so they wouldn't be scrubbed out of the system. The interesting bit will be to see if I can find out more about you."

"Don't find out too much," he blurted.

She ran into a wall right away, which relieved Cole. But then she showed him how a person with sufficient security clearance could bypass the block, and in a moment, his military record popped up on her screen. "Want me to keep digging?"

"There's more?" he asked.

Nissa laughed. "You have no idea." In a few minutes, she had his transcript from the Naval Academy. He'd gotten straight As and a few A pluses, graduating near the top of his class. "Well, look at you, smarty pants," she commented.

Cole rolled his eyes, and she kept digging.

His high school transcripts were equally impressive.

"Where were you when I was busting my butt to get through calculus?" Cole asked. "You could have just hacked my high school's computer and handed me the A."

"I didn't become a decent hacker until the agency taught me the tricks of the trade."

The next thing that popped up on her screen sobered her. She tried to close the window before Cole could see it, but he was too fast for her and swore under his breath behind her. She was looking at court records of a deposition he'd given as a teen against his father in a domestic abuse investigation.

"I'm sorry, Cole. I shouldn't have pried."

"I asked. My fault."

She shut down the search and leaned back in her chair, studying him as he moved into the living room and paced restlessly. "Do you want to talk about it?" she asked.

He glanced up at her, his eyes colder than she'd ever seen them. They were positively glacial—enough to send chills of trepidation down her spine. This must be how he looked when he killed someone. His voice was equally icy. He bit out, "My father was a bastard. My mother wouldn't leave him."

"Did he hit you?"

"Not after I hit him back. I was fifteen and finally bigger than him."

She winced. "Is that why you've been so protective of me? Because I'm a woman?"

He glanced at her briefly, then away. "No."

"Care to elaborate on that?"

"No."

Rats. He'd gone all strong and silent on her. "Do you still have contact with your parents?"

"My old man died about ten years ago. Heart attack. My mother died of a malignant brain tumor three years ago. It took her fast and she didn't suffer for long."

"I'm sorry," Nissa said in genuine sympathy. "Did you ever work things out with your father?"

Cole looked up at her, and his eyes were utterly emotionless. "We did, indeed, come to an understanding. I told him if he ever laid a hand on my mother again, I would kill him. And he had just enough brain cells left to believe me."

And, now she knew exactly why he'd become a SEAL. To protect his mother.

Her computer dinged to indicate an incoming message, and she opened the email. Three male babies had been born to a woman by the name Rosalie Martin in New Orleans in the ten-year window she'd requested.

"I've got three possible names for the boy in the picture," she announced. "Let me run them through the system and see if any of them still live in the local area."

This time, her computer dinged almost immediately. Cole came over and leaned over her shoulder close enough that the scent of his aftershave made her a little light-headed.

"What does this symbol mean?" He reached past her to point at a letter *D* in a circle by one of the boy's names.

"Deceased. Both of the surviving boys have Louisiana driver's licenses, though. Let me pull up addresses."

One of the boys, Stanley Martin, lived in Gretna, a

neighborhood south of the Mississippi River in New Orleans. The other one, Peter Martin, lived in Lakeview.

"Where's Lakeview?" she asked.

"North of the city, just east of Metairie, along Lake Pontchartrain." Cole added, "Any guesses as to which one is our guy?"

"The name Peter is obvious, and he lives on the same side of town as Petrov. However, Stanley can be an Anglicization of the Russian name Stanislav, and a good part of Petrov's criminal operation operated out of Gretna. I wouldn't rule out either one."

Cole asked, "Can you check the fathers' names on their birth certificates?"

"I can, but those are easy enough to fake. The birth mother can write in any name she wants. And Petrov wouldn't have let her use his real name."

"How do you want to proceed with checking these guys out?" Cole asked.

"We need to investigate both men as if they're the son. See if either of them has any ties to Petrov."

"When were they born?" Cole asked.

"Good question. Let me find out." She typed in a request and got back a startling answer. "They were both born on May 5th exactly thirty years ago."

"Twins?"

"Seems so."

Cole asked the next obvious question. "Then why was only one boy in the picture with the woman?"

She frowned. "Do you suppose it's possible she only told him about one child? Was she maybe trying to protect the other one?"

"Huh. Interesting theory. If we're going to find an answer we're on a short clock, since the National Guard is opening the city tomorrow. I suggest we visit both men's homes today and have a look around."

"You really are casual about breaking and entering, aren't you?"

Cole grinned. "I promise not to steal anything."

Nissa grinned back. "I don't promise. I'd love to get a look at both men's computers. If one or both of them is Petrov's son, there's bound to be some communication with Markus. And if we can figure out who's Petrov junior, maybe we can find a lead on daddy dearest." Then she asked, "How safe is it to break into private homes during daylight?"

"I'm a SEAL. I'm sneaky."

"Yes, but I'm not."

"Stick with me, kid. I'll make a spook out of you, yet."

She snorted. "Good luck with that. I jump at the sight of my own shadow."

"I noticed. But really, there's nothing to be worried about. I told you I'd look after you and keep you safe, and I will."

"Thanks."

"No problem."

And the smoking-hot attraction was there again, hanging heavily between them, just like that.

Chapter 10

Cole was so off-balance around this woman he could hardly think, let alone operate. In some ways, she was so young and naive, like when she was scared of the dark. But in others, she was shockingly wise, like when she'd been totally cool about his family's sordid past.

When that deposition had popped up on her computer screen, he'd died a little right then and there. It was a part of his past he'd done everything in his power to bury and forget over the years. Both of his parents were long gone, along with their dysfunctional marriage. All that was left in him was a deep suspicion of the institution of marriage, in general.

After all, he was his father's son. Who was to say that some woman wouldn't infuriate him enough to lash out someday, just like his father used to do? Although, the idea of striking a woman caused a gut-deep recoil of horror in him. The idea of hitting Nissa, for example. It would be like kicking a puppy. And he liked dogs. A lot. In fact, his only response to the idea of her getting hit was a visceral need to harm anyone who *ever* harmed her.

He drove north into Lakeview, but ran into flooded streets a half dozen blocks shy of the address of Peter Martin. "We're walking from here," he announced. "Or wading as the case might be."

Nissa groaned. "Please, God, let there be no alligators or snakes in the water."

Cole grinned. "I can't promise you either."

"You're killing me," she groused.

"I'll shoot any gators that decide you look like a tasty snack."

"I'll hold you to that," she declared, scowling.

The water never got more than knee-deep, however, and no critters were out and about this sunny morning. They arrived at Peter Martin's address, a new building with modern lines that looked out of place among its neighbors. Cole let them inside a home as sparse and modern as the exterior of the building. Everything was beige or brushed nickel where it wasn't stained black by floodwater. They waded around the ground floor among the sodden furniture. The rancid smell of mildew was starting to permeate the place.

"This place is going to be a total gut job," he commented.

"Help me look for a computer," Nissa said absently.

She was doing that thing again where she studied the room intently. As he looked around, he noted sight lines through windows, places to hide from gunfire, objects that would make for decent improvised weapons.

"What do you see when you look around this place?" he asked curiously.

"An organized man. Anal retentive. Secretive."

"Secretive?" Cole blurted. "How do you get that?"

"Closed cabinets. Bare walls. Bare tabletops. No clutter that would reveal anything about whoever lives here. No pictures anywhere. A propensity for putting everything in drawers or cupboards. Monochromatic color palette."

"Maybe that just means the guy has boring taste."

She shook her head. "People reveal a lot about themselves in the spaces they live in. Markus Petrov, although secretive also, is much more of an extrovert than this guy. Petrov loves to display his wealth and power within his home. He decorated his private living spaces with extravagant colors, big furniture, lots of pictures of himself. This guy is the complete opposite."

"I don't see a desk down here. There's just the living room and kitchen on this floor. Let's check upstairs," Cole said.

They squished up the stairs, water draining out of their boots as they climbed out of the floodwater. The second floor revealed an office and what looked like a spare bedroom.

Nissa wasted no time moving over to the computer sitting on the desk. "Have you got a battery pack?" she asked him.

He nodded and connected it to the desktop computer. The screen powered up. A three-inch vertical stripe on the left side of the screen was ruined, with black lines and pixilated fragments.

"Moisture damage," Nissa commented as she typed. "The good news is the hard drive is working."

"Are you planning to take it?"

"No. I'm just going to copy its contents onto this thumb drive," she muttered as she plugged the thumb drive into a USB port. "While it copies, let's check out the top floor."

The third floor was, not surprisingly, a master suite with a bedroom, bathroom and another computer in an alcove.

Nissa grinned as she looked at it. "Now that's a sweet gaming setup."

"Gaming? How do you know?"

"Twin large-screen monitors. Surround sound speakers. Auxiliary joystick. High-end headphones. And look at that computer. That baby's state-of-the-art."

"Maybe this is the hard drive we should be copying," he replied.

"Oh, we're going to copy it, too." She plugged in another thumb drive as he hooked up his last battery pack. "And, we're leaving a little gift for Mr. Martin, as well."

He watched as she plugged a tiny drive of some kind into an open port on the back side of the desktop tower. The device was barely the size of his pinkie fingernail and blended in with the jumble of cables and connectors. "What's that?"

"Cloning device," she answered. "Any time this system's running and online, it will send a phantom signal to my computer."

He followed her back to the second-floor office and watched her drop to her knees beside the first computer to install another tiny dongle. She commented, "I'll see every keystroke, every email, every website he visits."

"That's a little scary."

"Welcome to my world." She grinned at him and then disappeared under the desk, her luscious backside sticking out. Her pants tightened across her rear end, and an urge to reach down and caress her nearly overcame him.

Her muffled voice came out from under the desk. "You may kidnap and kill people, but I watch them. I learn every detail of their lives, every dirty little secret."

"Yeah, I noticed."

She mumbled, "Hey, I'm really sorry about that stuff I found on you. But the truth is, I'd have run a background check on you at some point, anyway. It's just as well that you were there to see what I found."

"Why would you have run a background check on me?" he asked, surprised.

"Well, I'm, umm, interested in you. I check out every guy I date."

He stared down at her tush in shock. Date? She was considering dating him? Was he considering dating her?

He sure as hell was considering sleeping with her. But did he want more? How *much* more? A brief image flashed through his mind, of them living together, maybe having a few kids, a normal life with a minivan and family activities, coming home to Nissa every night…

He waited for the distaste for normal to come. For the fear of being held down in one place to flood him. For the terror of being committed to a single woman forever to overcome him.

And he waited.

And waited.

Until at length it dawned on him that none of that was going to come this time.

What in the hell did that mean?

Nissa was thoughtful as they made their way south across the city toward the second house. If she were a betting woman, she'd guess the place they'd just left was the home of the unrevealed Petrov son. Still, she couldn't wait to see the next place.

They had to detour well west of downtown to the Huey Long Bridge, but they eventually crossed the Mississippi River. It was a scary proposition with muddy waters swirling high around the bridge girders, far too close to the road surface. She white knuckled the door handle as Cole made his way carefully across the structure.

The flooding was more widespread on this side of the river, and it took them nearly an hour to find a reasonably dry route into the vicinity of Stan Martin's home.

The guy's home turned out to be a big brick warehouse. "Is this the right place?" she asked doubtfully.

"Let's go inside and find out," Cole answered.

A padlock and chain on a big sliding door took him a few minutes to pick, and he shoved the rusted metal door open. It was, indeed, a warehouse. Whatever was usually stored in here had been moved out, though, likely because of the water that had flooded the place. Watermarks ran nearly four feet up the interior walls. All that was left of the floodwaters now, though, was a layer of black sludge that was slick as ice to walk on.

The entire back half of the building was overhung

by a second floor that might be a living space. It was to that they headed. Carefully.

The steps were metal mesh, and she clattered up them, gratified to observe that Cole wasn't managing to move up them any more quietly than she. A locked door blocked the top of the stairs. She stepped aside to let Cole do his magic, and in a minute the door swung open.

Cole started to step inside, but she grabbed his arm and cried, "Stop!"

"Why?" he replied tersely.

"Look at it."

The interior of what was, indeed, a residence was spotless. Totally spotless. Everything was shiny and white—polished white marble floors, white walls, white quartz counters, shiny chrome and even white furniture.

"We have to take off our boots and socks before we go in there and track in mud. And while you're at it, roll your pants up," she directed Cole.

"Sheesh. You sound like my mother."

"Well, we can stomp around and leave black boot prints everywhere, or we can just leave a note for Stan to let him know we've broken into his place to have a look around."

Cole grinned at her and rolled up his pants. "This is a first for me. A barefoot mission."

She tried not to stare as his sculpted calves came into sight, bulging with muscle, and smooth bronze skin. She tried not to dwell on the fact that her own legs were scrawny and pale by comparison.

They repeated pretty much the same process as they had at the last house. She looked around, and the pristine white of the place was completely unrelieved by any color or clutter. If Peter Martin had been secretive, Stan Martin was obsessive. Obsessively clean, obsessively organized, obsessively precise. Even the hangers in his closet were perfectly spaced two inches apart. Not a smudge or a single fingerprint marred the perfection of his housekeeping, either. The apartment was mostly one large space with only a bedroom and bathroom separated from the rest. Hence, it was no problem to spot the computer on a glass-and-chrome desk in one corner. It was to that she moved.

She had no problem copying the hard drive, but leaving behind a cloning dongle was going to be a problem. Stan had one of those sleek monitor and computer all-in-one models that was completely devoid of cables and bulky ports that would disguise even her tiny thumb drive.

Frowning, she rummaged in her pouch of computer gear. She found what she was looking for, a vibration transmitter. She had to lie down on her back underneath the table and reach way up to the back of the glass desk to hide the device behind one of the chrome cross supports at the back of the table.

She scooted out from under the desk and stood to examine her work.

"Satisfied?" Cole asked her.

"It'll do. Now we just have to hope that Stan or Peter reveals himself to be the son in contact with Markus."

"What do you think the odds are that we can figure out where Petrov is in the next few days?" Cole asked.

She shrugged. "It'll all depend on what I can pull off this computer. The hard drive is almost done downloading. We can head back to your office and have a look at the data, and then I'll be able to formulate a better answer for you."

"What's your gut saying, Nissa?" he asked.

"I think Petrov is still in the area. I can't believe he'll abandon the money still in the bank accounts we're watching. It's messy to leave it behind and provides a possible trail for us to follow once he disappears for good. He's not the kind of man to leave loose ends behind. He'll erase every bit of evidence of his existence before he goes to ground once and for all."

Cole nodded. "Seen everything you need to see in here?"

"Yes. Peter and Stan are definitely twins."

"How do you know?"

"They arrange their drawers and closets the exact same way. They both are neat freaks, and they both are insanely secretive. For two men, born the same day, in the same town, to women of the same name, and with the same last name themselves to be so similar and not be brothers would be nigh unto impossible."

"Fair enough."

Cole locked the door behind them while she worked at lacing on her boots again. He stomped into his boots, and they retraced their steps out of the building. The muck on the floor was still wet enough that their footsteps from before were already filling in with water and slime. In a few hours, there would be no trace of their having been here.

They slipped outside, and Nissa gratefully took a deep breath of fresh-smelling air. The smell of mildew and ruin was becoming all too familiar to her. At least all the sneaking around and dangerous stuff was over. Now she could sit back, wait for her cloning devices to start reporting, and in the meantime, analyze some nice, safe data. No more SEAL missions for her, thank goodness.

Stan Martin stepped out of his panic room thoughtfully. So. That woman and the SEAL with her knew his father was alive, did they? Well, well, well. Wasn't Markus going to be interested in that bit of news?

He looked around his apartment critically. They'd done a half-decent job of not marking the place up, at any rate. Still, he pulled out cleaning spray and a cloth and scrubbed down all the surfaces they might have touched. If only he'd had working security cameras, he would know everything they'd touched. As it was, he just had to clean the whole place. God, he couldn't wait for the electricity to come back on so his air filters could do their job. He hated the smell of filth rising from the warehouse below.

They would pay for coming into his house and mauling his things. He would make sure of it. Markus was going to be livid that someone outside the family knew he was alive. There was going to be hell to pay, all right. He'd hate to be that Nissa woman and her thug friend. Yes, indeed. The two of them were royally screwed.

Wary of bugs the intruders might have planted, he retreated to his safe room to pull out his cell phone. Service had returned this morning, thankfully. He placed a call to a memorized phone number he was strictly forbidden from writing down.

"Papa, it's me. We have a problem..."

Chapter 11

Nissa worked through the remainder of the afternoon, testing the feeds from her remote cloning devices. She hooked her laptop to Peter's computer and she borrowed Cole's desktop computer in the loft to monitor Stan's. She set the two up side by side. And now it was a waiting game to see who each man contacted electronically and what they said.

Cole cooked something downstairs that smelled Italian and delicious while she dug into the data from the twins' hard drives. Most of it was innocuous, but she isolated a series of emails from each man that might be using a code of some kind to disguise the true meaning of their messages. She started listing words that didn't quite seem to be the right word in sentences, and sure enough, the two lists from each man had more overlap than could be coincidence.

The next task would be to track down the recipients of the coded emails, particularly the recipients in the week prior to the hurricane's arrival, after the criminal side of Petrov's organization had been taken down. If the recipients worked for Petrov, they could only be members of his spy ring or perhaps a few members of his crime ring that the big FBI sting had failed to net.

And if she got lucky, one of the recipients was Markus Petrov, himself.

"Dinner's ready!" Cole called up to her.

She went downstairs to a pan of the best-tasting lasagna she'd ever had, and a salad. Her appetite was sharp after the day's running around, and she dug in with gusto. Afterward she helped wash the dishes and tidy the kitchen, and then Cole went outside to turn off the generator for a few hours. He'd rigged the computers to recharge whenever the generator kicked on automatically to cool the refrigerator and freezer. That way her monitoring of the twins' computers would be continuous.

She moved into the living room and had just sat down on the sofa when the lights went out and plunged the house into darkness. She didn't hear Cole come inside, but all of a sudden, a shadow moved in front of the window and she jumped about a foot in the air. "Dang, you're quiet!"

"I should hope so. My life routinely depends on it."

"Right. I forgot for a second." When she was in his home with him like this, watching him do domestic things like cooking and washing, it was easy to see him as a regular guy and not the trained killer that he was.

She watched with interest as he lit several pillar candles on the tables and shelves around the room. A soft, freakishly romantic glow filled the room. The entire evening stretched before them. How were they going to pass the time? It wasn't like they could watch a movie on TV. It was only the two of them, together.

And, just like that, her heart was racing again, and acute awareness of him as an insanely hot man made her jumpy as all get-out. He sat down on the other end of the couch and propped his bare feet on the coffee table. Crud. Even his feet were perfect.

"So, Nissa. I've been curious about something since we met. Where does your name come from? It's really unusual."

"It means signal in Hebrew, but I don't give my parents that much credit for symbolic depth in naming me. My grandmother was named Vanessa, and they say I'm loosely named after her."

"At least you're not named after Nessie, the Loch Ness monster."

She rolled her eyes. "I got called Messy Nessy all the time as a kid."

"Why Messy?"

"My hair."

He frowned and reached out to lift a golden wave and let it sift through his fingers. Her heart fluttered wildly. "What's wrong with your hair?"

"Nothing at the moment. But any time we go outside, I've been keeping it braided, which contains its wilder tendencies. You haven't seen it loose and exposed to humidity."

"It was plenty humid in the bayou."

"Yes, but I kept it tightly under control out there."

"Do you always stay tightly under control?" His voice was low and serious, and although there wasn't the slightest overt sexual overtone, nonetheless, her insides turned to jelly.

She half whispered, "Not always."

He sighed. "What on earth are we going to do about this attraction between us? You can't tell me you don't feel it, too."

"I definitely feel it," she confessed.

"We've both tried hard to ignore it, and we did manage to get through the operational portion of our mission without giving in. But your job's nearly over. As soon as we get a bead on Petrov, my guys and I will apprehend him, you'll make a simple identification and then you'll leave."

Her heart clenched at the idea of leaving him and going back to Washington, DC. "I've gotten so used to being with you day and night, I won't know what to do with myself if I leave you."

"I know the feeling," he admitted.

Their gazes locked, and he leaned toward her very slowly. She met him halfway. His mouth stopped about six inches from hers. "Tell me, Nissa. What do you like to do when you lose control?"

She leaned in the last few inches. "I kiss the boys."

Their smiles merged into a soft, wondering kiss. She couldn't believe this remarkable man wanted anything to do with her, but who was she to argue? His mouth slanted across hers, and he drew her partially across his lap, fitting their mouths together even more perfectly. He seemed to be in no hurry tonight, and prepared to take his time getting to know her in this way.

Given the panting lust she'd been living with constantly for the past several days, this wasn't what she'd expected. She'd thought he would fall on her, tear her clothes off and launch straight into gnarly sex. She hadn't realized how nervous she'd been about that prospect until this very second, though.

But as she gradually relaxed and the tension slowly drained from her neck and shoulders, she realized she'd needed this easy, no-pressure approach. It was as if he'd read her mind.

"Thank you," she mumbled against his delicious mouth.

"For what?" He nibbled at her lower lip and then laved the spot lightly with his tongue.

"For not just jumping me and going for it."

He kissed his way across her jaw and paused to sample the tender spot just below her left ear. "Give me a little more credit than that. Although…" he took her earlobe between his teeth and nipped just hard enough to make her gasp and to send bolts of electricity through her body "…the thought had occurred to me."

"What thought?" she gasped, arching up into his hard body and clinging to his broad shoulders.

"The thought of ripping off my clothes and jumping you. The idea has occurred to me on more than one occasion."

"Thank God. I would hate to think I'd imagined all those vibes between us."

His mouth closed on hers again, this time with considerably more heat. He murmured against her lips, "You didn't imagine them."

He lifted her slightly and shifted his weight, and all of a sudden, she was lying on the sofa with him sprawled out beside her. His thigh draped across hers and his arm was a delightful weight across her belly. His muscular body was as irresistible as ever, and a driving need to feel his flesh came over her. She scooted over a bit and rolled to face him, plunging her hands under his polo shirt and pushing up the soft cotton. She inhaled sharply at the feel of hot skin over hard muscle.

He became all motion and heat and masculine energy, then. His big, hard palms slid under her T-shirt, returning the favor and stripping it off over her head. He pushed her gently to her back as he kissed his way across her collarbone. He cupped her breast with his hand, which was tanned against the white lace of her bra, measuring and testing the resilience of her flesh in his palm. His knee landed between hers, and in an effort to appease the hungry ache between her thighs, she squeezed his leg with both of hers.

She didn't realize her entire body was undulating beneath his until he laughed a little against her temple and mumbled, "You're going to test my restraint hard tonight, aren't you?"

"Who says I want any restraint out of you?" she retorted, staring up at him. His eyes were silver in the candlelight, his hair glistening sable. The more she looked at him, the more gorgeous he became. Or maybe that was just her seeing behind the facade to the real man beneath.

"Well, then." He pushed away from her and stood up, scooping her in his arms and striding swiftly to the back of the house and his bedroom. He put a knee on the mattress and laid her on it, following her down, kissing her and murmuring words of praise and desire as he stretched out beside her.

The remainder of their clothes went flying, and then

his erection was pressing against her belly, and she was pressing herself against him in wanton desire.

"You're sure you want this?" he asked.

"Absolutely," she declared, grateful that he had enough respect for her to obtain consent, even after she'd practically thrown herself at him.

"If you don't like anything or want to stop—"

She cut him off. "I'll let you know. Right now, the only thing I don't like is that you're talking and not kissing me."

He grinned and gathered her close, kissing her voraciously now, surging against her hungrily. He was big and imposing and could overpower her any time he liked, but in spite of that, she felt perfectly safe with him. The only thing that gave her pause was how very physical a guy he was. She was deeply skeptical of her ability to keep up with him when it came to athletic sex. However, she was going to give it her best shot or die trying…and what a way to go.

She wrapped her legs around his hips and hung on tightly as he leaned away from her for a moment and opened his nightstand drawer. She heard a quick rip of plastic and he reached between them to put on a condom. Then, he surged over her, smiling, his weight crushing her into the mattress, and she sighed in delight.

She reached for him, drawing him to her, desperate to be in as much skin-to-skin contact with him as humanly possible. Now that they were on the verge of finally doing this, he seemed in no rush at all to move things along. He kissed her leisurely, and she kissed him back urgently, her fingers roaming across his back and shoulders, and settling in the short hairs at his nape.

The tendons in his neck flexed powerfully, reminding her of the warrior this man was. No matter that his mouth was gentle on hers and his weight propped carefully on an elbow in spite of her best efforts to convince him to let go of his formidable control.

Finally, she huffed against his mouth.

"What?" he asked.

"You're making me crazy, Cole."

He pushed up onto both of his elbows to stare down at her in the darkness. She felt, more than saw, his stare. "How so?"

"Will you quit messing around and make love to me already? I won't break, darn it."

"I didn't want to scare you."

"Hah. You couldn't scare me if you tried," she declared. The truth of her own words sank into her soul. She trusted this man. Utterly and completely.

"That's because you've never seen me neutralize someone."

She laughed. "You can try to talk me out of doing this with you, but you'll fail, Cole. I want you."

He went very still, as if having to absorb what she'd just said. And maybe as if not entirely believing her.

She added, "You forget what I do for a living, mister. I see the after action reports from guys like you all the time. Your work is no mystery to me. Men like you attack only when ordered to or to save your own lives. And neither of those make you a killer or a bad person. They only make you a soldier following orders."

She felt the intensity of his stare and asked in more

than a little frustration, "Are we really going to debate morality and ethics while I'm naked in your bed?"

It started as a low rumble in his chest and rolled forth as full-blown laughter. "Good God. I've never met a woman like you. Most women who go for SEALs get all turned on by the idea of sleeping with a guy who's capable of violence."

She pushed him onto his back, and he gave way to her puny strength good-naturedly. She sat upright, and glared down at him, demanding. "Are you calling me a groupie?"

"I guess not."

She surged over him, putting a hand on either side of his head. "Don't ever mistake me for some shallow chick who just wants your body—" She broke off. "Well, I do totally want your body. But I'm not shallow."

He wrapped his arm around her neck and pulled her down to him. "Got it. And I'm sorry. You're just so far outside my experience, I'm not sure what to do with you."

"Make love to me, you idiot. Don't hold back, don't try to be someone you're not. I want *you.*"

"Well, then." He rolled her over in a quick reversal of their positions. And make love to her, he did.

He pushed the covers entirely off the bed, baring her to his gaze, and to his mouth and hands, which he made liberal use of to explore her body. Every last ticklish, sensitive, panting inch of it. Cole Perriman was no amateur when it came to knowing his way around a woman, and he unabashedly played her body, teasing and tantalizing her into a frenzy of lust that left her vision hazy and her brain completely fogged.

He murmured words of pleasure and encouragement, for which she was abjectly grateful. She was a mere mortal, and making love to a superhero was intimidating, no matter how much she adored and trusted him. How was she ever going to measure up to him?

Wave upon wave of pleasure rolled over her as he stroked her core in time with tantalizing swipes of his tongue across her nipples. They hadn't even done the deed yet. Finally, she grabbed his shoulders and dragged him up her body—or more accurately, he let her drag him up, since he was about a hundred times stronger than her—and she hooked her right heel around his hips. She panted, "If you don't take me right now, I'm going to explode."

"Mmm. Just how I like my woman. Hot and bothered."

"I'm burning up and losing my mind!"

He laughed down at her, but as the humor faded from his shadowed features, their gazes met. Naked intimacy flowed between them. And that was when she felt him at her core, pressing forward, entering her with slow certainty, filling her with his hardness and heat, a stretching sensation of delight that had her arching up eagerly into the invasion.

His stare never left hers, and in his eyes she saw the intense enjoyment of her body clutching his, the possessiveness as he started to move within her, the drugging ecstasy as a climax clawed at both of them, and he fought like hell to hold it off.

She took no mercy on him and joyfully found her first release, shuddering with pleasure and crying out into his mouth as he kissed her and inhaled her orgasm. Still he moved within her, and still he stared down at her. Gradually, wonder and even amazement filled his eyes as she climaxed again, and yet again.

And still he stroked within her, using his strength and stamina and extreme fitness to both of their vast delights. Surfing the pleasure storm he created within her, she surged against his sweat-slick body over and over, reveling in the way his abs contracted against hers, the way the muscles in his arms and neck strained, the way he engulfed her with his size and strength, overwhelming her senses in every way.

He looked like a god making love to her but he smelled like fresh rain, forests and man. He tasted like the sky and sea, and his breathing sounded like a storm in her ears. It was the greatest thing she'd ever heard. And the feel of him—oh, the feel of him was indescribably wonderful.

She took his body deep into hers and opened her heart to him joyfully, letting him look into her soul as she stared up at him, coming sharply and then shuddering down the back side of the climax for longer than she'd known possible.

He absorbed her pleasure in silence, but his eyes blazed like twin stars in the night sky, piercing her soul and stripping her bare. And into the heavenly abyss of his creation he surged faster and faster, thrusting one last time, sheathing himself to the fullest within her, and then throwing his head back and coming with a cry that was as primal as it was uninhibited.

Her entire being shattered. She shattered in gratitude that this man had given this most intimate part of himself to her, that he'd seemed to enjoy making love to her as much as she'd enjoyed it, that they'd somehow, miraculously, found each other.

"Where have you been my whole life?" she panted.

"I found you as fast as I could," he mumbled.

She clutched him against her as he collapsed on top of her, his head resting on the pillow beside hers, his breath hot against her neck. He was breathing hard as if he'd just sprinted a mile full-out.

After a blissful eternity, he pressed up on his elbows above her. "I'm sorry. I'm crushing you," he murmured.

"Crush me. It's lovely."

"You're lovely. Hell, you're perfect."

"Cole Perriman, I'm a lot of things, but perfect is not one of them."

He rolled to one side, taking her with him, in an embrace that was both affectionate and protective—all the things she'd ever hoped for from a man and never gotten before.

"Whatever you, are, good, bad, or ugly, Nissa Beck, you're perfect to me."

She couldn't argue with that. Not one bit.

Chapter 12

Cole stared up at the ceiling of his bedroom as Nissa slept on his outstretched arm. He'd done some dumb things in his life, but this had to rank right up there. The mission was not over yet. But he'd given in to his raging desire for Nissa and put his personal feelings ahead of the job.

Hell, he didn't even know what his feelings regarding her were. He definitely had a major crush on her. But it had been so long since he'd cared for anyone that he didn't remember how to do this. Or maybe he'd never known how to care for anyone at all.

He'd loved his mother, but the way he felt about Nissa was entirely different. His mother had been a distant figure he'd never really understood. She'd been closed off and withdrawn for so much of his life—he'd never really known the woman she'd been before his father had sapped all the life out of her.

But Nissa was a vibrant, dynamic woman, full of life and curiosity. She was soft in all the ways he was hard, sensitive in the ways he was tough, warm in all the ways he was cold.

As the hours of the night passed slowly, he could find no end to this situation that was positive for them. Tonight had to be a one-time thing. He had to get up in the morning, walk away from her and not look back. Maybe after he retired he could look her up, and if he was lucky, she wouldn't have moved on to another relationship yet.

Jealousy of whatever lucky bastard ended up with her flared in his gut. He wanted her for himself, dammit. But he of all people knew that timing mattered. They might have found each other, but the timing was all wrong.

It was near dawn when a beep from upstairs startled him out of the meditative state he'd resorted to when sleep utterly refused to come to him. That sounded like an alarm of some kind.

"Nissa, wake up. Your computers just got a hit."

She roused like a kitten, adorable and sweet as she stretched and rubbed her eyes sleepily. "Do I have to get up? Can't we sleep some more?"

"You tell me. Your laptop just beeped three times in about a minute."

She grumbled under her breath and sat up. He devoured the sight of her naked back, slender and feminine. A back whose every contour he'd explored, whose taste he knew now, and whose feel he would never forget.

Another beep sounded overhead.

"One of the twins must be sending emails," she mumbled. "Stay here. I'll go check it out."

He shamelessly watched her pert backside as she sauntered out of his room. He saw her shadow swing into the bathroom and she emerged in a moment, swathed in his bathrobe, which swallowed her petite form.

A floorboard squeaked upstairs as she moved to his desk, and he waited patiently to hear what she'd found. In a few minutes, she returned to stand beside the bed.

"Are you awake?" she whispered.

He opened his eyes to gaze up at her. "I am. But for the record, if you do ever need to wake me up, touch my foot and then stand back. SEALs are known to wake rather violently."

"Duly noted."

"What did you find?" he asked.

"I think Peter was sending coded messages again. The words he chooses aren't quite right for the syntax in which he uses them. There's just something off about the emails from him and Stan. I'll work on decrypting the code in the morning."

He held a welcoming arm out to her. If he was only going to have this one night with her, he damned well planned to make the most of it. "Come back to bed, Nissa."

She slipped out of the robe and into his arms, coming to him joyfully, bringing all her light and charm with her, and sharing them with him. He was humbled by the gift.

And as she drifted off to sleep sprawled across his chest this time, he cursed the fates for bringing him this woman when he couldn't make her his. Tomorrow, he would tell her they couldn't do this again. She would be hurt and angry, but it was the only honorable thing to do.

Man, being honorable sucked sometimes.

He woke up to bright sunshine creeping around the edges of his blackout blinds. Wow. He hadn't slept this late in forever. Half-conscious, he became aware of something soft and wonderful passing over his body lightly. It was a massage, but as if given to him by an ethereal fairy barely discernable to his physical form.

Something warm and gentle and loving joined the light fingertips touching his skin, and he realized with a jolt to full consciousness that a mouth was moving across his chest, exploring his body with little licks and nips that were tantalizing and sexy as hell.

He shouldn't do this. Last night needed to be a one-off deal. No repeats today or ever. He'd promised himself.

But as Nissa's mouth traced a path of pillage and destruction down his stomach his resolve wavered.

Be tough. Be cold. Emotionless. In total control of mind and body.

Nope. Not happening. His body had a mind all its own right now, and his stiff flesh was eagerly anticipating the arrival of her mouth any second.

"Nissa," he ground out from between clenched teeth. "We can't."

Her laugh was sultry and soft, and his erection jumped almost painfully. "Sure we can. We already have. And I want to return the favor from last night. I want to make you feel at least half as amazing as you made me feel."

Her tongue flicked around the base of his main problem and he groaned aloud. *Must. Resist.* No torture training he'd ever experienced came even remotely close to this in agony.

"Relax, Cole. I've got this." Her hand closed around his aching shaft, and her mouth closed upon its ultrasensitive tip. And, she did, indeed, have it.

His self-control shattered all at once, flying off in a thousand shards of discarded intentions. He surged up into her grasp and lost his mind as she played his body like a musical instrument.

She stripped away every last layer of sane thought, leaving him a mass of ravenous lust. For her. He'd had sex with women before, but he'd always been the one in control, the one calling the shots and holding back a little. But Nissa left him nowhere to hide, nowhere to retreat emotionally. She drew forth feelings and desires he didn't even know he had.

To want someone like this, with every cell in his body, with every breath, with every thought—it was unlike anything he'd ever dreamed existed.

His entire body coiled in anticipation of climax, and he reached down for her, drawing her up his body, a delicious slide of skin on skin.

"What am I going to do with you?" he muttered against her mouth.

Her lips curved into a smile beneath his. "Whatever you want."

He groaned and rolled over, kissing her with abandon, inhaling everything about her into himself, making her a part of him in ways he hadn't known he could until this very moment. Their bodies, now familiar to each other, joined easily, finding a shared rhythm as naturally as breathing.

His raging lust expanded, morphing into something more, something emotional, that made the act of making love practically transcendental. He stared into her beautiful eyes, transfixed by the emotions he saw in them, the adoration and frank enjoyment she took in him.

For once, he felt like a woman was making love with *him*, not with some symbolic military badass. For once, he wasn't a SEAL. He was a man. She made him whole in ways he hadn't even known he was broken.

The pace of their lovemaking accelerated and he rode the wave, loving every second of the building pleasure. Nissa's eyes glazed over as her climax neared, and he took fierce satisfaction in pushing her over the edge. He captured her shuddering cries of ecstasy in a deep kiss that claimed all of her pleasure for himself. And then his own body exploded, his orgasm ripping through him like a blast of dynamite.

If there'd been any semblance of control left before, it was torn away now. He sagged on his elbows, panting, just conscious enough to stop himself from crushing her. His head hung between his shoulders, his forehead touching hers lightly.

She undid him in every way it was possible to be undone. Surrendering to that reality was inevitable, and glorious…

…until rational thought began to intrude upon his overloaded senses. And that was when fear overtook him. It was insidious and ugly, worming its way into his psyche like a thief sneaking into his head.

What had she done to him? He was the ice man. Frosty. Mr. Control. And she effortlessly destroyed all of that, leaving him naked and vulnerable. He didn't *do* vulnerable, dammit!

His job, his life, his entire identity revolved around being not vulnerable.

He pushed away from her and came to his feet, striding away from Nissa and his bed. He took an angry shower, scrubbing off the sweet vanilla scent of her, scouring away the feel of the pleasure she gave him, doing his damnedest to soak away any memory of what they'd had between them.

Making love with her had been a mistake. A terrible miscalculation that he mustn't repeat. Ever.

When he emerged into the bedroom, Nissa had rolled onto her stomach and dozed off. Tangled in the sheets, with her curly hair untamed, she looked like a siren in his bed.

She was as dangerous as one of the mythical females, too. Nissa would destroy him if he let her.

Using every bit of stealth at his command, he moved around his bedroom silently, dressing. He closed the door quietly behind him and raced out of his home, frantic to put as much distance as possible between himself and her.

He jumped in his truck and backed out of the driveway, sighing with relief that he'd made a clean getaway. Well, not entirely clean. She'd shown him a scary truth about himself. His icy armor was not as ironclad as he'd thought.

But he would fix the breach. He *had* to, or else how would he survive?

* * *

Nissa woke up slowly, deeply relaxed and rested. She took her time rousing, rolling onto her back and enjoying the cool air wafting down from the air conditioner vent overhead onto her bare skin.

Deep silence enveloped her, and she knew intuitively that she was alone in the house. She couldn't feel Cole's presence. She wasn't worried, though. Not after the extraordinary night and morning they'd shared. She had no doubt whatsoever that she'd rocked his world every bit as much as he'd rocked hers. She'd seen it in his eyes when they'd made love.

Smiling lazily, she climbed out of his big bed and made her way to the shower. It had been used this morning, but the bath mat was mostly dry. He'd been gone a while, then. She let the hot water pound away the residual soreness of athletic sex with a man of Cole's general fitness and stamina. After her shower, she dried her hair, straightening it as best she could.

She stared into her small suitcase. She had one pair of clean underwear left, and one clean shirt. When Cole got home, she would ask to use his washing machine. But if she was going to be here a while longer, she would love to get a few more items of clothing.

She cranked up her laptop and pulled up a map of New Orleans. A nice shopping area was only a few blocks away. According to the description, the series of small, artisan-owned shops offered a variety of items including clothing, lingerie and toiletries.

She streamed a local news channel next. It was playing live footage of the masses of residents streaming back into New Orleans, creating traffic jams and congestion galore. She made herself a sandwich and had just finished rinsing off her plate when the generator kicked off. Rather than stay in the house as it heated up over the next few hours until it was time for the generator to come on again, she decided to go see if any of the shops were open for business.

Her hair was a lion's mane within a few blocks and she sighed, pulling it back into a ponytail. It looked like a poodle's pom-pom tail like this, but there was no help for it.

A few of the shopkeepers had, indeed, returned, although they were mostly cleaning up debris out front or carrying down merchandise from upstairs storerooms where it had been stashed to avoid possible flooding.

She talked a few of them into selling her skirts and tops, soap and matching perfume and her best purchase of all—barrettes and hairbands to help corral her runaway hair. She even found a couple of pairs of cute sandals decorated with crystals, bows and ribbons. Thankfully, the internet was working in this area after a fashion and they were able to run her credit card, albeit slowly.

It was a rare treat to indulge her inner girly girl. The CIA demanded conservative business attire for its employees, and her closet at home was populated almost entirely by gray, brown, navy and black suits and equally boring blouses.

Sunshine was warm on her face, and the humidity today just enough to make the air feel soft on her skin. She felt great as she carried her purchases back to Cole's place. Life was pretty darned close to perfect. She'd found an amazing man—an actual adult one— who seemed to genuinely return her interest, they were closing in on Markus Petrov and she had some attractive, feminine clothes that reflected her true personality for a change.

It felt incredible to break out of her shell like this. She should have done this years ago. Who knew that getting out in the field and away from a desk would be so good for her soul? Or maybe it was the man who'd helped her overcome her fears who'd been so good for her soul. Either way, she felt like skipping as she rounded the corner to Cole's house.

She spent the afternoon babysitting the computers upstairs, occupying herself by combing through the files on both Peter and Stan Martins' systems. While most people seemed to think hacking was sexy stuff, she knew from her work at Langley that the vast majority of peoples' lives were intensely boring and that most of what hackers looked at was useless and equally boring data.

Of course, the good news was she knew how to filter through the mundane mass to find the significant tidbits, and she put those skills to use now.

As the afternoon aged into evening and still Cole hadn't returned, her general sense of joy dimmed a little. Where was he? And why hadn't he been in contact with her all day?

Bah. She was just being insecure. He was no doubt tied up helping out with opening up New Orleans to the general population.

She made herself a peanut butter and jelly sandwich and carried it upstairs to continue working. She'd run into an encrypted file on Stan's computer that looked like a spreadsheet of some kind. She knew from his emails that he ran an import-export business out of the warehouse below his apartment. And, she knew from her work at the CIA that import-export firms were ideal covers for smuggling and trafficking operations. She went to work on forensically decoding the spreadsheet.

The numbers listed on the document were staggering. Tens of millions of dollars passed through Stan's business. Surely the guy wasn't making all that money importing antiques. He had to be laundering money for someone, the obvious person being his alleged father, Markus Petrov.

Peter, on the other hand, turned out to be an accountant. Even better, he worked from home, which meant she had files on all of his clients. She dug through two dozen or more sets of financial records without anything popping out at her, but then she ran across the books for a strip club in the French Quarter, a joint called the Who Do Voodoo Club. Its cash flow was off the charts.

She figured out how to wirelessly send a document to Cole's printer and printed the financial statements of the club. And she printed the decoded spreadsheet from Stan's business.

She lay them down on the desk side by side and glanced back and forth between the two. She wasn't looking for any kind of a connection, but she noticed that a big income report at the strip club was followed a few days later by a big amount received by the import business. And the amounts were within a few thousand dollars of each other.

Huh. She looked a little more closely and found a dozen transactions that corresponded almost identically with one another. If Petrov owned both of these businesses, he could definitely be laundering illegal money from the club through the legal import-export business.

She rummaged around in Cole's desk and found a highlighter, which she used to mark the corresponding transactions.

She'd found a promising money trail. Now all she had to do was find out where the import-export business did its banking. She could follow the routing numbers and track where Stan moved the money to once it passed through his cleaning process. Then, they should get a good idea of where Markus was if they tracked the money he pulled from those secondary bank accounts.

It always boiled down to following the money.

Excited, she picked up her cell phone and dialed Cole's number. Funny, but the call went to voice mail. Of course, given his line of work, he might be doing something sneaky and not be answering phone calls at the moment. Disappointed, she left a short message to call her back when he had a minute and hung up. Where could he be? It wasn't like him to just disappear like this.

A feeling that something was wrong took root in her belly, and nothing she did, no argument she made to herself, could dislodge it.

Chapter 13

Cole was in a foul mood, and he knew it. He did his best not to take it out on his men, but he caught them rolling their eyes when they thought he wasn't looking. Tough. They were SEALs and he expected excellence from them. If he was hard on them, it was for their own good.

He spent the afternoon helping man one of the entry points to New Orleans. Returning citizens were required to show some form of identification to prove that they lived in the city before they were allowed to pass the police barricades. The idea was to keep looters and thieves out of the city and only let in bona fide residents.

He'd returned to SEAL Ops and was eating a dry sandwich off a tray someone had brought over from the mess hall when Bastien LeBlanc, wearing his police uniform, burst into the ready room, looking like he had a serious burr up his butt.

"There you are, boss. I've been trying to call you on your personal cell phone."

"Had my personal phone turned off. Sorry."

Bass frowned, but Cole damned well wasn't going to explain to the Cajun that he was avoiding talking to the woman he'd slept with that morning, and who happened to be his CIA liaison. "What's the big crisis, Bass?"

"We need to talk in private."

What the hell? He led Bass to the conference room and closed the door. "Talk."

"I got a call from an informant today. He said word's out on the street that people from the Petrov crime ring are looking for a woman by the name of Nissa. Petite blonde."

Cole was aghast. How in the hell did Petrov's people know about her? "How?" he managed to choke out. "Why?"

"My informant didn't know a whole lot, other than the remnants of the Bratya—that's Petrov's crime ring NOPD and the FBI busted up a few weeks back—are jonesing hard to find this blonde named Nissa. They've even put word out to legitimate people like merchants, hotel staff and restaurant workers. There's apparently a big reward for information leading to finding her."

Cole's blood ran cold. He'd missed something important in the past few days of working with Nissa. No big surprise. She distracted the hell out of him. This was exactly why getting involved with a coworker was a disastrous mistake!

Hell, maybe the ship had been wired with cameras.

God knew, he hadn't been looking for those when he searched the *Anna Belle*. He'd been so tense about the damned vessel capsizing he hadn't stopped to think about anything but finding Petrov and bugging out.

But surveillance was the only reasonable explanation for her name and physical description being out on the street. How else would anyone in the Petrov organization even know she existed?

"What gets me," Bass was saying, "is how they know what she looks like. I could believe them hearing her name from an informant, maybe finding out she's been tracking Petrov from an insider at Langley. But they wouldn't know what she looks like."

"A camera," Cole declared. "Nissa and I broke into the homes of two men we believe to be Petrov's twin sons. One or both of them must have had some sort of surveillance running while we were there." He swore under his breath. Sloppy, sloppy, sloppy. He'd assumed, because all the power was out, that electronic surveillance methods would be deactivated. This was *his* fault. He'd been distracted and not on top of his game, and now Nissa was in danger because of his lapse in sanity.

"Where is she now?" Bass asked.

"My place."

"How safe is she there?"

"As long as Petrov's men don't know where to find her, she should be all right."

"You need to keep her off the street and under wraps until we catch Petrov and take down the last pieces of his organization once and for all."

Cole pulled a face. He already knew that without Bass having to tell him. "I guess I'd better head back to my place and put her on lockdown, then."

"Why the unhappy face?" Bass asked. "I thought you two were hitting it off great."

"Butt out," Cole snapped.

"Yes, sir," Bass replied, clearly startled. "Butting out, sir."

He glared at Bass as he threw open the conference room door and stalked out. The guy couldn't take a hint, apparently, because Bastien followed him down the hall. The men in the ready room took one look at his expression and leaped out of his way, making a path, and Bass followed in his wake, much to Cole's irritation.

Cole stepped outside and fished his truck keys out of his pocket, pausing to snap at Bass, "What are you doing following me?"

"I'm going with you."

"Why?"

"You're going back to your place to guard Nissa, right? You're not exactly objective where she's concerned. I figure you could use the backup."

Cole swore at him, but he couldn't truthfully disagree with the guy. As his outburst wound down, he huffed. "Fine. Get in the damned truck."

Smiling cheerfully, Bass jumped in the passenger seat. The dude was incorrigible. Although Cole reluctantly had to admit he was glad for the help. If nothing else, Bass's presence forced him to keep his mind on business and not on bedding Nissa again.

He pointed the truck toward his house and asked, "How bad is crime in the city?"

"Not as bad as after Katrina, but the NOPD is staying busy."

"Why are you off duty, then?"

"I just pulled a twenty-four-hour shift. I got sent home."

"What the hell are you doing here, then? You should be sleeping."

"I slept about nine hours before my shift. I feel like a new man."

Cole couldn't fault the guy. SEALs could go a lot longer on a lot less rest than that. They parked behind his house, opened the front door…and Cole frowned. He couldn't feel Nissa's warm and bubbly energy.

"Nissa!" he called.

Nothing. Maybe she was taking a nap. He strode into his bedroom—the bed was neatly made and unoccupied. He poked his head in the bathroom and even jogged up the stairs to the loft to be sure she was gone.

"Where in the hell is she?" he burst out.

"Call her cell phone," Bass said practically.

He'd thought it went without saying that she would stay put in his house. Of course, he'd been in such an all-fired hurry to sneak out of here this morning and get the hell away from her that he hadn't actually spoken with her to convey any specific instructions.

Scowling, he pulled out his cell phone and dialed her number. The circuit was busy. He tried again. Same result. He swore under his breath. With the return of civilians to the city, they must have overloaded the limited cell coverage that was up and working. "Can't get through to her," Cole bit out.

Bass nodded. "We cops have been relying on our radios to communicate. The working cell towers are totally overwhelmed."

Cole stepped out on the front porch and looked both ways. No sign of her. She could be absolutely anywhere. Frustrated, he flopped into the porch swing he'd hauled out of the garage and rehung yesterday.

Bass sat down beside him. "See, this is why I don't get involved with women. Minds of their own. Unpredictable, they are."

Cole grunted. "You have no idea."

Bass grinned at him. "Oh, I enjoy the ladies. I just make sure not to have any deep feelings for them."

"Only way to be around them," he agreed. Except a twisting sensation in his gut told him he wasn't being entirely honest with Bass or with himself. He definitely had feelings for Nissa. And right now, they were borderline homicidal.

They sat on the porch for perhaps ten minutes before he spotted a familiar form strolling toward them. "There she is," he announced. The burst of relief in his chest was quickly morphing into fury.

"Hi, you two!" Nissa exclaimed. "To what do I owe the honor of this surprise visit?"

"Inside," Cole snapped, jerking his head.

Nissa's smile evaporated. She looked at Bass and asked, "What's wrong with him?"

"We've got some news. An informant gave me some information—"

Cole cut him off, irritated. "Let's take this inside."

Nissa and Bass went ahead of him, and Bass lifted shopping bags out of her arms, asking, "What treasures have you got here, Niss?"

"I went grocery shopping," she explained as they stepped inside his house. "I got all kinds of treasures. I found fresh peaches and a quart of milk and eggs. The store owner brought a truckload of food back to town with him. Charged me a fortune, but I can make a peach pie—"

"Nissa." Cole cut her off sharply. He didn't want to hear about her shopping trip and the food she'd found. It was all so normal and domestic, none of the things he wanted or needed in his life, dammit!

She broke off and stared up at him quizzically. "What's happened?"

"Tell her, Bass."

"An informant contacted me today. Word's out on the street that Petrov's old gang is looking for a woman. A petite blonde named Nissa. They've put word out with merchants, hotel and restaurant staffs and are offering a substantial reward for any information or sightings of her."

Cole was gratified when she dropped into a chair, looking stunned. She mumbled, "So I guess the fact that I used my credit card at a half dozen stores this morning and just went out grocery shopping is a problem."

Bass was more sympathetic than Cole would have been when the guy said, "It's probably fine. Petrov's people don't know everyone in New Orleans. Had you gone into a strip club or illegal gambling joint, then I'd definitely be worried. His gang controlled a whole bunch of those."

Nissa went quiet and pale. Cole knew he ought to say something to comfort her, but he was not in the mood to tell her she hadn't been reckless when she, in fact, had been. Bass joked around about her gambling habits and deep passion for watching strippers until he got a wan smile out of her. But then, Bass had a way with the ladies. The other guys all agreed he could charm the panties off any female he met.

As for him, Cole stewed, angrier than was at all rational over her endangering herself like she had. She should have known—

He cut himself off, forcing reason to the fore. She'd had no way of knowing that one or both of the twins' homes had some sort of operational surveillance. That had been *his* job. And, she had no way of knowing that the Petrov gang would put out the criminal version of an all-points bulletin on her.

Why was he so furious with her, then?

He shoved away the thought as she asked, "How does Petrov's gang know about me? I've only been in the city a few days. And most of it was when New Orleans was evacuated."

"The apartments," Cole answered curtly. "One or both of them had cameras, obviously."

She was silent for a long time. He hoped she was good and scared—scared enough not to go traipsing around the city by herself any more. But when she spoke, her words were the last thing he expected. "We can use this to our advantage."

"How?" Cole blurted.

She answered, "They know I know Petrov is alive. Why not double down and use this manhunt—or womanhunt as it were—to our advantage? Let's use Bass's informant to put word out on the street that I know what Markus Petrov looks like and that I'm tracking him."

"Why on earth would we do that?" Cole demanded.

Bass, however, grinned. "You think like a SEAL, Nissa. That's brilliant."

Cole was shocked. He was always the one who saw the new angle, the sideways solution to a problem. What was he missing here? He took a deep breath and counted backward from ten to one in his head, setting aside the entire stew of emotions roiling in his gut, the irritation, anger, fear and whatever else he hadn't identified yet.

"Bait," he blurted. "You want to use yourself as bait to draw out Petrov."

Nissa nodded. "The guy has a gigantic ego and prides himself on nobody knowing what he looks like. He's also counting on that as he prepares to disappear and go somewhere else to set up a new life. If I know what he looks like, I can find him. Or, at a minimum, I can force him to undergo rounds of painful plastic surgeries. And I think that idea pisses him off almost as much as the notion of being bested by a mere woman. The guy is famously a misogynist, after all."

Bass asked curiously, "How do you know he's a misogynist?"

"He killed my colleague's mother for refusing to sleep with him, and the mother of his sons also died young enough that I have to suspect murder. Petrov doesn't value women's lives. And then there's the whole strip club, brothel, sex-trafficking angle of his crime ring. Men who respect women don't do that."

Cole burst out, "Then why do you want to throw yourself into his path? He'll kill you without a second thought!"

She shrugged. "That's what you're for. I'll be bait, and you can catch him and keep me safe."

"It's a hell of a risk you're suggesting," Cole retorted.

"If I were one of your men, would you hesitate to use me as bait to draw out Petrov?" she demanded.

"No. But my guys are Navy SEALs. Not only can they handle themselves in dangerous situations, they signed up to take risks with their lives."

"I work for the same government you do," she stated.

"But not in the same capacity. No. I won't set you up as bait to draw this bastard out."

She responded, "He's going to slip away on us. As soon as full power is restored to the city, he's going to transfer his money out of town, set up another untraceable escape and flee for real this time."

"At least he'll be out of the United States," Cole snapped.

"Come on, you know how spy rings work," she replied. "He can keep running his espionage operation from halfway around the world. He'll have to find a new source of funding, and maybe mother Russia will have to pony up the bucks to finance him going forward, but they'll be happy to do it for a big, wide-ranging, long-established spy ring like his. We have to stop this guy right now. This is our only chance."

"Track his money like you were already going to. Figure out where he's going, and we'll go get him there. But I'm not putting you at risk!"

Bass spoke quietly. "I think she has a point, sir. What if he goes somewhere we don't have access to, or that's too politically sensitive for us to run an operation in?"

"We have access to everywhere! We're SEALs, dammit."

Nissa took up the argument. "Not if he goes back

to Russia. You can't run a SEAL team in there and snatch him."

"We have assets in-country to deal with him."

Nissa snorted. "You forget who I work for. I know exactly what capabilities assets in Russia have before they're burned or arrested, tortured and executed. One of our assets—my assets—*might* be able to kill Petrov inside Russia, *if* we devote a crap-ton of resources, time, money and planning to the job. But to snatch him inside Russia? Question him at enough length and in enough detail to unravel his spy ring? Not a chance, Cole. And don't tell me I'm wrong. I work the Russia desk every day in Langley."

Cole scowled and paced into the kitchen and back, too agitated to stand still.

"What's hanging you up about making a run at Petrov now?" Bass asked reasonably.

"I won't put Nissa's life in danger."

"My life is already in danger," she replied soberly. "All I'm suggesting is that we make me a more obvious and pressing target to Markus Petrov, personally. We need *him* to come after me, not just his thugs. And that means we have to make it personal to him."

Bass snorted. "You've already made it personal by finding out who his kids are."

Nissa glanced over at the Cajun. "He would sacrifice his children without a second thought to save his own hide. That's why we have to make this about him. Him and me."

Cole hated the idea. Passionately. But he couldn't fault her logic. He was surprised when Bass hand-signaled him subtly to exit the room. But he trusted the guy enough to mutter, "I'm going outside for a minute. I forgot to lock the garage door."

"I'll come with you," Bass said casually.

Cole doubted Nissa was fooled for a minute, but she made no comment as they stepped outside.

"What's up?" he asked Bass shortly.

"Why are you so opposed to Nissa's suggestion? You know it makes sense."

He crossed his arms and stared down the mostly empty street.

"Have you slept with her?" Bass asked quietly.

Cole whirled, livid. "That's none of your damned business."

"You have, haven't you?" Bass threw up his hands. "Hey, man, I'm not judging you. She's obviously as smitten with you as you are with her."

"I am not smitten—"

"Save it, Cole. This is me you're talking to. I've known you for fifteen years, and I've never seen you react to any woman like you do this one. I'm happy for you, man. It's about time you ditch that icy facade you hide behind and allow yourself to be happy."

He stared at Bass in utter shock. Never, in a million years, would he have expected Bastien LeBlanc, confirmed bachelor extraordinaire, to say something like that.

"However," Bass continued grimly, "if you do have feelings for Nissa, it's not only possible, but probable, those feelings are clouding your judgment. I'm merely suggesting that you take a step back and think about her idea before you dismiss it out of hand. She makes a good point. This may be our only shot at capturing Markus Petrov. Are you sure you want to throw that away because you're unwilling to put a woman you love at risk?"

"I don't love her!"

Bass threw up his hands. "Not my circus, not my monkeys. I'm not trying to get in the middle of whatever's going on between the two of you. But I am telling you that I think your judgment is compromised."

Bass might as well have kicked him squarely in the nuts. Cole's breath whooshed out of his chest at the shock of Bass's declaration. Cole had always prided himself on being a man of logic and reason, not ruled by impulses, and surely not by emotions. Hell, he'd walked out on Nissa this morning with every intention of never coming back because it was the right thing to do!

"So you're telling me that if I don't use her as bait, I'm guilty of fraternization and conduct unbecoming an officer?" he said heavily.

"C'mon, Cole. Don't be an ass. You know I'd never throw you to the wolves. We've been to hell and back together. I'm just telling you to separate your emotions from your decision here. You know as well as I do that her idea is a good one. And, if she were a man from the CIA, you wouldn't hesitate to set that guy up as bait to draw out Petrov."

If she were a man from the CIA, he wouldn't have slept with her and completely compromised himself. Reluctantly, he had to admit that Bass had a point. He hadn't worked with many women over the years, and the few he had worked with were as tough as they came, women operators who ran with his SEAL team and could keep up with the boys in pretty much every way it counted.

The door behind him opened and Nissa poked her head out. "Are you guys hungry? I'm going to make some sandwiches."

Bass replied, saving Cole from having to speak, "I'm always hungry, kid. Better make a big pile of sandwiches if you're feeding me and Frosty."

"Coming up." She disappeared back inside.

"Have a little faith in her," Bass said quietly. "She can do this."

"She's scared of her own shadow!"

Bass shrugged. "Being scared is normal and healthy if it doesn't stop you from doing what has to be done. I've seen a lot of courage in her, too. Hell, I was scared to climb on the *Anna Belle*. But she went. She was scared to go into Petrov's house, but she went there, too. She didn't let fear stop her from doing what she needed to do."

Bass shrugged and followed Nissa inside the house. Cole heard the two of them laughing in the kitchen. Bass, a gourmet chef in his spare time, must be helping her make the sandwiches.

Cole was arrested by Bass's observation about Nissa. The guy was right. She had gotten a lot more confident in the time they'd been together. Something rebelled inside him at the idea of Bass seeing her more clearly than he did. It was his job to know her the best. She was *his* woman—

His woman. And there it was. The crux of his problem with setting her up as bait. No matter how hard he hid from it, the truth was he wanted her for himself in the long term. He wasn't willing to risk her life by letting her run some suicidal sting operation. Because like it or not, he did have feelings for her. Real feelings. Strong feelings. Feelings he was unwilling to give a name to. But that didn't make them any less real.

Everything Bass had said to him was dead true. He was compromised, and his feelings for Nissa were clouding his judgment. And, like it or not, he knew what he had to do.

He went inside the house and strode to the kitchen. "All right, Nissa. If you want to be bait to draw out Markus Petrov, I'll approve the operation."

She and Bass both spun to grin at him.

"However," he continued grimly, "I'm taking myself off the mission. Bass or Ashe will be in charge of a team of their choosing and run the op."

Chapter 14

"No!" The word was out of Nissa's mouth before she could stop it. "I want you!" Alarmed at how that sounded and at the sharp look Bass threw at Cole in response, she amended, "I trust you, Cole. I want you to be in charge of using me as bait."

"I will technically be in charge. It's my team that will run the operation."

She planted her hands on her hips and glared at him. "You know what I mean. I want you there, personally in charge of things."

"Not going to happen," he bit out.

"Why not?"

He glared at her, spared a pained glance for Bass and then answered, "Because I have personal feelings for you. My judgment can't be trusted."

"Of course it can," she disagreed. "If you care about

me, you'll have that much more of a vested interest in keeping me alive."

"That's not how it works." He refused to make eye contact with her, and she was supremely confused. What had changed between their passionate lovemaking last night and this morning and now? For something surely had.

Cole was speaking. "Bass, have you got anywhere to be right now?"

"Nope. I'm off duty until tomorrow."

"Would you mind keeping an eye on Nissa while I go out for a little while? I need to stretch my legs."

"No problem, sir." Now why did Bass sound so subdued when he said that? And why had he added the *sir*? She looked back and forth between the two men. It felt as if they were holding an entire silent conversation over her head, and she was missing the whole thing.

Cole disappeared into his bedroom and emerged in a minute in running shorts and a T-shirt, running shoes in hand. Before she hardly knew what was happening, he'd left the house and silence fell in his wake.

"What the hell is going on?" she demanded of Bass.

The Cajun shrugged and smiled lamely.

"Don't give me that dumb guy act. Spill it." She shook a finger at him for good measure.

Bass sighed. "He's worried about you and doesn't like the idea of using you to draw out Petrov. He thinks he might make a bad call that could get you hurt because his feelings for you might get in the way."

"That's ridiculous. He's a smart man, rational to the core."

"Not where you're concerned, *chère.*"

She stared at Bass. "Really?" she asked in a small voice.

"Really. You've knocked that man clean off his feet."

Huh. She sure couldn't tell that from how he'd been acting. He'd been surly at best with her, and obnoxious at worst. Thoughtfully, she lifted a sandwich off the pile she and Bass had made. "How long is he likely to be gone jogging?"

Bass laughed. "Cole Perriman doesn't jog. He'll be turning five-minute miles if he's having a slow day. As for how far he'll run? No idea. He's pretty freaked-out. He could go ten or twelve miles before he calms down. Maybe more."

"Good grief. I keep forgetting you guys are super-human."

Bass shrugged modestly. Then in a blatant move to change the subject and distract her, he commented, "Cole said you got a bunch of data off the hard drives of the Petrov sons. Any progress on reading them?"

She gestured for him to join her at the dining table. "Indeed, I have made progress. I've got decent evidence that the son, Peter, is Markus's accountant. And Peter is passing cash to Stan—the other son—to launder through his import-export business."

"Where's the money going after Stan's done with it?"

"That takes us back to Peter's computer. I've found some bank account numbers. If I can break into those accounts, I should be able to track where exactly he's sending money."

"How do you break into the accounts?"

"Under normal circumstances, I'd write up a warrant request and pass it by a federal judge for permission. Then, I'd contact the bank, vet the warrant with their lawyers, and then they'd show me the transaction records."

"How long does that take?"

"Depends on how backed up the courts are. And in this case, whether or not any judges have returned to New Orleans after the hurricane."

Bass leaned back. "The governor declared martial law temporarily. That executive order hasn't been lifted yet. Seems to me you'd be on legally safe ground to go ahead and bust into the account, given that no judges are available and the executives of the local banks aren't in town, either."

"It would be illegal for me to hack the account."

"Could you do it if you had to?" he asked.

"Well, yeah. The agency has tools for that sort of thing. I can get into a bank's records without too much trouble."

Bass shrugged. "Do it."

"But—"

"This guy's trying to kill you. Seems to me like a straightforward case of self-defense for you to do everything in your power to find him before he murders you."

"You're a bad influence, Bastien LeBlanc."

He grinned. "That's what all the ladies say." He pushed her laptop across the table to her.

She hesitated a moment more, but then memory of Cole's grim expression came to mind. If she happened to find out where Petrov was planning to flee to, maybe they could avoid using her as bait. She signed in to the CIA's servers and downloaded a program designed to bypass banking security using a back door built in especially for government agencies.

Given that she had the account number, it didn't take long for a record of deposits and withdrawals to pop up on her computer. A series of large money transfers had been made recently to another bank account. She took screen shots of the new account number, and entered that into her CIA financial search algorithm.

"Now what?" Bass asked.

"Now we wait to see where that account leads us."

They repeated the procedure a half dozen more times, tracing the trail of nearly thirty million dollars. At long last, they ended up in a bank account located in Montenegro.

"Where the heck is that?" Bass asked.

"It's a little chunk of what used to be Yugoslavia. Located on the Adriatic Sea east of Italy, about halfway down the boot. Pretty little place. Mountainous, prosperous, and interestingly enough, it has no extradition treaty with the United States."

"Sounds like a great place for a Russian spy to retire to," Bass commented.

"Indeed." She stared at the computer screen in front of her. Obscure though it might be, the Montenegrin bank Markus had chosen was not up to speed with the latest financial security measures. She was actually inside his account at the moment, not just observing data from it.

She looked up at Bass. "How mad do you want me to make Markus Petrov?"

"What do you have in mind?"

"How interested would he be in finding me if I emptied his bank account?"

Bass stared at her for a minute and then started to laugh. "I love it. Also, he'd have to take you alive to find out where you've moved his money. The downside is he'd likely torture you if he caught you."

"That's better than killing me immediately. It would give you and your guys a window of time to rescue me in case things go wrong and I end up in his hands."

Bass shook his head. "It's scary how much like a SEAL you think. But I have to warn you. Cole's going to lose his mind if you intentionally provoke Petrov."

"He's not in charge of this operation anymore. You are. It's your call, Bass." She was taking advantage of Bass and the situation Cole had put him in, but she didn't much care at this point. She was willing to pull out all the stops to capture Markus Petrov.

Of all people, she understood that the man would never stop hunting her as long as she was still alive. She knew what he looked like, and she knew too many details of his life. She posed an unacceptable threat to Petrov. He had to eliminate her. This was a kill-or-be-killed scenario. Him or her. Only one of them was walking away from this confrontation.

She typed into her computer decisively, transferring every last cent out of the Montenegro account and into a CIA account she used from time to time to pay cyberinformants.

Quickly, before she could change her mind, she typed a memo to her boss informing him and the agency of the funds transfer and where the money came from. The notification was required by law, lest agents pocket money they lifted from criminals and spies around the world.

"It's done," she announced.

Bass nodded. "How long will it take him to figure out all his money is gone?"

"I highly doubt that's all of his money," she replied. "It's probably only a tiny percentage of his overall wealth. But it's a big enough chunk of change to tick him off pretty royally, I should think. I give it twenty-four hours until he gets some sort of notification of the withdrawal. Another two hours or so to get a hold of his bank and verify that it's not a mistake."

"And then he'll be on the warpath," Bass finished for her.

"Exactly."

"Okay. I'll need to find a defensible place to stash you. Someplace that looks vulnerable to Petrov's men, but with plenty of spots for my guys to ambush his people. I have a place in mind, actually. A warehouse the SEALs have used for training before. I'll brief my team tonight, and we'll get to work prepping it. In the morning, I'll need you to go over there so we can run various rescue scenarios with you. I need you to know what we'll be doing and where we'll be firing our weapons so you don't freak out when the real deal goes down."

"Sounds fun."

Bass rolled his eyes at her. "Let's see if you think that tomorrow when bullets are flying past your nose."

Okay, that sounded less fun.

The front door opened, and Cole came in, red cheeked and sweaty.

"Feeling better?" Bass asked lightly.

"Feeling calmer," Cole replied.

"Great. I've got some stuff to do, but Nissa can fill you in." Bass brushed past Cole pausing only when he got to the front door. "I'll pick you up first thing in the morning, Nissa."

"See you then," she called past Cole to Bass's retreating form.

"Where's he taking you?" Cole asked, using a kitchen towel to mop his face and neck.

"A warehouse the SEALs have used for training before. He wants to run scenarios with his guys and make sure I know what to expect."

"Good for him," Cole said neutrally enough.

"Umm, while you were gone, Bass and I might have done something to make Markus Petrov mad."

Cole turned, all muscular, six foot three of him. He'd never looked more forbidding than in that moment. "What did you do?" he asked ominously.

"I stole thirty million dollars from Petrov's bank account in Montenegro."

Cole's jaw dropped. She would take that as an admission of surprise. She spoke quickly to head off any explosions to come. "We figure that if I know where his money is, he can't kill me. He'll have to torture its location out of me and force me to give it back. That'll give Bass and his guys time to rescue me if I happen to end up in Petrov's custody."

Cole strode over to her and grabbed her shoulders in his big hands. Even mad as hell, she noted that he was gentle with her. "Did you hear what you just said? The man will torture you. As in maiming and harming and scarring you and causing you unbearable agony until you break and tell him what he wants to know."

"I'm familiar with the concept, Cole."

"Do you have torture training?"

"Well, no."

"Do you know how to resist it? Just what horrors against your body and mind to expect?" His words pounded at her.

"No," she answered a little less confidently.

"Do you realize that rape will be the least of your problems? What are you going to do when he starts pulling out your teeth, ripping out your fingernails and slicing the skin off your body in long strips?"

She stared up at him in dismay.

"What if he decides to put power drills through your hands? Or cut off a few fingers? Or he decides to drive spikes through your knees? Are you prepared to deal with that?"

"All right, already. You made your point. I'm not a superhero."

"You're not even a soldier."

"Look, Cole. I'll admit I'm scared to do this. But what other choice did we have?"

"There's always another way, Nissa. For that matter, we could let the bastard go. There are other ways to identify his spies. We'll find them eventually."

"But how long would it take us? How much more damage will they do to our country in the meantime? How many American lives will be lost? I'm one person. Even if I die—horribly—in the process of stopping this man, it'll be worth it. And it's not like I have a family that would be left behind."

"What about your parents?" Cole demanded.

"They're both deep into senile dementia. They barely know who each other are, let alone me. They won't miss me."

Cole paced several complete laps around his small

house before stopping in front of her again. His voice ravaged, he ground out, "What about me?"

She stared at him, completely at a loss for words. He would care if she died? As in *care*? As in real feelings and a deep, personal sense of loss? "Really?" she asked in a tiny voice. "You'd miss me?"

He shoved a hand through his short hair. "I took myself off a mission, for God's sake, Nissa. Do you have any idea how big a deal that is?"

"I'm starting to understand."

"It's a huge deal. Especially for me. I never, ever lose my cool. But I had one of my guys get right in my face today and accuse me outright of being compromised. And he was not wrong."

Bass. That must have been why the two men had stepped out on the front porch earlier. So Bass could confront Cole.

"Tell me something, Cole. Why did you leave this morning without saying goodbye?"

"You were asleep," he replied lamely.

"Wanna try that again?" she asked. "Keeping in mind that I'm a highly skilled intelligence analyst and trained to spot deception?"

He glared at her. "Cripes. Is this what it's like for my men to talk to me?"

"I wouldn't know," she answered smoothly. "And I'm still waiting for an answer to my question."

"Fine. I was running away from you."

"Why?"

"Making love with you scared the living hell out of me."

Hurt twisted in her stomach. "Why? Was I that needy?"

"No, Nissa. I was." The words sounded pulled from his throat entirely involuntarily.

"I don't understand."

"Good." He added sharply, "And don't ask me to explain."

She studied his back thoughtfully. He had more feelings for her than he was prepared to deal with. He was flipped out by whatever she'd made him feel. Son of a gun. A slow smile spread across her face. She'd gotten past all those walls of ice he'd erected to keep out the world, apparently. Her. Boring Nissa Beck. Who could have seen that one coming?

"I care about you, too," she said softly. "A lot."

"Don't."

And with that one clipped syllable, he retreated to his bathroom. She heard the shower go on. It ran for a long, long time.

Yes, indeed. She'd gotten under his skin but good.

Chapter 15

Cole felt like the walls of a trap were closing in on him, and no matter what direction he turned, the box he was locked inside was getting smaller and smaller.

He wanted to shout and lash out and hit something, but there was nothing and no one to aim his fury and terror at but himself. He'd tried to punish his body by running a dozen miles at a grueling pace, but it had only made him sore. It did nothing to relieve the terrible pressure building up inside his chest.

He spent the evening pretending to read while Nissa sat at the kitchen table digging through more of the files from Peter's and Stan's computers. Although he stared at words on pages, his mind was fully occupied with running scenario after scenario for ambushing Petrov's people in the warehouse.

He knew the building Bass was thinking of. It was

used for storing Mardi Gras floats and had a network of high catwalks perfect for snipers and lots of hiding places for SEALs. Field of fire control—making sure none of the SEALs ended up shooting toward each other and killing each other—would be an issue, and they would have to think about the best place to park Nissa. She would have to be exposed enough to lure in Petrov's men, but inaccessible enough to exits to make her hard to pull out of the building—

"I'm turning in for the night," Nissa announced, breaking into his thoughts.

"Sweet dreams."

"Feel free to join me. That futon upstairs or the sofa down here can't possibly be as comfortable as your own bed."

It wasn't, but no way was he about to admit that to her. He would sleep on a bed of nails before he would tempt and torture himself by sleeping next to her. "Thanks. I'll be up awhile, still."

She retreated to his bedroom, and he listened to the sounds of her getting ready for bed and settling down to sleep. There was something deeply domestic about listening to her brush her teeth and hearing the bedsprings squeak a little. It was relaxing. Peaceful. This was the first time in his life he'd shared his living space for more than a few hours, and he actually liked it. But then, he liked his roommate. Way too much.

There was more to it than that, though. As he listened to the rustle of blankets, the soft sigh Nissa let out as she got comfy and drifted off to sleep, he could picture himself doing this years from now. It was the first time he'd ever been able to picture anything that came after the SEALs. Furthermore, a life like this in place of his military career seemed like a decent trade. Maybe add a few kids to the picture in a few years—

Yeah. He could see himself doing this, and even being happy.

But then an image of his mother's battered face, his father's drunken rages flashed through his mind, and he recoiled from the idealized version of possible reality that he'd painted for himself. Nothing was ever as perfect as it seemed like it would be from the outside looking in.

Take the two of them right now. People would see the attractive woman in his bed, the spectacular sex they'd had, the crazy attraction between them and assume they were the perfect couple. Everything would be perfect between them, and there would be no problems.

Little would they know that he was scared out of his mind. Or that Nissa apparently had some sort of death wish.

What was up with that, anyway? Was she trying to prove she was as good as a SEAL? Or was it something more subtle? Was this a cry for attention, this need of hers to be a hero? He made a mental note to ask her about it first thing tomorrow.

He stretched out on the sofa, staring at the ceiling in soul-deep frustration. He had no idea what to do about her. At all. Although, none of that would matter if she got herself killed in the next few days.

In spite of his resolve to get to the bottom of her insistence on throwing herself in front of the buzz saw that was Markus Petrov, when he woke up in the morning, it was to an empty house. Then he remembered

Bass had promised to pick her up this morning. How in the hell had she managed to get up, get dressed and sneak out without waking him?

Kudos to her for stealth, but how hard had he been sleeping not to hear her? He shouldn't have run those last three miles or so yesterday. Cursing, he jumped up, dressed, grabbed a bite of food for the road and headed for his truck. He might not be in charge of the operation, but he could certainly supervise the training and preparation of Bass's team for the mission. He was damned well going to run his men through every scenario he could come up with until they all knew what to do backward and forward. And that included Nissa.

Traffic was horrendous as returning residents had to dodge debris and closed streets, and it took him a solid hour to get to the training site, a cavernous building in the warehouse district that stored gaudy Mardi Gras floats during the off-season. He'd always found the floats creepy as hell, with their fantastic creatures, garish colors and outlandish decorations. Fully lit and crawling with revelers, they didn't look spooky. But crammed together in a shadowy jumble like this, they looked downright sinister.

He heard voices, a short silence, and then a barrage of blanks firing from weapons. In a SEAL training facility, they would use live bullets, but in this rented space, they couldn't actually shoot up the floats. Hence, the blanks.

The noise and muzzle flashes would be important for Nissa to experience so she wouldn't panic and do something stupid if an actual rescue was necessary. As long as she sat still and let the SEALs do their work around her, she would be perfectly safe. But if she jumped unexpectedly, she could move into one of the guys' field of fire and take a bullet.

He moved to the edge of an open space in front of a glass-windowed office. Inside, he spied Nissa sitting on a chair in the far corner. Bass was standing beside her, leaning down and talking in her ear. A twist of jealously tightened in his gut before reason kicked in. Bass was probably talking her through what his guys were doing so she wouldn't freak out.

He watched with a critical eye the incursion by four of the SEALs while two laid down suppression fire outside. When the mock attack was finished, he strode forward. "Burkus, you were slow reacting to the incoming guys on your right, and Leonidas, watch your field of fire. It wasn't as tight as it could be."

Bass stepped out of the office. "Hey, boss. You wanna take over running the hostiles while I run the rescue team?"

"Sure." Using all the worst scenarios he'd envisioned last night when he couldn't sleep, he put the team that would be responsible for Nissa's safety through its paces. Hard. All the men were sweating and winded after several hours of nonstop firefighting. But he was confident that they all knew what to do if it came to a fight.

He called a ten-minute break for the team and ordered everyone to reload their weapons and rehydrate. To that end, he carried a water bottle over to Nissa. Although her job had been mostly to sit and occasionally to run a short distance with a rescue team, she looked pretty wrung out as he approached her.

"You holding up okay?" he asked her.

"This is stressful stuff. I keep imagining what

it would be like with real bullets flying around me. Sometimes the shots your guys take actually touch my hair, and I can feel them flying past my face."

"These guys are professional shooters. They practice hour after hour, day after day. They know themselves and their weapons inside and out. Which is to say, they won't miss. We actually run exercises exactly like this with live fire, meaning real bullets, all the time back at our own training facility."

She stared at him, looking appalled. "Who plays the kidnapping victim?"

"We take turns."

"Does anyone ever get shot?" she asked between slugs of water.

He pulled a scornful face. "I told you. We're pros. We don't miss."

"If you say so," she said doubtfully, passing the empty water bottle back to him.

"Ready to go again? I've got a few more scenarios I want to run before we call it quits."

"I'm all for your guys being as prepared as possible to protect me," she murmured.

"Me, too," he muttered under his breath.

Her eyes lit with gratitude. Dammit, he hadn't meant for her to hear that.

"Okay, let's reset!" he called out to the team. "Hostiles with me!"

He set his "bad guy" team for an all-out charge on the office, screaming and shouting and causing all the ruckus they could. It wasn't likely the way Petrov's men would come in, but he needed to let Nissa see a berserker charge at least once.

Both teams of SEALs had a field day, firing blanks

wildly at each other in a free-for-all that he knew from experience was a ton of fun and a great way to blow off steam.

But then one of the men, Chief Petty Officer Burkus, called out, "Medic! I'm bleeding!"

"Cease fire!" Cole yelled.

Another shot rang out, and he hollered angrily, "I said cease fire!"

Another man called in dismayed surprise, "Medic, I'm hit. I've been shot."

What the hell? Had one of his guys accidentally loaded live ammo? Sombody's head was going to roll for a dunderheaded mistake like that. Two of his guys were wounded—

Several more shots rang out in quick succession, and two more of his guys went down.

And that was when it hit him. Somebody *else* was shooting at his men. Somebody armed and with intent to kill.

Nissa.

His blood ran cold with soul-gripping, throat-clenching terror. The bastards had come for her. And every single one of his men was armed only with blanks in their weapons. They were sitting ducks. Worse, Nissa was a sitting duck.

"Take cover!" he shouted. "Incoming fire! This is not an exercise!"

The SEALs dived every which way. He was all the way across the open space from the office, but no power on earth was keeping him away from Nissa's side. The devil's own spurs dug into his sides, driving him forward with speed he didn't even know he had.

He barely managed to remember to zigzag randomly, so freaked-out was he. But his long years of training kicked in, and his body automatically did the right thing. Targets who were dodging like he was made themselves all but impossible to hit, and if he did take a bullet, the odds of it being lethal were close to zero.

Sure enough, several shots rang out. A chunk of concrete flew up beside him, grazing his arm, but he ignored the burning sensation. One of the big windows in front of him shattered, and he heard Nissa let out a scream. If she was hit, that shooter was going to die slowly and painfully.

He dived through the office door and was relieved to see that she'd done like she was supposed to in the sniper scenario and had crouched behind the desk, taking cover behind its bulk.

"Stay down," he ordered her sharply.

She nodded at him, her eyes the size of saucers.

He joined her behind the desk. "Find that shooter!" he shouted. "Team One, search pattern Delta, and maintain cover! Team Two, pattern Alpha! Weapons hot and mike up, everyone. Report as able, frequency three!" He'd just sent the team protecting Nissa into a fan formation around the office, but staying under cover. The second team, the guys playing hostiles, had been sent to search through the warehouse in a grid pattern for the sniper or snipers.

He switched his radio to the third preset frequency and repeated his orders over the earbuds and throat mikes that were standard-issue for every SEAL. He added under his breath, "Go hand to hand if necessary. Ideally we take any shooters alive, but not at the cost of anyone's life. You are green lighted."

Nissa stared at him and whispered, "Doesn't that mean your guys are authorized to kill?"

"Correct," he bit out, scanning the open space in front of the office. His medic was lying on the ground beside one of the downed men. From his frantic ministrations, Cole gathered the gunshot was life threatening.

"Nissa, call 911. Tell them twenty unarmed SEALs are pinned down in a real gunfight at this address and requesting full SWAT response and at least four ambulances."

She fumbled in her pocket for her cell phone and made the call, relaying the message verbatim. He noted wryly that she added a single word to his message. *Hurry.*

The first cops would be here in five minutes. Full SWAT would take ten. The building would be ringed with cops in about the same ten minutes. That was a lifetime when it came to a gun battle.

A shot rang out, and the other window in the office shattered. He threw himself over Nissa and smashed her flat. From on top of her he bit out, "Are you hit?"

"I can't tell. I'm too squashed to register anything else."

He muttered, "We have to get you out of here."

"I'm not running out into the open where I'm a sitting duck," she whispered frantically.

"No, you're not. I have a plan." He would kill to have his full kit of gear with him right now, but he didn't. And so he did what any self-respecting SEAL would. He improvised. He pulled out his pocketknife and stabbed it into the wall at his back.

"What are you doing?" Nissa whispered.

"Making a back door for us."

To her credit, she reached up and opened the shallow center desk drawer, feeling around over her head.

"What are *you* doing?" he asked as he sawed through drywall to expose a two-by-four wall stud. He could probably just smash his fist through the flimsy drywall, but that would make a lot of noise and announce what he was up to. He chose the slower—but quieter—route of cutting a hole.

"I saw a pair of scissors in here earlier…aha!" She opened the scissors wide and used one blade to help him saw at the wall.

"It's going to be a narrow opening. I'll go through first, clear the area and then bring you through," he said low. "Stick to my back like glue, and do whatever I do when we get out there."

"Why aren't we sitting tight here and waiting for your guys to clear the warehouse? Or waiting for the SWAT team to get here?"

"Because whoever shot at you and my guys was good enough to sneak in here and take up a shooting position without anybody noticing. This isn't some amateur thug patrol. Whoever's out there is professional." Which was to say, the shooter was too dangerous to wait out.

He regretted saying that as Nissa's eyes glazed over with fear.

He lifted out a big chunk of drywall and eyed the opening. It would be a tight fit, but he thought he could make it. "Look at me, Nissa."

Her eyes were dilated and black with fear, and she was visibly trembling, a sure sign her adrenaline was off the charts. If she could control it, that would work in her favor. But if she let her fear get the best of her, she could very well die in the next few minutes.

He spoke slowly so her adrenaline-laced brain could absorb his words. "I promised I'd keep you safe, and I'm going to do that. Don't fall apart on me now. I need you to be tough, keep your wits about you and listen to me. Can you do that?"

He rarely had to drag civilians into combat, and it was a worst-case scenario that all SEALs dreaded. Normally, they cleared the path for their exit on the way in, and by the time they got to whatever civilian they planned to rescue, they could escape unopposed.

"I've got a shooter in the northwest corner," one of the men breathed into his earbud.

Good Lord willing, that was the only hostile in the building.

Lying on his side, Cole squeezed between the wall studs, grateful for shoddy construction that had the studs a good twenty-four inches apart. He came to his knees clutching his Ka-Bar knife. What he wouldn't give for even a handgun right now!

He looked around carefully, scanning low and then high in search of any shapes that might be human, any movement, any indication at all of a threat to Nissa. Without taking his gaze off the rows of floats in front of him, he reached back to wave Nissa through the gap. She joined him, and in the deep, dangerous silence of the place, he heard her breathing light and fast beside him. She was on the verge of a full-on panic attack.

No help for it, though. They had no time for her to collect herself. He gestured for her to grab his belt, and then he moved out.

Chapter 16

What on earth was going on? Nissa crept along behind Cole in a state of complete disbelief. Who was out there shooting SEALs and shooting at her? Surely, Petrov's men hadn't found her so quickly. But if they had, what did it mean?

Cole moved at a fast walk-jog down the length of a big float in the shape of a swan. He ducked under its arching fiberglass neck and crouched at its base. She did the same, looking around fearfully.

She had no business being in a situation like this. None. It was all well and good to run around with a SEAL team on an extended camping trip. But this crisis was real. Men were bleeding, maybe dying, and someone was out there trying to kill her.

It had been great in theory to offer herself up as bait to Petrov. But after seeing this reality—Cole had been totally right. She'd had no idea whatsoever what she was volunteering for.

Who knew that knees actually did knock together when a person was terrified enough? Or that her hands could shake so badly she barely had the strength to hang on to Cole's belt? Or that she could feel like throwing up and fainting at the same time?

Cole stood up, easing along the side of the float. He darted across an open aisle, all but yanking her arm out of the socket. He stopped just as abruptly, and she slammed into his back. She started to apologize, but bit back the words just in time. He was running silent and obviously wanted her to do the same.

She did her best to mimic his catlike tread, moving with bent knees and placing each foot lightly so as to make no sound. In her ears, her steps were painfully loud though, in spite of her best efforts to be quiet.

She totally sucked at this stuff. In fact, she was a total fraud. A person like her had no business at all being out here in the field with special forces operators. She was a desk jockey through and through. On top of that, she was scared of her own shadow. In every way that mattered, she was the antithesis of Cole.

It had been sheer self-delusion to think they had anything in common, let alone that they could form a lasting relationship. This was the real Cole, the silent, lethal predator at home in crises and combat.

In her borrowed earbud, she heard a few of his men whisper status reports and sightings of multiple armed figures moving stealthily through the building. It was a killing field in here! A giant game of cat and mouse with real lives on the line. The horror of it overwhelmed her until she hardly had the strength or will to move.

Cole paused in front of her at an intersection of two narrow aisles, apparently listening. A huge sleigh-like float loomed in front of them. It had a half dozen molded fiberglass seats leading up a set of risers to a big, throne-like chair that was gaudily painted. Mimicking Cole, she strained to hear something and started as she thought she heard a quiet scuffle—of a boot, maybe.

Cole's back muscles went rock hard against her fingers. Very slowly, he reached back with his left hand and removed her hand from his belt. He showed her an open palm that she interpreted as a command to stay put.

Something moved in front of him, but she couldn't see over Cole's bulk. However, she felt Cole coil like a tiger in front of her, ready to strike.

The icy danger that poured off him was perhaps the scariest thing she'd encountered since this whole nightmare commenced. Never in her life had she felt such cold determination from anyone. His concentration was total, his intent apparent. He was about to attack someone. Violently.

All of a sudden, he leaped out into the aisle, and she briefly glimpsed a man dressed in black from head to toe. Even his face was covered with a balaclava that left only his eyes showing, and they had some sort of black grease smeared around them.

The man in black jumped at Cole, and the two men grappled hand to hand in the most violent sparring she'd ever seen. Vicious kicks and punches flew. Eyes were jabbed at, groins kneed and elbows thrown.

This was an entirely different kind of fighting than her self-defense classes. This was a life-and-death struggle. It only lasted maybe thirty seconds, and then Cole got behind the guy and had him around the neck with his left arm.

The guy in black tried to bend forward and flip Cole over his shoulder, but Cole slipped off to one side, rolled to his back and pulled the guy in black backward to the ground on top of him. She spied Cole's hand across the guy's mouth.

She caught a glimpse of Cole's face, a grimace distorting it, the aversion for what he was about to do as clear as day on his features.

There was a quick swipe of something dull under the guy's chin, and the man in black stiffened. The scenario froze in front of her for several seconds, then the guy went limp.

Cole pushed the inert form off him and crouched beside the assailant, pressing two fingers against the guy's neck, checking for a pulse. His fingers came away covered in blood.

Ho. Lee. Cow. Cole had slit that man's throat! She stared in horror at the dead man at her feet. But then Cole grabbed her upper arm and yanked her away from the corpse. She stumbled along beside him, stunned at what she'd just witnessed.

She'd known intellectually that SEALs were capable killers, but knowing it and *seeing* it were two entirely different beasts.

Cole paused in the shelter of a giant clown face and touched his throat. He breathed, "One down, south center."

His hand slid down her arm to grasp her palm. He

gave it a brief squeeze and then placed her hand on his belt once more. They continued forward, him on grim alert, and her in deepening shock. She'd just witnessed a murder. Sure, it had been a kill-or-be-killed situation, and she didn't blame Cole for having done what he did. But she'd just seen a human being die.

The wail of distant sirens became audible. Thank God. At least the police would have bullets in their guns.

Something moved ahead of them, and she tensed. But instead of attacking the figure, Cole flashed a hand signal and then moved forward swiftly. It was one of the other SEALs. Her legs all but collapsed in relief.

The other SEAL nodded briefly at Cole and then flashed about six hand signals in quick succession. She only knew a couple of them, but gathered the guy had spotted a hostile up ahead. Maybe that was the signal for twenty feet? Or maybe twenty yards? She wasn't sure.

Cole nodded and sent the guy a bunch of signals back. The other SEAL melted into the shadows ahead of them while Cole held his position. In about thirty seconds, she heard the sounds of scuffling, and then a muffled cry. It sounded like someone shouting out in pain but with a hand smashed over his mouth.

She was huddling so close to Cole's back that she heard a voice in his earpiece along with her own. It announced, "One down, south exit."

Exit? Were they close to a door, then? Did that mean they could get out of this house of horrors and the killers roaming it? A spark of hope ignited in her chest. Maybe they were going to make it out of this disaster alive, after all.

Cole and the other SEAL led her to a metal door, and Cole's man went to work on the padlock holding a length of chain around the handle and around a matching steel cleat beside the door.

It was impressive how quickly and quietly the guy was able to remove the lock and lift the chains without a single metallic clank of noise. There was a quick exchange of hand signals, and then Cole leaned close to whisper directly in her ear, "I'll go first, you right behind me. I'm going to land on you outside, and then Bill's going to jump over both of us. Don't trip him."

She'd barely processed all of that when Cole threw the door open, letting in a blinding spill of light to the dim warehouse. He bolted outside, all but dislocating her right arm as she clung to his belt. She jumped after him and had barely cleared the doorway when a massive weight flattened her on her back.

Sharp stones ground into her flesh through her blouse, and what breath she had whooshed out of her all at once. She lay perfectly still as a big dark shape hurdled overhead and crouched in front of her and Cole.

"Clear," the SEAL called Bill announced under his breath.

Cole pressed up and away from her and dragged her to her feet. No sooner was she upright than the two men flanked her, each grabbing her by the elbow and all but carrying her as they sprinted down a narrow street flanked by brick walls. She ran for all she was worth.

They rounded the corner and skidded to a halt in front of two police cars parked sideways with four grim-faced cops crouching behind them, weapons pointed at them.

Cole and Bill threw their hands up in the air and

both dropped their knives. Belatedly, Nissa followed suit, raising her hands. But she was unable to tear her stare away from the black bores of those shotguns pointed at her. Renewed panic roared through her, and an urge to turn and run.

"I'm Commander Cole Perriman, commander of the SEAL team pinned down inside. We've eliminated at least two hostiles. None of my men are carrying live firearms. The man with me is Petty Officer First Class Bill Thompson. We have identification on us."

The shotguns pointed up toward the sky and she ran beside Cole and Bill to take cover behind the cop cars. The SEALs pulled out their wallets and showed their military ID cards to the cops, and she did the same. Although all she had to show were her driver's license and generic government ID card. CIA analysts didn't get a badge or membership card for the cool kids gang to show anyone.

A black van careened around the corner and no fewer than twelve armored SWAT operators piled out, its leader heading for Cole. "You Commander Perriman?"

"Yes."

"How will we tell your guys from the hostiles?"

"None of my men are carrying live firearms. In fact—" Cole pressed his throat mike. "SWAT inbound. All SEALs stow or drop any guns or pistols. Go knives only. Surrender as SWAT approaches you."

The SWAT commander nodded tersely and he and his men disappeared through the open door into the warehouse.

One of the police officers spoke up. "Sir, SWAT will clear the building from back to front. They could use you around front to identify and vouch for your men as they come out."

"Where will the ambulances go?" Cole asked.

"North side of the building."

"Radio them that we're coming around the building to join them," Cole ordered.

The cops nodded and one of them murmured into the radio mounted by his shirt collar.

Cole wasted no time taking off at a brisk run down the street. He hadn't said anything about her staying behind with the police, and her terror level was so high that she had no intention of trusting anyone else right now. So she raced along just behind him, and not surprisingly, Bill stayed at her side. She was hauling butt, full-out, but Bill managed to look casual, and she actually caught him looking around, scanning the buildings and rooflines for hostiles as he ran beside her. Show-off.

They careened around the north side of the warehouse to a chaotic scene. A dozen police cars and a half dozen ambulances were on-scene. Two men were just emerging from the warehouse, carrying a prostrate body between them.

Cole, holding up his military ID, called out, "Those men are mine! I'm vouching for them." He raced over to the ambulance with Nissa on his heels. The wounded man was a SEAL, apparently shot in the belly. A SEAL medic handed over control of the pressure pad on the wound to the EMTs and stepped back.

"Who are you?" called a cop who looked like someone in charge.

"Perriman," Cole shouted back.

"Roger. They told me you were coming around."

Cole turned to the SEAL medic. "Report."

"Cowboy took a round in the right side, back to front. Through-and-through shot. Not fatal, but bleeding heavily from the exit wound. It'll need cleaning up and cauterizing, and he may need a pint or two of blood. But he'll live."

"My other guys' injuries?" Cole demanded.

"I was pinned down with Cowboy, and he needed my full attention, anyway. I don't know how hurt the other SEALs are."

"How many of our guys got shot?" Nissa blurted.

The medic glanced over at her. "Four that I'm aware of."

Another SEAL came out of the warehouse just then, raising only one arm and cradling his other arm against his chest. EMTs rushed over to him along with the SEAL medic. Nissa started to follow, but Cole put a restraining hand on her arm. "Stay out of their way and let them do their job."

She nodded, heart in her throat. These men had been shot protecting her. This was her fault! She'd been so cavalier about using herself as bait to catch Petrov and his men that she'd never considered the danger she was putting Cole's men into. She'd been so focused on proving how badass she was to Cole that she'd lost sight of the cost of the real goal—catching Petrov while *not* getting anyone killed. She was totally unfit to be out in the field making these life-and-death decisions.

She'd gotten people hurt because she was so caught up in her mad attraction to Cole Perriman and in proving that she was worthy of him. Who was she kidding? She wasn't cut out for this stuff.

Fraud. Fraud. Fraud. The word whispered through her mind, an accusation and sickening condemnation.

The medic trotted back to Cole. "Jeeby took a shot through the forearm. Flesh wound, but ragged. Gonna need a bunch of sutures."

"Who else is hit?"

"Leon Burkus got winged by a bullet in the leg and got cut by a knife in a hand-to-hand engagement but is ambulatory, and Willoughby got grazed in the head by a gunshot. Nothing serious, but a lot of blood, apparently. He reported having trouble seeing through it."

Nausea rumbled through Nissa. It was all her fault. All of it. Every single wound. "I think I'm going to be sick," she mumbled. She stepped around the side of the ambulance and emptied her stomach beside the tire.

Hands lifted her upright. Cole. Great. He got to see her puking her guts out because she couldn't handle any of this. Her humiliation was complete.

He passed her a water bottle without comment. She rinsed her mouth and spit, the humiliation still acid in her stomach.

"Two more men coming out," someone called from behind Cole.

"Stay here, Nissa. I've got to finish making the IDs on my men for the police. I wouldn't want them to shoot the wrong guys."

As he moved away from her, violent trembling set in and she was just as glad he wasn't beside her to witness her completely falling apart like this.

An EMT poked his head out of the next ambulance over. "Are you okay, ma'am? Do you need to lie down?"

She mumbled something in the negative and continued to watch the warehouse, praying fervently that all of Cole's men walked out of there alive. Two of the ambulances left the scene with their flashers going as they whisked Cole's men off to the hospital.

Eventually, SWAT team guys started to emerge. Within the next ten minutes or so, all the SWAT guys gathered outside. An all clear was given, and the police swarmed inside the building like an army of dark blue ants.

Bass came over to the ambulance whose bumper she was sitting on. "How're you doing, Nissa?"

"Shaky."

"Understandable."

"What's going on now?" she asked.

"Crime scene guys are going in to figure out what the hell just happened."

Cole came up from behind Bass and she managed to meet his gaze for an instant, but then had to look away. Her guilt was too much for her to overcome. She couldn't look at him.

Bass asked Cole, "What the hell did just happen?"

Cole shrugged. "As best I can tell, Petrov's goons figured out where Nissa was and made a run at her. I have to admit it was a good plan. Good timing. All of us were unarmed, and that warehouse was the ideal spot for an ambush."

"Well, yeah. That's why we use it for training," Bass retorted. "How many of Petrov's guys were in there?"

"Four."

"Did we take any of them alive?" Bass asked curiously.

"Interestingly enough, they all managed to make sure they died fighting."

"Fanatics?" Bass asked quietly.

Nissa's blood ran even colder than it already was at hearing that word.

Cole frowned slightly. "In a manner of speaking. My guess is they were scared enough of Petrov to go down fighting rather than go back to him having failed or rather than risk letting us question them and facing consequences from him later."

Good grief. Just how vicious was Markus Petrov?

"Bass, I need to stash Nissa somewhere. I can't take her back to my place because it's obviously under surveillance by Petrov's goons."

She rounded on Cole. "How do you know that?"

"How else did these jokers find you? I figure one of the shopkeepers yesterday took Petrov's reward and told him about seeing you. The shopkeeper must have reported that you were on foot, which narrowed the search area considerably. Petrov must have had his guys check out anyone who lives nearby and my name popped as a soldier. He must have put two and two together and had his guys watching my place. When you left this morning, they had to have followed you here. I can't think of any other way they found you so fast."

"Or maybe they have an informant," she offered.

"Not on my team," Cole disagreed sharply.

It was her turn to shrug. "Did you guys have to notify the police that you would be running an exercise here today so they didn't panic at the sound of gunfire?"

Bass and Cole traded grim looks. "Yes," Bass answered.

She didn't voice the obvious: that maybe there was an informant for Markus Petrov on the police force.

The Cajun reached into his pants pocket. "These are the keys to my place, boss."

Cole took the key chain with a nod of thanks.

"What do you think about me and a few of the boys camping out around your place to see if we can pick up the surveillance on it?" Bass asked.

Cole nodded again. "Do it."

"Do you want a team at my place with you?" Bass followed up.

Cole tilted his head, considering. "I think at this point that would draw the wrong kind of attention. It would be smarter if she and I just go to ground and disappear."

"I'll bring you food," Bass said. "I can come and go freely from my own house and no one will think anything of it."

"Thanks, man."

Bass and Cole traded quick slaps on the shoulder, and then Cole was guiding Nissa toward a beat-up navy blue pickup truck that looked like it had been through a few too many seasons of mudding.

He muttered, "We're going to walk around the far side of Bass's truck and crawl in the passenger door."

"Why?"

"Possible informant in the police department. There are cops everywhere at this scene."

"Got it," she muttered back. Suddenly, the back of her neck felt prickly as she counted police by the dozens around them. And every last one of them could be Petrov's man.

Cole eased the truck door open and crawled in first, snaking across to the driver's seat. She followed close behind, climbing in awkwardly.

Cole righted himself enough to start the engine and guide the vehicle away from the crowd of police cars.

She banged her head on the dashboard and he snapped. "Put your head in my lap," Cole ordered impatiently.

She complied, startled and unsettled. Sure, she'd had her face in his crotch before, with outstanding results as a matter of fact. But this wasn't sexy at all. The steering wheel barely cleared her face, and the seat belt receptacles dug into her side painfully. Cole's muscular thigh flexed beneath her cheek as he stepped on the gas pedal and then the brake pedal.

She braced herself against the dashboard grimly and counted the minutes until she was freed from this awkward and embarrassing position.

Cole drove for perhaps ten minutes and then the truck slowed. It made one last turn, threatening to dump her onto the floor, and then the interior of a large metal shop-style building appeared overhead through the windshield.

"You can sit up now," Cole said.

"Well. That was fun," she declared sarcastically, pushing away from him with alacrity.

"It was necessary, in case you're right and Petrov has a cop informant who was there to see me leave. He had to see me leave alone."

She climbed out of the truck and looked around at the interior of a neat auto repair shop with two gorgeous antique sports cars in the middle of being restored. On the far side of the space was what looked like a building within a building. It was to this that Cole led her. He used Bass's keys to let them inside, and it turned out to be an equally tidy home tucked inside the shop.

She looked around intently, taking note of the complete lack of feminine touches. "Bass's bachelor pad?" she asked.

"Yup. Make yourself at home."

She perched on the edge of the sofa, unsure of what to say or do with Cole in this brusque, no-nonsense mood of his. Not that she blamed him. Her stupidity had led the bad guys straight to him and his men.

In all the time she'd known him, this was the most intimidated she'd been of being alone with him. Now that she'd seen him in action, she had a much richer sense of just who she was dealing with. The amount of self-control he had was stunning. She knew all SEALs were capable of killing, that Cole himself was capable of it. But she'd had no idea that he disliked doing it so much. Cole's face at the moment he'd slit that guy's throat had reflected distaste. Revulsion, even. But he hadn't hesitated when he'd been forced to kill to save her.

"Hungry?" he called from what must be the kitchen.

The idea of food right now made her faintly ill. "No, thanks."

She heard the ding of a microwave, and then Cole came out into the living room carrying two bowls of what turned out to be gumbo.

"You haven't lived until you've tried Bastien Le-Blanc's gumbo. And your stomach could use the food. It will give all that acid floating around in it something to work on besides your stomach wall."

How did he know about the acid roiling in her gut?

Hesitantly, she tried a spoonful of the rich stew of rice, shrimp, sausage, celery and who knew what else.

"Oh my God, that tastes incredible," she groaned.

"Would I lie to you?" Cole asked.

"I don't know. Would you?" she retorted.

He stared at her over his bowl of gumbo. "What's that comment supposed to mean? I just saved your life."

"What just happened? Really? Was the plan all along to show me how lousy my idea was? Were you out to prove how stupid I am?"

Cole surged to his feet, fury written in the tight lines of his face. "You think I would *ever* set my men up like that? I would never—not even for you, Nissa. If that's what you think of me, you don't know me. At all."

Chapter 17

Nissa watched in dismay as Cole stormed out of the room. She slumped back against the cushions, defeated. Of course, he wouldn't ever intentionally put his men in harm's way if it could be avoided. It was just her fear and guilt and shock talking. If she was brutally honest with herself, she was lashing out to cover up her own responsibility for that fiasco.

With a sigh of resignation, she followed the path of Cole's retreat down the hall and found him pacing in a bedroom.

"I'm sorry, Cole. That was out of line. And I'm sorry for getting you and your men into that mess. It's all my fault."

"What the hell are you talking about?"

"I'm the one who stole Petrov's money and pissed him off. And I'm the one who suggested using me as bait to draw him out."

"If you'll recall, I approved the operation."

"Well, yes. And as I recall, you didn't like the plan one little bit. I forced you into going along with it."

Cole paused in his pacing to glare at her. "Do you seriously think you could force me to do anything, Nissa?"

She gave his question serious consideration. Eventually, she sighed. "I suppose not. After all it's not like I have any hold over you or like you owe me anything." She took a deep breath and continued, "I've misread the situation between us badly, and I apologize. I took advantage of you, and that wasn't fair to you."

"I beg your pardon?"

She raised her hand to stop him from saying anything more. She had to get this out all at once or she would never be brave enough to say it again. "You've been nothing but a gentleman toward me since we met, and you've taken care of me and kept me safe. I really appreciate that. I confess that I was wildly starstruck at the idea of getting to run with a SEAL team. In particular, I was wildly impressed by you. You're an extraordinary man, Cole Perriman. But I was wrong to think that I could ever be worthy of you. And for that, I apologize."

All of a sudden he was in front of her, looming large. "What in the bloody hell are you talking about?"

"I'm apologizing for maneuvering you into bed with me. I took advantage of you, and I'm sorry."

"You did no such thing. No female maneuvers me into bed without my full consent. I'm not some horny eighteen-year-old who can't control my lusty urges."

She blinked up at him, confused. "But… I don't understand."

Frustration glittered in his light blue gaze and he ground out, "I wanted to sleep with you in the worst way. I'm the one who maneuvered you into bed."

She snorted. "No you didn't."

"There you have it. Our time together was a mutual thing."

Was he right? On that one score, at least, was she blameless? "So you don't regret making love with me?"

He laid his hands gently on her shoulders. "Nissa, you are a colleague. And in spite of what you seem to think of me, I respect women and fully support women working in my field. However, being involved with you romantically skirts dangerously close to fraternization. Without question, a personal entanglement with you jeopardizes my career. But I could no more stop myself from being with you than I could choose to stop breathing."

She stared into his eyes, searching for truth in his words. He stared back as if willing her to believe him. She didn't see the slightest hint of evasion or inaccuracy in his crystalline eyes. "Really?"

His arms swept around her and dragged her up against him as his mouth swooped down to capture hers. All of it was there instantly, the incendiary attraction, the irresistible pull for more, the incredible fit between them. She groaned and threw her arms around his waist, giving herself over to her desire and relief with a new humility.

"I don't deserve you," she mumbled against his lips.

"Hah. I'm the one who doesn't deserve you. Hell, I just killed a man in front of you." He lifted her off her feet and turned in a one-eighty before slowing and backing her up toward the big bed.

"You were protecting me."

"I'm still sorry you had to see that." His hand slipped under her shirt and raised it over her head, and she returned the favor, stripping off his black turtleneck.

"I'm not sorry," she disagreed. "If you had to do that on my behalf, it's only fair that I share the memory of it with you."

"Aww, baby, the difference is I won't dwell on it and you will. But for me, it's just my job." He paused in the act of laying her down on the bed. "I'm a soldier, Nissa. At the end of the day, I'm trained to kill. I don't know if I'll ever be able to put away that part of myself and be the kind of man who can have a real relationship with a real woman like you."

She stared up at him in shock. Was that what he thought of himself? That he wasn't worthy of being loved? "Just because you're a soldier doesn't make you unlovable, Cole."

He stared down at her looking patently unconvinced.

She reached up to cup his beautiful face in her hands. "Do you hear me? You can have a real relationship right now, just the way you are. You deserve a real relationship. Maybe not with me, but with someone worthy of you."

He frowned at that. "What's wrong with you?"

She squeezed her eyes shut. He wasn't really going to make her say it, was he? She would give anything not to have to admit to him that she was a fraud. It would be the end of any shred of respect he might still have for her. And yet...

If she was ever going to have a real and lasting relationship with him, it had to be built on a foundation of total honesty.

She took a deep breath. "I'm a fraud."

He pulled back, studying her intently. "How so?"

"I'm not like you at all. I don't run around in the field—I don't even like running around in the field. I'm not the least bit brave or strong."

One corner of his mouth twitched upward. "Yeah, I got that memo."

Indignant that he wasn't getting the point, she exclaimed, "I'm afraid of everything!"

"I know."

"You know?" she repeated blankly.

He kissed the tip of her nose. Was that a chuckle making his chest shake like that?

"Are you laughing at me?" she demanded.

"Yes. Yes I am."

"But...why?"

"Because everybody gets scared. Bravery isn't the absence of fear. It's being afraid and doing what needs to be done anyway. You may get scared, but you're one of the bravest women I know."

She stared up into his eyes in amazement. Was he right? Was she being too hard on herself?

"Do you get scared?" she asked.

"Hell yes. I was scared to death when I realized we were under attack in the warehouse and I had no way to protect you."

She laid her palm on his cheek and gazed up into his beautiful blue eyes. "But you did protect me. You risked your life for me."

He stared down at her, relief, regret and real care for her warring in his expression.

"Thank you, Cole." She stood on her tiptoes and

kissed him until his mouth opened against hers and his arms swept around her.

He efficiently stripped her jeans off, and where her lingerie went was anybody's guess. My, my, my, that man had clever fingers.

They tumbled across the bed, and she smiled up at him, profoundly relieved that he wasn't holding himself apart from her anymore.

She pushed on his shoulders and he gave way, rolling onto his back. She snapped open the military buckle on his belt and shoved his camouflage pants down. She, too, could get rid of underwear and socks efficiently, and she sat back in satisfaction when he sprawled naked in front of her.

Good golly, Miss Molly, that man was pretty. He was also completely unconcerned about his nudity. Which she found intensely erotic and intensely intimidating. She wasn't nearly as comfortable with her body as he seemed to be. She commented enviously, "It must be nice to be so at ease in one's skin."

He reached up to smooth away the frown from her forehead. "Why wouldn't you be at ease in your skin? You're a beautiful woman."

"Hah! I'll cop to being scrawny, and maybe to having interesting hair, but not to being beautiful."

He surged up over her, pushing her down into the pillows. "Are you kidding me?" he demanded. "What isn't to like?" He kissed his way across her shoulder. "This is a great shoulder. I like how your collarbone creates this little hollow for me to kiss."

He moved lower and her breath caught on a gasp.

He murmured, "And I like this warm valley between your breasts. It smells like you and tastes like vanilla."

His hands went around her hips and he easily raised her torso to meet his exploring kisses. "And I like your stomach. It's flat and smooth, but it's soft. You're not all muscle and ridges, rather, you're gentle and womanly. Sometimes I get an urge to rest my head on your stomach. Like this."

Her hand drifted to his hair, and she stroked his head in minor disbelief. "Why do you like this?" she asked after a while.

"I find peace here."

Huh. He found peace in her body? She could live with that.

He rose up over her then, and his gaze was anything but peaceful. Desire was turbulent in his eyes as he positioned himself over her and his velvet heat touched her center. She stared up at him and had to ask, "Are you sure about this? I'm done with trying to finagle what I want out of you. What do you want, Cole?"

"I want this." He reached across her for a condom, and then slowly, slowly, he entered her, his gaze burning with cold fire as he stared down at her. Her breath hitched as he filled her totally. "And I am sure about this, Nissa."

She arched up into him, reveling in the hardness of his warrior's body against hers. "But why?" she whispered. "I'm nothing."

He withdrew partially to stare down at her in what looked like disbelief, and she clutched at him in quick desperation for him not to leave her. But then she forced herself to let him go and unwrapped her arms and legs from around his body. She would not force him to stay with her if it wasn't where he wanted to be.

"Never let me go. Please," he pleaded.

Shocked, she wrapped her entire being around him then—arms, legs, heart and soul—and made love to him with every fiber of her being.

Their lovemaking was urgent at first, but gradually they slowed to more deeply savor the moment and each other. She pushed the hair off his forehead and he smiled down at her before kissing her slowly and deeply. She met his tongue with hers; she met each of his kisses with one of her own. Her hands roved across his back and shoulders, and eventually, she grabbed his hips and pulled him closer, showing him what she wanted as her hips surged upward eagerly.

He chuckled under his breath. "Tease."

"Torturer."

He kissed her lightly. "Impatient."

"Control freak."

He laughed outright then. "Guilty as charged."

Their smiles mingled as he did, indeed, take control of their lovemaking, setting up a steady, unhurried rhythm that drove her out of her mind. She cried out against his shoulder as wave after wave of pleasure broke over her. But still he kept up that steady stroke, never wavering in his clear purpose to give her pleasure. And frankly, she was totally on board with the idea.

He roused her to such a fever pitch with every thrust of his body, that finally she came again. She'd never experienced anything to compare to the continuous chain of orgasms he brought her to.

She could only hope his eventual release would be so epic that it would make up for all the ones she got to enjoy. To that end, she clutched him with her internal muscles and rocked her hips in time with his, finding the rhythms of his body and matching them instinctively, doing her best to milk all the pleasure from him that she could.

Everything in his being and body strained toward her, and she reveled in the sight and feel of him as she drove him toward the edge. It was glorious having this much power over a man like him. But then, he had every bit as much power over her.

Their perspiration-slicked bodies tangled together so closely she couldn't tell where she ended and he began. Their breath mingled and pleasure entwined until they were practically one being. One spirit.

And in that moment of exquisite sympatico, Cole stared down at her and she up at him. He gave one last, mighty thrust, and then his entire body arched and hers did the same, as taut as a high wire that she balanced upon precariously. He cried out, beginning a long, shuddering fall, and that was all it took. She toppled off the thin wire of control and fell with him, down, down, into an abyss of pleasure so deep and intense it felt like he'd torn out her very soul and replaced it with his own.

Her undulating cries joined his groan of release as pure ecstasy rippled across her skin and passed through her like a seismic shock. Her entire body tingled and she felt more alive than she had in ages.

Cole's big body relaxed against hers, and she struggled to catch her breath. "I suppose you're not even winded by that," she groused.

He kissed her forehead lightly. "I'm wiped out."

"Thank God. Me, too."

He rolled onto his back and tucked her against his side, her head resting on his shoulder. She threw her arm across his chest and placed her hand over his heart. It was thudding hard. She smiled in satisfaction and dropped a lazy kiss on his chest.

"Get some rest, Nissa. You're going to need your strength."

"Oooh. Are we going to do that again?"

"I sincerely hope so. But we also have to repeat this morning's exercise."

She frowned a little, unsure of what he was saying. "You mean we have to repeat the training scenarios with your men?"

"No."

"Then what are you talking about?" she asked cautiously, not liking where this could be going. Suddenly, all the pleasure that had zinged through her body moments ago fled.

"We have to set you up as bait again. Except next time, I plan to draw out Petrov himself. And furthermore, I'll be there to look out for you."

She sat up and stared down at him. "Are you crazy? Four of your men got shot. We can't do that again!"

"Nissa, if four of my men had been *killed*, I would still use you again. We have to catch this guy. You said so, yourself. Not only is he a clear and present danger to national security, but now you're on his radar. It's him or you, Nissa. And I intend for it to be him who goes down."

No. No, no, no, no, no. Nissa hated that idea. No way was she putting Cole and his men into danger again. "There has to be another way!" she blurted.

"I'm open to suggestions," Cole said evenly. But there was steel beneath his words that even she, in her agitation, couldn't miss.

"This guy is dangerous!"

Cole snorted. "In case you haven't noticed, so are the SEALs."

"But he's desperate. Cornered."

"Exactly. We have to keep the heat on him until we break him."

She scowled down at Cole. "What do you propose we do? Call him and tell him to meet us at the O.K. Corral at high noon?"

"Well, I was thinking more in terms of meeting him at one of his strip clubs and closer to midnight."

"Are you freaking kidding me?" she exclaimed.

"No."

"That's insane."

"It's audacious. And Markus Petrov is nothing if not audacious. His attack on the warehouse this morning proves that."

"All the more reason to stay the hell away from him!" she declared.

Cole sat up, and she gulped as his abs flexed into a six pack so hot she had trouble tearing her gaze away from it. "Do you want to catch this guy or not?" he demanded.

"Of course I do."

"Do you trust me?"

She hesitated, seeing the trap he was laying for her.

"Do you?" Cole challenged.

"Well, yes."

"Well, then. What's the problem?"

"I can't take responsibility for getting any more of your guys hurt, or Heaven forbid, you getting hurt. I saw the way you charged across the warehouse to get to my side when the shooting started."

"You saw that, huh?" he replied neutrally.

"It was a suicide move, and you know it."

"Cutting out through the wall at the back of the office was an unpredictable move that the shooter wasn't prepared for. It worked, didn't it?"

"You got lucky," she accused.

"You know what they say. It's better to be lucky than good."

"Don't give me that crap. You know that's not true."

Cole swung his muscular, gorgeous legs out of bed. He stood up and went hunting for their clothes, donning his as he found them and tossing hers to her. She'd managed to get her panties and bra on before he loomed over her fully dressed and back to being every inch the military officer.

"I take calculated risks for a living, Nissa. And given that I've survived a long damned time as a SEAL, I must be decent at what I do. Have a little faith in me, for crying out loud."

Enough faith in him to trust her life to him? That was a big leap of faith. But truth be told, she wouldn't trust anyone else to protect her.

"If I agree to do this, do you promise to personally look out for me?"

"Nissa, I was always personally looking out for you. Just because I put Bass in charge of the operation didn't mean I wasn't there every step of the way watching every move he made."

"Does he know you were prepared to step in and take over the op from him at a moment's notice?"

Cole shrugged. "You're my woman. It went without saying."

"Are you guys really that Neanderthal about women?"

He scowled. "I'm the guy who selected and supervised the training of the first female SEALs, I'll have you know."

"And yet, I'm your woman?"

"Why are you trying to pick a fight with me?"

His question cut through all her indignation and cut right to the heart of the matter. She was, indeed, diverting away from the main issue. Of course he'd seen right through it. She said quietly, "You're right. I'm fighting because I'm scared to death and I'm embarrassed to let you see how scared I am."

His rigid spine relaxed, and he gathered her into her arms gently. "Nissa, I don't expect you to be invincible. It's okay for you to be terrified. I wouldn't want you to be just like one of my guys. You're my safe haven from all of that military stuff."

She inhaled the masculine scent of him, loving it. "Promise me one more thing, Cole."

"What's that?"

"Swear you won't do anything stupid and get yourself hurt or killed on my behalf."

He laughed shortly. "I'm not going to promise that. I'd lay down my life for you without a second thought."

She stepped back and stared up at him in horror. "Then I'm sorry. I can't help you."

Chapter 18

Frustration roared through Cole. They were so close to catching Petrov and *now* she had to get cold feet?

He said grimly, "Nissa, with or without you, my mission is to apprehend Markus Petrov. You remain tasked to my team to identify Petrov. Technically, you are under my command. Don't make me pull rank and force you to help me capture him."

She recoiled from him even farther. "You wouldn't force me," she accused.

"Please don't test me." Honestly, he didn't know how far he would make her go if push came to shove. Answering that question would involve him figuring out exactly how he felt about her and furthermore, figuring out where the line between his personal life and professional duty was drawn.

Her eyes narrowed and she opened her mouth, no

doubt to tear him a new one, but the sound of the front door opening derailed her explosion.

"Cole! Nissa! You guys home?" It was Bass.

Saved by the bell. Cole whirled and went out into the living room to waylay Bass long enough for Nissa to finish getting dressed. She strolled out a moment later, her wild hair the only sign of their recent lovemaking.

"What's up, Bass?" Cole asked.

"We got IDs on Petrov's men—the ones from the warehouse."

Meaning the four corpses from the warehouse. He was thankful that Bass had exercised a bit of taste in describing them. "Who were they?"

"Two of them worked at a restaurant in the Quarter. I ran a quick records search on the joint, and you'll never guess who manages the place. Stan Martin."

"Nice. What kind of restaurant is it?"

"High-end. Continental cuisine. Has a couple private dining rooms, and is rumored to be a site for mob meetings."

"Which mob?" Nissa asked. "Italian or Russian? Or some other flavor altogether?"

Bass shrugged. "NOPD doesn't know. It's not the kind of place informants can stroll into and make it out of alive. Clientele is selected carefully and is well-known to the staff."

Cole frowned. "Is it a private joint, then?"

Bass shook his head. "No, but it's the sort of place that doesn't hang out a big sign and invite in the tourists. You'd have to know it was a restaurant to even go there. It's a completely unmarked building."

Nissa piped up. "That sounds like exactly the kind

of place Markus Petrov would go to meet with his top lieutenants."

Bass nodded. "That's what I was thinking. How would you two feel about a stakeout? I'm on duty until midnight with the police and can spell you after that."

Cole frowned. "You worked all morning at the warehouse, went through a shoot-out and then are working all afternoon and evening as a cop. The last thing you need is to spend the night having to stay awake on some boring stakeout. I'll handle watching the restaurant. You come home and get some sleep, bro."

Cole glanced over at Nissa, unsure of what to expect from her. He would love to have her go on the stakeout with him since she would recognize Petrov on sight and he would not. But she'd made her position pretty clear earlier. She was out.

"Will it be dangerous?" she asked Bass. Avoiding talking with him, was she? Wry amusement coursed through Cole.

"Nah. It's just a stakeout. All you'll be doing is figuring out if this is a place Petrov or his men hang out."

Cole added, "In the interest of full disclosure, it will be about as exciting as watching grass grow."

She met his eyes only briefly, then her gaze skated away. "All right. I'll do it. Nobody else would know Petrov's face like me."

She had used the one existing photograph of Petrov that was thirty or more years old and had run dozens of simulations to predict what he looked like now. More important, she'd carefully memorized the structure of his facial bones, the shape, color and size of his eyes. Even if he'd had some sort of face altering plastic surgery in the past three decades, she ought to be able to recognize him.

Technically, she could just show the aged simulations of Petrov to Cole and his men, but she was the expert. He would rather have her make the identification.

Cole looked at his watch. "We've probably got just enough time to pack some snacks before we have to head out. I'd like to be in place in front of the restaurant by about four o'clock."

"That's pretty early," Nissa commented.

Cole shrugged. "Petrov should be pretty agitated by losing four men and failing to kill you this morning. He may call some sort of meeting with his people, and it may not be at the usual dinner hour."

"Good point," Nissa mumbled.

Bass said jovially, "I'll take care of putting together a picnic. You two grab whatever you need from around here for a stakeout party. And I've got just the car for you to use. It's parked out back."

The vehicle turned out to be a banged up midsize sedan about a decade old. More important, though, it had dark side and rear windows, and a powerful late-model engine under the hood. Knowing Bass, the engine was in perfect running condition. That man was a magician with anything mechanical.

Bass handed Cole a basket of food and drinks and, with a lopsided grin, handed Nissa a plastic grocery bag that appeared to hold random car parts. The guy muttered something to her too quietly for Cole to hear, and her face turned bright pink.

Cole slid behind the wheel of the car while Nissa buckled her seat belt. As they pulled out of Bass's mini car lot, he asked, "What's with the bag Bass handed you back there?"

"He gave me some sort of old oil pan that he rigged up for me to, uh, relieve myself into if the need arises."

Cole grinned at her red face. "The guy thinks of everything. And there's nothing to be embarrassed about. Bodily functions are a necessary part of life. And it's not like you and I aren't intimately familiar with each other's bodies."

"Your frankness about physical stuff takes a little getting used to."

He shrugged. "Modern hinkiness about such things makes no sense to me."

"It's a leftover from our Puritan roots, I suppose," she replied.

"I'm no Puritan."

"A fact for which I am intensely grateful—"

She broke off, and he glanced over at her. He was amused to see her face was scarlet.

It took him a moment to realize why she was blushing. And then it dawned on him. She was embarrassed about being uninhibited in bed. He smiled broadly. "I enjoy you immensely in bed. There's nothing to be ashamed of."

"Umm, thank you, I think."

"Oh, I definitely meant that as a compliment."

She rolled her eyes. "I don't have near the experience you do."

He parallel parked the car a little way down the street from the unmarked restaurant, commenting as he looked back over his shoulder, "I'm not exactly a gigolo. Unlike some of my guys, I have not made a habit over the years of leaping into the sack with every willing female who comes along."

"Really?"

He frowned at her. "Do I strike you as that kind of man? I think I'm a bit insulted."

"No, not at all. But what other explanation is there for you and me?"

"Why can't you accept that I happen to find you attractive? Do you really think that badly of yourself?" He was tempted to lean across the gearshift box and kiss her to prove just how attracted he was to her, but they were working, and the confines of this car could get very tight in the next twelve hours or so.

Nissa stared down at her entwined fingers, which were worrying at one another absently. He was at a loss as to how to prove to her how much he cared for her. He'd made love to her with his all his heart, wearing it solidly on his sleeve—or on his bare arm as the case might be. What more was there to do?

Vexed, he sighed and turned his attention to the building across the street. It was old and brick, with elaborate wrought iron grills over the front windows. A narrow upstairs porch sported wrought iron railings, as well. Tall casement windows rose behind them.

He pulled out binoculars and was able to look in the second-story windows, spying a room with round tables through the two left-hand windows. The third window looked in on what must be a private dining room, however. A long table was set with twelve place settings. The ground floor was too dark to see into at the moment.

"Place looks deserted right now," he commented. "If

Petrov's coming here any time soon, I think we beat him into position."

"Now what?"

"Now we wait." Waiting was a big part of his job. Surveillance could be painstaking, boring work, but was vital to understanding the layout of a site and the patterns of the people inside. Sometimes the SEALs were handed surveillance from other sources, but just as often, they had to gather their own intel before launching an operation.

"How long do you expect to be here?" she asked.

"All night if necessary. Hence the food and drink, and your relief kit."

The early crowd of diners came and went from the restaurant, and Nissa passed the time by looking up on the internet the history of the building they were watching. It turned out to be one of the oldest standing structures in the French Quarter, built in the early 1800s by smugglers and pirates. Apparently, the entire block had been built by a group of them, and the current restaurant was one of the original residences that made up the complex.

It amused him that Nissa couldn't ever turn off her inner researcher/analyst. Of course, it also meant she was constantly popping up with strange trivia and factoids. No doubt about it, the woman was really smart, and he found that extremely attractive.

Sex for sex's sake was good up to a point, but as he'd learned in the past few days, there could be much more to it than just a physical connection. And that other connection, the emotional one, turned out to be a great deal more addictive. He truly was at a loss to know what to do with her. Was he ready to leap out of his military career and into a new life as a normal guy? With her?

A while later, as the sun set in the west behind them and twilight fell, Nissa interrupted the silence to ask him, "Did you find out how Petrov's snipers got into the warehouse this morning?"

He glanced over at her quizzically. "That's a strange question. Why do you ask?"

"Well, I watched Bass and his guys do their thing for a couple of hours before the shooting started. I didn't see any approaches to that office they had me sitting in except to walk in like you did from either the front or back doors. But Petrov's guys seemed to appear out of nowhere. From what I remember, it seemed to me like they were up on the catwalks shooting down at us."

Everything had been such a whirlwind since those first gunshots rang out and he'd panicked and run for Nissa that he honestly hadn't had a moment to stop and think about it yet. It would take the police forensics guys a few days to piece together exactly what had happened. They would look at the angles of entry wounds on his guys and find out exactly where the men had been standing when they'd been shot, and then a determination could be made as to where Petrov's men had been hiding.

"What makes you think Petrov's men were shooting downward?" he asked.

"I've watched a fair bit of video footage of firefights in my day and the sound of a gunshot from up high is distinctive."

Now that he stopped and thought about it, she was exactly right. He glanced over at her. "When have you watched combat footage?"

"I'm an analyst. I analyze whatever they put in front of me. It turns out I'm pretty good at looking at live feeds and spotting little details that the guys with boots on the ground miss in the heat of battle. I've seen a bunch of film of Russian special forces teams doing their thing over the years."

"Really? I'd love to pick your brain sometime about their procedures and how they roll. For that matter, some of Petrov's guys may come from the Spetznaz. Can you give me any insights as to how they might operate that I haven't already thought of?"

"I can tell you flatly that you SEALs don't have much to learn from them. They tend to be extremely hierarchical and enlisted troops as a rule despise officers. In turn, officers trust enlisted troops about as far as they can throw them. Communication can be stilted at best and nonexistent at worst. The one positive thing I'll say about them is that they're excellent at improvising and working around equipment or intelligence failures. When a plan goes awry, they adapt very well."

"Good to know. Let's hope none of Petrov's men are trained special forces guys."

She shrugged. "I would expect his personal bodyguards to be at least that well trained. It's possible he uses mercenaries from some other country where the special forces types are actually extremely competent. Don't underestimate him or his men. They'll fight tenaciously and do whatever it takes to stay alive…or in Petrov's case to stay alive *and* escape."

"Duly noted."

"If it's not a violation of your security procedures, could you tell me something about the SEALs?"

"Ask me. I'll let you know if I can answer or not."

"Do you guys use live intel analysts to watch your helmet cameras' feeds?"

"Sometimes. Just as often it's a team of SEAL supervisors who watch the feeds. In the case of a high-profile operation, the feed may go all the way up to the Situation Room at the White House."

"I assume that's not considered ideal by you and your guys?" she asked.

He snorted. "Correct. The higher level the observers, the more they want to interfere and tell us how to do our jobs."

"Are you the guy who has to keep those other peoples' noses out of your missions, or does that happen at a higher level than yours?"

"It depends. Sometimes I'm the guy arguing with the guys in civilian suits, sometimes it's my bosses. Sometimes it's all of us."

"Sounds like a pain in the patootie."

"Oh, yeah," he replied. "Particularly in a gunfight. It's already chaotic, and then you've got these idiots yelling helpful suggestions in your ears. I can hardly hear my own men, sometimes, and the last thing I need is civilian Cub Scout ideas."

"Speaking as one of those Cub Scouts who doesn't want to get in the way, what would you tell me if I was the one talking in your ear?"

"Trust us to get the job done and leave us alone. My only priority is to stay alive and accomplish the goal as fast as possible so I can get my guys out of the line of fire. I'm the guy seeing the operational situation firsthand. And yes, I can miss details here and there, but I catch the big stuff that could get me and my guys killed."

"Fair enough. Still, that very thing is why people like me are asked to watch the feeds. We don't have any skin in the game, as it were, and can objectively observe the scenario. We might take note of minutiae that's not important to you."

He admitted a little begrudgingly, "I've worked with a couple outside observers over the years who were pretty good. They caught stuff that was helpful to me and my guys."

She laughed. "I'm glad to know not all of us analysts are worthless."

"Speaking of which, what else did you see yesterday that my men and I might have missed?"

She shrugged. "I wasn't exactly an objective observer yesterday. My neck was on the line just like yours." She added drily, "It turns out that makes quite a significant difference in how a person views a gun battle."

He snorted. "Ya think? If you think that's bad, you ought to see how your perspective distorts when you're responsible for the lives of the men with you."

"I can't even imagine it."

Cole rarely stopped to think about the enormous pressure of his job, but every now and then, the reality that peoples' actual lives were in his hands still struck him, even after all these years. It was an awesome burden. He'd born it gladly for all these years, but he honestly wasn't that sorry to lay down that part of his job, now that he thought about it.

"Does that look like Markus Petrov?" Nissa said abruptly from beside him.

He looked up sharply at where she was pointing. A middle-aged man, accompanied by two big men who could easily be bodyguards, was just entering the restaurant. "I didn't get a good look at his face," Cole said. "Did you?"

"No, I didn't," she answered in frustration.

"Let's give it a minute and see if he sits where we can spot him through a window," Cole suggested.

A light went on upstairs in the room that looked like a private dining room, but from their vantage point down at street level, much of the room wasn't visible to them.

Over the next ten minutes, a half dozen more men of similar age, and similarly accompanied by big burly men, entered the restaurant. Shadows were visible occasionally moving past that upstairs window, but no faces came into plain sight. Cole trained his binoculars on the private dining room, hoping to glimpse someone as the minutes ticked past, but he saw no one.

"Oh my gosh, that's Peter Martin going into the restaurant!" Nissa exclaimed.

He pointed the binoculars at the ground floor entrance. Sure enough, Cole recognized one of the Petrov sons from his driver's license picture.

"This is certainly getting interesting," he murmured. Dialing his cell phone without looking away from the restaurant, he called Bass. "I need you and your guys to get over here. It looks like our buddy and all his friends are gathering. I'd hate for you to get left out of the party."

In spite of the lightness of the message's delivery, Bass answered soberly, all business. "We'll roll immediately. About a block behind where you're parked is a side street. I'll meet you there, and then we can go to the party together. I'll be there in ten."

It was more like fifteen minutes before Cole's phone beeped with a text message that Bass was three minutes out. But New Orleans wasn't back to ops normal yet by any means.

In the meantime, Petrov's other son, Stan, even showed up. It was great news. They were going to net the entire family tonight, and hopefully the rest of the Petrov organization, spies and all.

Exultant, he turned to Nissa. "Stay here in the car. I'm going to meet Bass and his team down the street and breach the restaurant with them. When we've got everyone secured and in custody, I'll call you to come inside and make the positive ID on Petrov. Okay?"

She nodded, her eyes big and scared.

"Don't worry, kid. We do stuff like this all the time. Sit back and enjoy the show. You're about to see something very few civilians ever get to witness."

"I just hope nothing goes wrong."

"What could go wrong? This is a routine op. Our targets are gathered in a public space with limited entrances and exits. We'll bottle them up and then enter at our leisure to secure them."

He got out of the car and leaned down briefly to say, "I'll see you on the other side."

Chapter 19

Nissa shivered as Cole strode away from her. She watched him in the passenger side rearview mirror until he turned the corner and disappeared from sight. She had a bad feeling about tonight. A very bad feeling.

But it wasn't like she could share that with Cole. He already thought she was dingbatty enough. The last thing she needed to do was confirm his low opinion of her as a flighty, emotional female.

She picked up the binoculars Cole had left in the passenger seat between them. They were heavy and clunky, but the interior of the upstairs dining room leaped into clear relief as she stared at it. Or at least a tiny sliver of the room came into view. What she wouldn't give to be able to look in that window squarely. She eyed the buildings to her right, but they appeared locked up tight. And unlike Cole, she was no expert at breaking and entering. Huffing, she turned back to watching the restaurant.

The old bricks and crumbling mortar reminded her a lot of the warehouse she'd spent the morning training— and nearly dying—in. Maybe the warehouse had been a particularly old building, too. It would be the sort of space that smugglers or pirates would have built in early New Orleans to hold their booty.

As she waited for Cole, Bass and the other SEALs to assault the restaurant, she watched waiters moving around the dining room upstairs, beginning to serve Petrov and his companions their supper. She circled back to her earlier question, considering idly how the shooters had gotten into the warehouse. What if there were still secret passages the smugglers used to get in and out of the warehouse unseen? It would explain how Petrov's men had gotten right into the middle of the SEALs undetected and had been able to spring that ambush.

Underground tunnels were the obvious thing, but they would likely still be flooded after the recent hurricane. Hmm. Upstairs passages, then? Maybe false walls with narrow tunnels between them? Eagerness came over her to go back to the warehouse, measure its interior dimensions and compare them to the building's exterior dimensions.

Another twenty minutes passed without any activity, and impatience rolled through her. Where were Cole and his men? Sure, she knew they liked to take their time and get the layout of a place and do a little of their own surveillance before they just barged into any place, but this was starting to seem excessive.

And then it dawned on her that part of the team must

be making its way around the far side of the building and the rear exit from the kitchen. What had Cole said? They would bottle the place up and then go in at their leisure? Right.

She forced herself to sit back to wait for the show. She'd never seen a real operation up close and personal like this. She was just as happy to be sitting in a car a block away and not be right in the thick of the action. Even here, her adrenaline was pumping wildly and her entire body felt shaky.

All of a sudden, with no warning at all, she saw a trio of black shapes move swiftly in front of the restaurant door. Where had they come from? One moment they weren't visible, and the next, they were looming in front of the door flashing fast hand signals at one another.

A pause no longer than a breath or two, and the men slipped inside the restaurant. Honestly, she expected other diners and staff to stream out into the street, but nobody came in or left the place in the next sixty seconds. She did notice that the lights went out in the upstairs dining room abruptly, casting the space in sudden darkness.

Flashlight beams came from the private dining room's window, spearing the night outside like lasers. A few fast moving shadows were silhouetted by the bright lights, but then even those stopped.

Her cell phone rang, and Cole said tersely, "He's not here. If you could come inside and verify that, I'd be grateful."

"Not there? We saw him go in."

"Unless there's a trap door in the floor or he melted through the walls, the guy's not here."

Frowning, she climbed out of the car. *Gone?* That made no sense at all. She was sure that first man had been Petrov. Goodness knew, she'd studied the pictures of him exhaustively. No way had he had time to get plastic surgery and heal from it.

She climbed out of the car, staring up at the two-story brick building. It was an old building reportedly built by smugglers. What if, as she suspected with the warehouse, this building had secret passageways, too?

Instead of going directly to the building, she paralleled it across the street, staring in the windows where she was able to, eyeballing measurements of the interior walls versus the exterior dimensions. She didn't spot any potential passageways on first glance. Of course, tunnels could have been between interior spaces and not be visible from out here. That made more sense.

She reached the end of the block and crossed the street to double back alongside the restaurant and then go in. But as she crossed the street, she spied two figures just slipping out of a doorway ahead of her. It was the last building in the row of brick dwellings containing the restaurant.

She squinted into the shadows trying to make out the men's features. One of them was big and strong looking. The other man wore a hat pulled low over his eyes as if he was hiding his face. But he did glance up briefly toward a street lamp and Nissa caught a glimpse of his profile.

She would know that hawk nose anywhere. She'd stared at it in the photograph taped to her cubicle wall for the past year. *Markus Petrov.*

She pulled out her cell phone and speed-dialed Cole

as she stepped onto the curb. Petrov and his man turned away from her and started to move quickly down the side street, deeper into the French Quarter.

"Where are you?" Cole bit out when he answered his phone.

"I'm outside, following our friend," she murmured as quietly as she could. "We're heading north one block east of the restaurant."

Cole swore under his breath. "Do not approach them. You hear me? And don't let them see you!"

He said that like she knew the first thing about basic spycraft. Desk jockeys like her weren't taught things like tailing bad guys without being spotted. Sure, she'd read her fair share of spy novels over the years. But that didn't constitute actually knowing what she was doing.

"I'm on my way," Cole muttered. "Stay on the line with me and vector me in. I'll catch up as fast as I can."

It sounded simple enough, but Petrov and his man were obviously wary of being followed and turned several corners in fast succession in front of her. During one such abrupt turn when they disappeared from sight, she sprinted for the corner but paused long enough to shed her thin jacket and pull her hair down out of its ponytail.

Maybe changing her clothing and hair would throw off Petrov and his bodyguard from spotting her. Her hands shook as she stuffed the jacket in a trash can and turned the corner.

Big hands grabbed her and shoved her up against a wall and a gruff voice growled, "Who the hell are you?"

She squeaked past the choke hold Petrov's bodyguard had on her as best she could, but that was about all the noise she could force past the strangling hold he had on her neck. Rather than try to make conversation she kicked him in the shin as hard as she could.

"Oww!"

She thrust her hands up inside his grip and aimed her thumbs for his eyes, forcing him to turn his head away from her in self-defense. She kneed him as hard as she could and wrung a satisfying groan from him, followed by a string of curses in Russian as he released her throat. She pretended, of course, not to understand those.

"Fire!" she yelled at the top of her lungs. She ducked out from under his arm and darted back around the corner, only to run into something at least as hard and muscular as the assailant behind her.

She opened her mouth to scream again, but looked up and recognized Cole. "A man! Big and strong. Right around the—"

Said thug barreled around the wall and slammed into her, in turn slamming her into Cole. He and she both went down in a tangle as he tried to brace her from the fall and she tried to get off him and free him up as fast as possible.

It was a chaotic moment, but she rolled to one side and Cole jumped to his feet, driving forward and up into the bodyguard's gut with the crown of his head. It was a tackle worthy of a professional football player.

Both men went down, grappling and throwing fists and elbows every which way. She had to scramble on her hands and knees to get clear enough of the melee to climb to her feet. Watching carefully, she kicked the bodyguard in the kidneys as he rolled to expose his back to her.

He cried out and Cole managed to wriggle out from underneath the guy's superior weight. She kicked the thug again, this time in the back of the legs. He flailed and rolled to his knees, Cole doing the same.

Clasping her fists together, she swung her arms like a sledgehammer and smashed her hands into the back of the bad guy's head. She'd hoped to knock him out, but the guy was made of sterner stuff than that. Plus, she wasn't exactly a bundle of power.

But, her blow to the back of his head did stun him enough that Cole was able to get in a couple of hard uppercuts, one of which toppled the big man like a bowling pin. He fell onto his side and rolled slowly onto his back.

"You okay?" Cole asked her.

"Yes. You?"

He ignored her question. "Any sign of Petrov?"

"He went around the corner that the bodyguard jumped out from."

"C'mon, then," Cole grunted as he climbed to his feet. A trickle of blood ran from the corner of his mouth and the side of his face was all scraped up, but now was not the time to stop and mop off a little blood.

Cole ran around the corner and she followed on his heels. But he pulled up sharply in front of her and tried to back her up around the corner with his body.

"No, no," a male voice said from in front of Cole. "I want the lady to join us. I especially want her."

Cole raised his hands up in the air slowly. She took another step backward, ready to turn and flee, but the voice said, "If you run, young lady, I will be forced to shoot your companion and then come after you and shoot you, as well."

"Go!" Cole ordered her.

No way was she leaving him behind to get shot. She stepped out from behind Cole, and sure enough, Markus Petrov was standing there, pointing a large-caliber pistol at Cole.

"I told you to go," Cole ground out.

"And I'm not letting you die to save me," she ground back.

"How noble of you, Miss…Beck, is it? You're a hard woman to find."

"You should know, Mr. Petrov," she replied tartly. Her knees were shaking and she felt like she might throw up any second, but she would be damned if she showed fear to this jackal.

He smiled coldly. "Walk. Both of you. You know the drill. No sudden movements, or my excellent reflexes will take over and I'll kill you."

"If you kill me, you'll never get your money back," she declared.

"Oh, I will get my money back, and I will, indeed, kill you, my dear. But first you will talk."

The dark tone of his voice hinted at unknown tortures that made her gut turn to acid.

"Yes, indeed. I shall take great pleasure in making your friend suffer for harming my man. And then I will make you *sing*, little girl." He hissed the word in threat so thick it choked her.

The idea of having to watch Cole being hurt almost broke her on the spot. She wouldn't be able to do that, no matter how tough she knew Cole to be, no matter how trained he was to endure such atrocities. She was *not* trained.

However, she also wasn't ready to roll over and die.

She noticed that Cole was walking slower than he usually did, and she followed suit, sticking beside him. "Are you hurt?" she asked aloud.

No surprise, he nodded and stumbled against her a little bit. What did surprise her, though, was feeling something cold and hard poke her in the side. She palmed the handgun Cole passed her and surreptitiously tucked it into her waistband and pulled her T-shirt over it as Cole stumbled again, ostensibly distracting Petrov behind them.

Did that mean he was unarmed now? Why on earth had he given up his weapon to her? He was the trained commando! Of course, she knew the answer. He had gone all heroic and self-sacrificing on her. Darn him.

"Turn right," Petrov ordered.

They walked another block before he ordered them to kneel on the ground while he unlocked a door and let them into an anonymous house. It looked like any other home in the French Quarter—with tall, narrow windows and plenty of wrought iron. Nobody coming to look for them would have any idea how to find them. Once she and Cole were inside, they would be entirely at Petrov's mercy—unless she managed to shoot the guy, which was a long shot at best.

Petrov shoved Cole hard, and Cole stumbled through the door. In that moment, she kicked off her tennis shoe and pushed it to one side of the front door. Good Lord willing, Bass would recognize it as hers.

"Inside, Miss Beck."

She crossed the threshold into a dark, musty room that didn't look furnished at a glance. But as her eyes adjusted to the dark, she spied furniture pushed back against the walls under white sheets.

"I'll need you to lie down on the floor, boy toy," Petrov ordered.

Cole threw her a significant look and nodded infinitesimally. Was that a signal to shoot Petrov? Now? She gulped. Could she do it? Could she shoot and maybe kill someone? If it came down to a choice between Cole's life and Petrov's, it was no choice at all.

But the CIA hoped to question Markus Petrov. Where was she supposed to shoot him to disable him but not kill him? She had to injure him badly enough to get him to drop the gun, but not blow his head off. She had no training for this. She didn't know what to aim for, and heaven only knew if she could even hit her target.

But she had no more time to dither, because when Cole dropped to his knees, Petrov drew his arm back and swung it toward Cole, obviously to pistol-whip Cole.

Something exploded inside her—a burst of outrage and fury that she was totally unprepared for. It was accompanied by a burst of adrenaline so violent that time seemed to stand still around her.

As if in slow motion, she reached for the pistol in her belt, drew it, felt with her index finger that the safety was off, slid her finger through the trigger guard, aimed the pistol, and pulled the trigger all in one movement that couldn't have taken more than a few tenths of a second.

A tremendous explosion of light and sound rocked her backward, nearly knocking her off her feet.

What little weapons training she did have recommended firing the weapon until it was empty. She pointed in Petrov's general direction and fired again, double tapping the trigger this time.

The pistol kicked hard in her hands and she wrestled it down into firing position a third time. And that was when she finally became conscious enough of her surroundings to actually see Petrov in front of her. A look of infinite surprise was in his eyes as he looked down at his chest. Four black holes were clear in his white dress shirt.

Why wasn't there any blood?

She raised the pistol to point it at Petrov's face just as he raised his right hand from his side at an angle pointing downward.

In the slow-motion time warp she existed in at the moment, she saw a cold smile enter his eyes and curve his mouth upward. He pulled the trigger on his weapon once and Cole toppled over.

"No!" she screamed.

She pulled the trigger again and again until it clicked, empty, in her hands.

When she finally stopped firing, Petrov was gone, and Cole lay flat out on the floor in a trickle of black liquid spreading beside him.

Chapter 20

Time resumed its normal flow all at once, slamming into Nissa like a physical blow, staggering her and nearly knocking her over.

She threw down the pistol and rushed to Cole, dropping to her knees beside him. "Oh God, oh God, oh God. Please be alive," she chanted. "I can't lose you. Not now. Not when I've just found you."

Her hands passed over him frantically, searching for a pulse. She felt a thud beneath his chin. Thank God. She nearly collapsed, weeping, then and there. But he needed her. She had to stay focused. Stay strong. She could do this.

She ran her hands over him again, searching for the wound. There. Her fingers found a small round hole in his shirt. His upper right side was hit, just below his right arm. Crap. Maybe his lung was hit. God knew what else the bullet had hit on its path into his torso and all those vital organs.

Sure enough, he took a gasping, horrible sounding breath. His eyes fluttered open weakly and his mouth opened to speak.

"Don't talk," she told him as she pressed the heel of her hand against the entry wound. "You're shot. Your right side is hit and you might have a collapsed lung. Don't move. I'm calling for help now."

Although the way her fingers were fumbling and trembling, it was a miracle she managed to hit a nine and two ones on her phone at all.

The police dispatcher was calm and directed her to step outside and get an address for the ambulance to find her and Cole. She hated to leave him, but he would die without immediate medical care. She ran outside, spotted the street signs at the corner, relayed the names, and then left the front door standing wide-open as she returned to Cole.

She was stunned to see Cole sitting up when she went back inside, unbuttoning his shirt. "What are you doing?"

"Checking my vest."

"Your vest? As in bulletproof?" she exclaimed.

"Well, bullet resistant. He was using a big-caliber Teflon-coated round if I had to guess. It actually punched through the vest enough to make me bleed. But I think my rib stopped the round."

"Why don't you let medics get here and decide that for you?" she replied tartly.

"Because Petrov's getting away. Can you reach in my pants pocket on my right side and get out my phone? I need to call Bass."

She didn't know whether to be relieved or outraged that he was still thinking about the mission. She pulled out his phone. "You can have this if you promise to wait for the ambulance to get here and get checked out."

"This isn't a game. Give me my phone."

"I'm not playing a game. No phone if you won't take care of yourself. I'm not losing you because you're too macho to admit you're hurt."

His gaze snapped to hers and she stared into his eyes, willing him to see how much she cared for him. His gaze faltered first. "Fine. Give me my phone."

She handed over the device and he dialed Bass quickly, ordering his man to pull the SEALs out of the restaurant as soon as police arrived to take custody of everyone in the place. Cole ordered the SEALs to spread out through this neighborhood in a manhunt for Markus Petrov.

"I don't think he went out on the street," she said after Cole hung up.

"What do you mean?"

She explained, "I'm fairly certain he used old smugglers' tunnels to get out of the restaurant. He emerged onto the street at the other end of that block of old buildings. And when he left here—I know I was busy firing my gun—but I never heard or felt the outside door open."

Cole went on high alert. "Give me the handgun," he ordered her under his breath.

She did so, and he quickly ejected the empty clip and rammed home a new one. He chambered a round and stood up, looking around the room suspiciously.

She continued thinking out loud. "Why did he enter this building in particular? How did he have a key to it? It's obvious no one lives here. He must own it or lease it. Maybe he uses it for meetings or to store inventory. But whatever its main purpose, I think this building must have another secret passageway or hidden room in it, too."

Cole stepped over to her and swept her up in his arms, gasping a little as she came into contact with his injured side. "You, my love, are brilliant."

He turned her loose and commenced inspecting the walls as she stared in total shock at his back. *My love?*

She followed Cole around the ground floor of the house. It was sparsely furnished with sheet-covered pieces and it only took them about five minutes to search it. No sign of any hidden passageways leaped out at them.

"Any chance there's a basement in this place?" she asked Cole.

"Doubtful. This city sits below sea level and the water tables are practically at street level."

"We're missing something," she declared in frustration. "I know he didn't leave through a door. At least not a regular door."

Something moved fast behind them and Cole whirled, pistol at the ready.

"Stand down, boss. It's me," Bass announced.

"Thank God," Nissa breathed. "Will you please make him sit down until medics get here to check him over?"

Bass stepped forward quickly. "Gunshot?"

Cole nodded. "Right side. Caught my vest but penetrated the flesh a bit. It's nothing serious."

"Let me be the judge of that," Bass retorted. "Show me your side."

Cole passed her the handgun while he opened his shirt and vest for Bass. "At a minimum, you busted a rib pretty good. You need to sit down and not do anything strenuous, or else fragments of rib bone could puncture your lung."

"As soon as we catch Petrov," Cole replied.

Nissa rolled her eyes. Of course he would feel that way. As much as she wanted to argue with him, she knew a losing fight when she saw one. Instead, she asked Bass, "Will you stay and help us look for a hidden room or secret passage? That way if Macho Man over there passes out, you'll be close by to save his sorry life."

Bass nodded tersely, already looking around the dark interior. "This is the oldest part of the French Quarter. Most of these homes were built by people with secrets to hide. Have you checked the slave quarters yet?"

"What slave quarters?" Nissa blurted.

Bass explained, "There should be a courtyard garden out back. Behind it will be the old stable and slave quarters. Assuming the barn hasn't been torn down and replaced with a new building."

Cole was already moving toward the French doors that led out into a small garden, walled on each side by the house. Nissa hustled to catch up with him, and Bass followed on her heels.

Cole eased one of the doors open and pointed down at the ground. Bass nodded right away. It took her a second longer to spot the footprints in the dust accumulated on the threshold. Fresh footprints.

Bass pulled out a handgun and moved swiftly in front of her to stand shoulder to shoulder with Cole.

The two men advanced with fast stealth toward a two-story structure that formed the rear wall of the garden.

The building was unlocked and they slipped past a large sliding door on a steel track. The downstairs was tall-ceilinged and outfitted like a garage. Cole moved off toward one side and Nissa spotted a wooden staircase on a side wall. She pointed at it and Cole and Bass eased up the steps in total silence, predators on the move.

She followed behind them, turning into what must have been some sort of bunk room in its heyday. Now it was used as an attic, crowded with jumbled junk. Cole and Bass moved forward through the boxes, trunks, paintings and racks of clothing, clearing each new space as they went. She stayed behind them out of their way.

Quickly, she performed a visual measurement of the interior space versus the exterior walls. As she half expected, the dimensions of this room didn't fit the building. She stepped up to the far end of the storage space where Cole and Bass were searching behind junk, and pointed at the wall urgently.

Cole nodded and began examining the wall, running his hands over the vertical wood slats covering it. In seconds, he froze and gestured for Bass to come up beside him. Using their fingernails, the two men together pried open a narrow door. There was likely a clever hidden mechanism for opening it, but they didn't have time to search for it. The two men used brute force to pry the door open and then propped it open with a box.

Cole stepped inside first, followed by Bass, then her. It was a tunnel. It angled downward sharply with narrow steps leading the way. The two big men had to turn sideways to navigate the stairs and she watched her steps with care.

They reached the bottom and the tunnel leveled out, running away from them into pitch blackness. As it was, all three of them were using flashlights with their fingers plastered over the ends to see at all.

Cole led the way, striding swiftly down the corridor for about twenty yards. He stopped abruptly, though, and Nissa peeked around Bass's back to see why they'd stopped. Water was pooling on the floor just ahead of Cole.

Bass whispered to her, "Move slow so you don't make splashing noises. Keep your feet under the water. Don't lift them out."

She nodded and followed the men into the water. It started out as a puddle on the floor but rapidly deepened to her knees. It was incredibly hard work pushing her legs and feet forward through the icy water. But if it meant capturing Markus Petrov, she could find the strength to keep going.

The water began to recede, and then ebbed to nothing. Cole picked up his pace, moving off into the tunnel quickly once more.

They'd gone several dozen yards when the tunnel ended as abruptly as it had begun. The three of them stopped, staring at a brick wall. What had they missed? She did a slow pirouette, examining the walls carefully.

She spied what looked like a steel coal bin tucked back in a dark alcove and pointed at it. Cole and Bass nodded and moved to flank it. At a nod from Cole, Bass threw the door open. Gunshots rang out, deafeningly loud in the confined tunnel, the flashes of light blinding Nissa.

She flung herself back against a side wall, out of the line of fire. Cole and Bass didn't fire back immediately, but let whoever was inside, presumably Petrov, shoot all he wanted.

Silence fell as sharply as the noise had erupted.

Cole said calmly into the void, "Markus, you're outmanned and outgunned. Do you want to die down here, or would you rather come out with us peacefully?"

More silence.

Nissa hated the idea of either Cole or Bass having to go into whatever lay behind that four-foot-tall steel door and duke it out with Petrov. She had no doubt the guy still had enough ammunition to kill someone.

She spoke urgently. "Mr. Petrov, if you come out peacefully now, the United States government is prepared to make a deal with you. We'd like to hear about the organization you've built. In return, you may be repatriated to your homeland if you'd like, or to some other country of your choice." Of course, she didn't have the authority by a long shot to offer him such a deal, but Petrov didn't know that.

"Who are you?" a voice demanded from inside the coal bin.

"I'm the woman you've been hunting. The one who figured out you weren't on the *Anna Belle* when she sank, who found your sons and who took your money."

"You've been nothing but a pain in my—"

Cole cut him off. "Do we have a deal? Are you cooperating and coming out alive or are you going to die in there?"

One more long silence ensued. Nissa was impressed by Cole's patience. He neither rushed Petrov nor broke the waiting tension. Cole was sending a message that he didn't care either way. He was just as happy to kill Petrov as to arrest him.

At length, Petrov growled, "I'm coming out."

"Weapons first, please. Make them safe and toss them out here," Cole ordered.

A pistol and a revolver thudded onto the dirt floor of the tunnel. Cole kicked them toward Bass, who leaned over, checked both weapons and tucked them in his waistband.

"Nice and slow, Mr. Petrov. On your hands and knees, please."

She nodded in approval at Cole. From what she knew of him, Petrov would respond positively to respect and very negatively to insults.

The man who emerged from the coal bin was covered in black soot.

"Verification, please, Nissa," Cole murmured.

She stepped close to the man now kneeling before her and flashed the light in his face. Resentful eyes stared back at her, white against the blackened features. "That's him."

Bass lifted Petrov to his feet and efficiently zip-tied the Russian's wrists behind his back. She noted that Bass also put metal handcuffs over the zip ties. Good call given how slippery this man had been for the past three decades. Bass then used a length of rope to tie Petrov's ankles together loosely, affording only enough room to allow Petrov to move at a slow shuffle.

"Is all of this really necessary?" Petrov snapped.

Cole apologized evenly. "I'm sorry. We're required to follow procedures. You understand how that goes. We'll turn you loose as soon as we can."

Petrov nodded arrogantly.

Nissa smiled privately to herself. The man had no idea the debriefing that awaited him. Before he was done talking, that arrogance would be long gone.

It was a long walk back through the tunnel, up the narrow stairs and through the garage to the street. Bass radioed for his team to bring a transport vehicle to their location, and in a few minutes, all of them climbed into a big flatbed truck with a canvas roof. The trip back to the naval base was quiet. No one questioned Petrov, and no one celebrated in front of the prisoner.

As soon as they crossed onto military land, Nissa made the phone calls she'd been waiting to make for two years. The first went to her boss to let him know that Petrov had been apprehended. The second call went through a classified switchboard that connected her to her coworker Max Kuznetsov. He had spearheaded the entire manhunt for Petrov. Max was relieved, but subdued at the news. After all, Petrov had murdered his mother.

She disconnected the call and Cole asked, "Are you going with the asset to his final destination?"

"Someone will have to escort him and hand him over. But if I can impose upon the SEALs for one last favor, I'd appreciate it if your men made the trip with him. He's dangerous enough that I wouldn't trust myself to keep him safely in custody. I would only trust him to SEALs."

That finally got grins out of the men in the truck. Cole nodded briskly to his men. "Bass, have you and your guys got this?"

"Yes, sir," Bass answered smartly.

Cole nodded. "I'll have the alert aircrew launched. They'll be ready to go in about an hour."

Bass replied, "I'll personally make sure he gets on that plane."

"Where are you taking me?" Petrov asked in alarm.

Cole leaned back and stretched out his legs, invading Petrov's space opposite him in the truck. "You didn't think we were going to keep you on American soil for your interrogation, did you?"

Petrov lurched for Nissa but didn't get far. "You said there would be a deal!"

"There will be," she said calmly. "As soon as we've heard everything you have to say."

"I will tell you nothing," Petrov spat.

Nissa laughed a little, without humor. "You don't know much about my employer, then. You'll sing like an opera star before it's over. Then, and only then, we'll trade you back to your mother country."

"You lied to me!"

Nissa shrugged. She was lying now, too. She highly doubted the CIA would hand him back to Russia any time soon. But honesty had never been part of the world of spies and espionage. To Petrov, she said, "I didn't tell you the full truth. But I didn't lie, either."

"Same difference," Petrov spat.

"I have faith that you, of all people, understand the art of splitting hairs."

"I will not speak anymore." To emphasize the declaration, Petrov stared fixedly at the floor.

Nissa spoke quietly. "Do your sons know you killed their mother? I'm expecting they will be eager to talk with us when they find out you have a history of killing women who cross you, including her."

His gaze snapped back to hers, furious. She was tired of playing games with him. "To the victor goes the spoils, Markus. You had a good run, but you've lost. You're done."

With that, the truck pulled up beside a small passenger jet. Bass and five of his men jumped out of the truck, helping Petrov down, as well, still cuffed and shackled. Bass and his team closed in around Petrov and crowded the Russian spymaster onto the plane.

She turned back to Cole in relief. "Hopefully, I never have to see him again."

"Mission accomplished," he sighed, just as he fell over onto his side, unconscious.

Chapter 21

Cole woke up slowly. He registered being in a soft bed. A steady beeping noise beside him announced that he was in a hospital and that his heart was still ticking. There was a tube under his nose. Supplemental oxygen, then. He moved his right arm and noted that a tube beside him moved, too. An IV drip.

Something moved swiftly toward him from the other direction and he tried to react, tried to raise his hands to defend himself, but was too weak, or too drugged, to respond.

"Hey, handsome," a familiar female voice said softly. *Nissa.*

She was still here? Why hadn't she gone with Petrov to interrogate him? "Why…" The rest of the words in his head refused to go to his lips.

"Your lung collapsed, after all. Doctors had to reinflate it and do a little surgery to stabilize your broken rib."

She'd misunderstood what he was asking. He shook his head weakly. "Why are...you here?"

"You mean why didn't I go with Markus Petrov to oversee his interrogation?"

He nodded, relieved not to have to speak aloud.

"Because you're hurt, silly. I would never leave your side without knowing you're going to be okay."

"I'll be okay. Go. Good for your career...to lead... the debriefing."

"Cole Perriman, you nearly died on me. Do you seriously think advancing my career matters one bit to me in the face of your safety?"

He stared up at her questioningly. The anesthesia was wearing off, and he was feeling more alert by the second. "It was your collar. You should get credit."

"It was your collar, Cole. You and your guys tracked him down and arrested him."

"Couldn't have done it without you."

"Fine. I helped. I'm not going to argue with you about it."

"Good." He smiled a little. "And besides, I'll always win."

"Hah! You wish!" she exclaimed.

There. She was smiling, her beautiful eyes sparkling with humor, the way he liked them best.

"How soon can I get out of here?" he asked.

"Doctors want to keep you overnight for observation. Then your rib will have to heal. That'll take a few months."

In a few months, he would be eligible to retire. He

was done in the field, then. He braced himself for grief, loss and regret, but none of it came. He frowned, confused.

"What's wrong?" Nissa asked quickly.

"Nothing's wrong. And that's what's wrong."

"I don't understand."

"I'm done as a SEAL. I should be devastated, but I'm not."

"Why not?" she asked cautiously.

"Because all I can think about is looking forward to spending time with you."

Nissa blinked down at him like the world's cutest owl. Her head was even tilted to one side as she tried to comprehend him.

He smiled up at her. "I'm sorry I can't get out of bed and do this right—" He paused to take a deep breath. "But would you consider spending the rest of your life with me?"

"I beg your pardon?" she blurted.

"Pretend I'm kneeling on one knee in front of you holding out a ring box with an obnoxiously huge and expensive diamond ring in it. Marry me, Nissa."

"But...but...but I'm a giant chicken and I'm not the least bit badass."

He struggled to sit up in bed and she leaped forward to support him. "Nissa Beck. You are the most genuine woman I know. And correct me if I'm wrong, but you emptied a gun into Markus Petrov's bulletproof vest. You found his hiding place, and you talked him out of it without violence. I'd say that makes you officially badass. And you rock my world in bed."

She was starting to blush, her cheeks pinkening brightly.

"As for you being a chicken, you've been braver than most would be pretty much from the first minute you set foot on the *Anna Belle*. For that matter, it takes nerves of steel to get involved with a man like me."

"You're easy as pie to be with."

"There you have it. I don't intimidate you at all."

She laughed. "Oh, you intimidate me. I just love you anyway."

He gestured her to lean down close to him. "For the record, I love you, too. But you scare me to death."

She lurched upright sharply. "Why?"

"Because you make me feel things I didn't know I could feel. Because you make me want to take a chance on a real relationship. I've never met a woman who did that to me."

"Really?"

"Yes, really. I'm serious, Nissa. Marry me. Make me the happiest man alive."

"Only if you promise to stay alive for a very, very long time."

"As soon as I get out of this place, I'm hanging up my SEAL trident for good. I'm yours forever."

"What if you miss the work too much?"

"All I'll have to do is think about what I got in return. You. Love. Happiness. A real home. Hell, a family of my own. All things I've never had and never thought I would have. You've made dreams I didn't even know I had come true."

She leaned down to kiss him gently and then looked deeply into his eyes. "In that case, I accept. If you're okay becoming plain old Mr. Perriman, I'm okay with becoming Mrs. Perriman."

And in that moment, he knew. He was no longer just a cold, hard soldier. At long last, he was a complete man. And Nissa was the reason why.

* * * * *

Be sure to check out previous books in the
CODE: WARRIOR SEALS *miniseries:*

UNDERCOVER WITH A SEAL
HER SECRET SPY

Available now from Harlequin Romantic Suspense.

And for more suspenseful stories from Cindy Dees,
try THE PRESCOTT BROTHERS *miniseries:*

HIGH-STAKES BACHELOR
HIGH-STAKES PLAYBOY

Available now wherever Harlequin books
and ebooks are sold!

Get 2 Free Books,
Plus 2 Free Gifts—
just for trying the Reader Service!

◆ HARLEQUIN®
ROMANTIC suspense

SPECIAL EXCERPT FROM

◆HARLEQUIN®

ROMANTIC suspense

Bea Colton is the only living victim of Red Ridge's Groom Killer, and Micah Shaw will do everything in his power to make sure she stays that way—even if he's risking getting his heart broken all over again.

Read on for a sneak preview of the next installment in
THE COLTONS OF RED RIDGE *continuity:*
COLTON K-9 BODYGUARD
by Lara Lacombe.

Micah leaned forward, his hand tightening on hers. "You're the first person to encounter the Groom Killer and live to talk about it," he said quietly. "I want to put you in protective custody, to make sure you're safe in case the killer targets you again."

Bea's heart began to pound. "Do you really think that's a possibility?" The Groom Killer went after men, not women. And she hadn't seen anything in the dark—surely the killer would know Bea couldn't identify them.

"I think it's a risk we can't afford to take." He gave her hand a final squeeze and released it, and Bea immediately missed the warmth of his touch. "I can start the paperwork—"

"That won't be necessary."

Disappointment flashed across Micah's face. "Bea, please," he began, but she lifted her hand to cut him off.

"I'll agree to a bodyguard, but only under one condition."

"What's that?" There was a note of wariness in his voice, as if he was worried about what she was going to say.

"It's got to be you," Bea said firmly. "No one else."

"Me?" Micah made a strangled sound, and Bea fought the urge to laugh. She knew how ridiculous her request must seem to him. They hadn't seen each other in years, and after the way he'd ended things between them, he probably figured she wanted nothing more to do with him.

Truth be told, Bea herself was surprised by the intensity of her determination. But she felt safe with Micah, and she knew he would protect her if the Groom Killer did come back around. Besides, maybe if they spent more time together, she could finally get him out of her system and truly move on. The man had flaws—he was only human, after all. Hopefully, seeing them up close again would be enough to take the shine off her memories of their time together.

It was a long shot, but she was just desperate enough to take it.

Don't miss
COLTON K-9 BODYGUARD by Lara Lacombe,
available March 2018 wherever
Harlequin® Romantic Suspense books and ebooks are sold.

www.Harlequin.com

LOVE
Harlequin
romance?

Join our Harlequin community to share your thoughts and connect with other romance readers!

Be the first to find out about promotions, news, and exclusive content!

Sign up for the Harlequin e-newsletter and download a free book from any series at

www.TryHarlequin.com

CONNECT WITH US AT:

Harlequin.com/Community

 Facebook.com/HarlequinBooks

 Twitter.com/HarlequinBooks

 Instagram.com/HarlequinBooks

 Pinterest.com/HarlequinBooks

ReaderService.com

**ROMANCE WHEN
YOU NEED IT**

Earn points from all your Harlequin book purchases from wherever you shop.

Turn your points into *FREE BOOKS* of your choice
OR
EXCLUSIVE GIFTS from your favorite authors or series.

Join for FREE today at
www.HarlequinMyRewards.com.

Harlequin My Rewards is a free program (no fees) without any commitments or obligations.

MYR17